MURDER IN HELL'S CORNER

Further Titles by Amy Myers from Severn House

MURDER IN THE QUEEN'S BOUDOIR
MURDER WITH MAJESTY
THE WICKENHAM MURDERS
MURDER IN FRIDAY STREET
MURDER IN HELL'S CORNER

Writing as Harriet Hudson

APPLEMERE SUMMER
CATCHING THE SUNLIGHT
QUINN
SONGS OF SPRING
THE STATIONMASTER'S DAUGHTER
TOMORROW'S GARDEN
TO MY OWN DESIRE
THE WINDY HILL
WINTER ROSES

MURDER IN HELL'S CORNER

Amy Myers

This first world edition published in Great Britain 2006 by
SEVERN HOUSE PUBLISHERS LTD of
9–15 High Street, Sutton, Surrey SM1 1DF.
This first world edition published in the USA 2006 by
SEVERN HOUSE PUBLISHERS INC of
595 Madison Avenue, New York, N.Y. 10022.

British Library Cataloguing in Publication Data

Myers, Amy, 1938-
   Murder in hell's corner
   1.   Marsh, Georgia (Fictitious character) - Fiction
   2.   Marsh, Peter (Fictitious character) - Fiction
   3.   Detective and mystery stories
   I.   Title
   823.9'14 [F]

ISBN-13: 978-0-7278-6393-5
ISBN-10: 0-7278-6393-2

All Severn House titles are printed on acid-free paper.

Typeset by Palimpsest Book Production Ltd.,
Grangemouth, Stirlingshire, Scotland.
Printed and bound in Great Britain by
MPG Books Ltd., Bodmin, Cornwall.

Author's Note

West Malling airfield was heavily bombed by the Luftwaffe during the Battle of Britain in 1940, as were other airfields in Kent and Sussex, in order to render them unusable prior to invasion by Germany. Although for the purposes of this novel the fictitious 362 Squadron was operating there, in fact no Spitfires flew from West Malling until the battle was virtually over at the end of October that year. During the battle only an army co-operation squadron, No. 26, flying Lysanders, was operative at this airfield. Robin J. Brooks' *From Moths to Merlins* provides an invaluable history of the airfield, which has now closed and is the site of a housing and business development. I would like to thank the aviation historian Norman Franks for so patiently and authoritatively answering my questions, and also Marion Binks, Douglas Tyler and Tangmere Aviation Museum. However, any blunders in the novel are solely down to me. My gratitude also goes to Edwin Buckhalter and my editor Amanda Stewart at Severn House for their interest in this project, and to my agent Dorothy Lumley of Dorian Literary Agency for her constant support. Lastly, my gratitude for the memories that the true Spitfire pilots of the battle left with me both in person and in their memoirs during my years in publishing with the firm of William Kimber.

One

'No, let's go this way.' Georgia Marsh fought back instant, irrational panic. She tried to speak casually, but Luke wasn't easily fooled.

'It's not like you to mind a shoeful of mud. What's wrong?'

'Nothing.' Stupid, but what else could she say? Luke was Marsh & Daughter's publisher; he was also her dearly beloved partner, but he was still trespassing in an area barred to all except herself and her father. How could she explain to Luke the Calm (apparently), Laidback (superficially) and Practical (when it suited him) that this overgrown dank path through the undergrowth, which disappeared so enticingly round a corner, offered only threat? Some places had an atmosphere implanted in them by human passions that still cried out to be heard, and one of them lay ahead. She was sure of it, and it scared her.

'You're very white,' Luke observed dispassionately, his eye keenly on her. 'How nothing is nothing?'

Georgia swallowed. Suppose it *was* nothing? She had been wrong before, hadn't she? It could just be the gloom ahead that deterred her, as she stood there in relatively sunny daylight. Anyway, if here be dragons, shouldn't she be facing them, returning fire for fire?

'OK, let's go, Indiana Jones.' Surprised by her sudden bullish attitude, she took the lead, picking her way carefully along the damp grassy path. It couldn't be that bad, she tried to convince herself. After all, these were the well-maintained

1

grounds of a flourishing hotel in so-called rural Kent, hardly the outposts of civilization as they knew it. Nevertheless she continued warily, glad that Luke was behind her; that way he couldn't turn unexpectedly and be presented by the sight of her white face. Then she came to the bend in the path . . . Onward, she ordered herself firmly, fighting her desire to turn and run.

After her first few steps, she knew she couldn't go on. Instead she stood there looking at what lay before her, as Luke came up to stand at her side. She felt as hypnotized as Wordsworth gazing at his fluttering daffodils, though hardly with the same emotions. In her case it was an instant relief that all that seemed to face her was the blue haze of a Kentish wood in May. The path before them sloped gently into a dell with banks on either side, protecting it, sheltering it from outside view. Bluebells clung to both sides in profusion, their colour only broken by the occasional grey rock which served to highlight it. Unlike the rest of the gardens of Woodring Manor, if gardeners penetrated here at all they were running after nature, rather than imposing their will upon it.

'Bluebells,' he announced with satisfaction. 'Aren't you glad you didn't chicken out?'

Georgia didn't answer Luke's question. She couldn't. Relief was giving way to an overwhelming sense of unrest that clung to her like a pall. Her instincts had been right. However lovely the sight, these bluebells were masking a tragedy whose roots were deeply embedded in this small valley. It reeked of some terrible event. It reeked of death.

'The Ash Grove,' she said abruptly.

'Beech and hazel, I'd say,' Luke replied idly, wandering down the path into the dell.

She tried to make her legs follow him but they refused. 'Around us for gladness the bluebells were ringing . . . Amid the dark shades of the lonely ash grove.' Isn't that how the old folk song went? That grove had been a place of grief,

2

death and loss, although the story behind it was lost in history. What did this one hide? She wanted to cry out to Luke to come back to safety, to leave the enchanted wood, and had to force herself to remain silent.

'You're bonkers, Georgia,' she told herself, and by the time he had strolled back to her she had almost convinced herself it was true.

'Time we found Peter,' Luke said, taking her arm. It felt good, though she hated to admit she needed the comfort of company. 'He should be here by now.' She had been staying with Luke overnight in his South Malling home, and her father was driving up that morning from his home in Haden Shaw near Canterbury.

'He's never in much need of finding,' she managed to laugh. Back to normal, now that the dell was behind her.

Woodring Manor was no architectural beauty, with its Victorian towers, mock beams and flamboyant touches of the Gothic, but it was certainly eye-catching, Georgia thought as they skirted the lake to walk up the slope to the terrace and hotel. It was set in the midst of nowhere at the end of a single-track lane running up from the Mereworth road, situated on the ridge of a low hill, with lawns and formal gardens sloping down to a small lake with a wooded wilderness beyond. For diners to appreciate this view, the former ballroom and dining room had been converted to a restaurant, with a delightful small bar-cum-conservatory at one end. It was there as she and Luke reached the terrace that she could see a group of elderly men sitting chatting in the armchairs – and with them was Peter, who had somehow manoeuvred his wheelchair into the circle. Being that much higher than they, he appeared to be leader of the group, which amused Georgia greatly – especially as, when they drew closer, she could see the men were all blazer-clad with identical formal ties, the design of which looked familiar.

'RAF,' whispered Luke in her ear. He was beginning to

read her thoughts with uncomfortable ease, Georgia thought. She now realized why Peter was chatting so much that he hadn't noticed their arrival: his father had served with the Royal Air Force, and that of course was where she had seen the tie before.

What did etiquette demand, she wondered. There was hardly room for them all to sit in here and yet Peter obviously had no intention of moving.

'Georgia, Luke,' he cried with great pleasure as he at last acknowledged their presence. 'Let me introduce Number 362 Spitfire Squadron, here to toast the memory of West Malling airfield, now alas with only a lonely control tower and a bronze statue to mark the spot.'

Spitfires? Did that imply Second World War or post-war, she wondered. Peter was obviously about to tell them, but just as he began to introduce the group the restaurant manager arrived to summon the veterans to their lunch. Georgia was left only with a jumble of names and impressions: a virtually bald, bright-eyed thin man, a red-cheeked life and soul of the party, a serious grey-haired academic type, a burly rugged no-nonsense sort, and an almost skeletal man with a bewildered look in his eyes. Not one of them could be under eighty-five, and one or two might be nearer ninety, she estimated, so that could mean they saw service during the Second World War. The quintet departed for lunch with courteous pleasantries to them, reaching for sticks, squaring stooped shoulders under loose blazers, and tossing names between them: Daz, Bob, Jan, were the ones she caught.

'Enough gongs and history between them to start a museum,' Peter said with satisfaction as she and Luke took the now vacant armchairs. 'Did you notice one of them had the DSO, and there were a couple of DFCs?'

'All World War Two?' Luke asked.

'I imagine so.'

'Unlike you not to have their full life stories by now,' his daughter remarked.

4

'You're quite right, Georgia,' Peter said without rancour. 'My usual charm didn't seem to work, though they're friendly enough.' A pause, then an innocent-sounding, 'Let's eat in the restaurant, shall we?'

'Hey, what happened to the quick bar snack?' Georgia asked.

'I'll treat you both,' Peter said firmly.

'No turning that down,' Luke accepted graciously. 'All right by you, Georgia?'

She nodded. 'I never stand in the way of Peter and piqued curiosity.'

'How well you understand me,' her father commented. 'I do admit to a certain interest. What do they talk about at such reunions?'

'The old days.'

'That's just it,' Peter said. 'They weren't when I arrived.'

'*Because* you'd arrived,' Luke pointed out.

'You think they stopped gassing about their war exploits just to be kind to a gent in a wheelchair? They'd never talk at all if so. They got inured to disabilities quickly in wartime.'

'I meant that you were an outsider,' Luke explained equably.

'All the better audience, in my experience,' Peter said. 'After all, I have a bond with them. My father flew in Burma.' Georgia's suspicions were confirmed. For some reason the bloodhound was on the trail of prey. It was her duty – mutually understood – to shoot it down at birth, if she could. If it survived, that gave it validity.

'Some people want to talk about their war experiences, some don't,' she said flatly. 'You can't take them by the scruff of their necks and insist they talk like Lewis Carroll's old man on the gate.'

Peter wore a look of hurt dignity. 'I trust I am sensitive enough to realize that. Just as,' he said thoughtfully, as Luke vanished to speak to the waiter, 'I detect you don't wish to

5

talk about whatever upset you out in the gardens. A quarrel
with Luke?'

'No. This place,' she told him bluntly, deciding to overlook her father's quick departure from sensitivity. 'At one
end of the lake, there's a series of feeder ponds in a wilder
part of the garden, and on the far side a sort of hidden
valley smothered with bluebells.'

'But not ringing for you, I take it?'

'Very definitely not.' She glanced at him, knowing he
would understand. 'It might just be me . . .'

'Or it might have the same effect on me. All right, I'll
go after lunch. Coming?'

She made a face. 'I suppose I'd better or Luke will
wonder why you're shooting off on your own to look at
bluebells.'

'I have a notion that Luke is not as unobservant as you
imagine in such matters. He might even feel left out.'

Georgia dismissed this impatiently. 'We've talked about
this before. Even if Luke the man would understand, the
publisher side of him might not. We go to great lengths
to separate what sparks off our investigations from the
facts that eventually make the book. We agree that they
have to stand alone, so why fill Luke with unnecessary
worries?'

'Because he's halfway in, halfway out of our family, and
it behoves me to say, dear daughter, that this can't go on
for ever.'

'I know,' she said crossly. It was her fault, she knew that.
But the status quo was much more comfortable than a
possible thorny way ahead – into a marriage like her last
one.

When they entered the restaurant there were few diners,
which was just as well since 362 Squadron obviously took
its reunion seriously. It was too small a group, Georgia
presumed, for a private room to be allotted to them, but a
virtually empty restaurant sufficed.

She watched the former pilots with interest, while she, Peter and Luke ate their own passable meal. One of them, the burly one, whom she had pinned down as Bob, had a sketchbook on his lap and was busy drawing unobserved, or at any rate disregarded, by his comrades. The ceremonial, even the permission to smoke – which no one did, of course – took place with moving dedication.

'Gentlemen, the Queen.' The toast was proposed by the thin man with the bewildered look. All five of them looked entirely wrapped up in themselves and their reason for being here. Even if the restaurant had been overflowing it would have made no difference to them, she realized. They must have pasts that made most people alive today seem pale shadows, and today 362 Squadron was reasserting its values. At one point the bright-eyed man stood up to make another toast – to whom she could not hear – and began to recite the well known, but still spellbinding lines:

> Oh, I have slipped the surly bonds of earth
> And danced the skies on laughter-silvered wings . . .

She knew the poem, but had never heard it voiced by men who had so danced the skies, albeit in their case so often a dance of death. Each one of them could surely say, as did the poet, he had put out his hand and touched the face of God.

'Written by John Magee,' Peter whispered. 'Canadian. Shot down and killed in 1941 aged only nineteen. Remarkable poem to write in wartime. And over there are five of them who flew for the same cause.'

'That's a lot,' observed Luke, 'when you come to think of it.'

'Five out of thousand upon thousand? Fifty-five thousand lost in Bomber Command alone, let alone the other commands. That's just in this country, not counting the other Allies and the Germans.'

7

'True,' Luke acknowledged, 'but if you take twelve or so in a squadron at any one period – and these men look all in their mid-eighties, which suggests it *was* at more or less the same time – where are the others? Squadrons didn't die out with the war, they went on. You know what I think? This isn't a squadron reunion, it's a reunion of *part* of a squadron.'

'Interesting,' Georgia said. 'You could be right.'

'We publishers sometimes have something to offer you struggling authors,' Luke said graciously.

'There's something else unusual too,' Peter pointed out. 'There are no women here.'

Georgia laughed. 'The last stand of the male preserve.'

'Up to a point,' Peter replied seriously. 'But these men are a fair age, and not what they used to be, physically. Where are the carers, the helpers, the wives, the daughters to see their poor old dads are OK? Even grandchildren often come to listen to what Grandpa did in the war.'

Georgia considered. 'Too close a group. They've just come to chat and bar the door to all intruders, or at least those without a rhinoceros hide like yours. They probably drink all they like, and the minions come to pick them up when midnight strikes the witching hour.' Unbidden, the thought of a witching hour in that dell crossed her mind, but was quickly sent packing.

'Perhaps.' Peter yawned – a trifle ostentatiously, Georgia felt. 'I need some fresh air. Feel like a turn round the grounds?'

'Again?' Luke asked plaintively. 'I've done my mud walking for the day.'

'I might need a push,' Peter said firmly.

The fitful sun had disappeared now, and as they strolled into the gardens from the terrace, Georgia decided to keep firmly away from the dell. Peter would do better alone, she told herself, and it was probably true. Instead, as they walked over the grass, she fixed her mind on 362 Squadron. Luke's comment had set her thinking. Why, if he was right, was that group here? Just because they remembered their time at West Malling in the war?

'Where was the airfield?' she asked.

'It's disappeared under the King's Hill business development,' Luke replied. 'Not to mention housing estates. I was sad to see it go. It had a splendid pre-war career, run from the mid-1930s by the Malling Aero Club. All the aviation celebs touched base here.'

'Amy Johnson?' Georgia asked.

'Yes, and Sir Alan Cobham's Flying Circus. Then the RAF took it over in '39, where it was conveniently placed for the Biggin Hill and Kenley sector in the Battle of Britain the following year. It went on to play a bigger role during the war, especially during the early part of the flying bomb campaign, but in August 1944 it was closed for operational purposes.'

'And that was it?'

'No. After the war it remained an RAF station until the early Sixties; the Yanks then took over for a couple of years, and one way or another it stayed an active airfield until the going was too tough and it was sold for development.'

'How come you know so much about it?' Georgia asked curiously. It was the first time she'd heard Luke express any personal interest in aviation, though his publishing list included local war histories and memoirs.

'One can hardly fail to, living round here. Anyway, my dad brought me to see the Red Arrows here in the 1970s . . . Where are you off to?' Luke looked round in surprise as Peter turned his chair and bumped along the path to the dell. Georgia was glad he hadn't asked her to come. Peter didn't always agree with her, and she found herself hoping that this time he wouldn't.

'To see those bluebells Georgia told me about,' Peter called back over his shoulder. 'Damn! I'm stuck.'

Luke gave her a quick glance as he went over to push

the wheelchair out of the mud. She heard Peter thanking him, which must have been an effort. Peter hated anything he couldn't do himself. She watched the chair progress to the bend in the path, but then it went a little further and out of her sight, and there was only the sound of the birds singing their May song. Luke stayed silent, which made Georgia feel guilty. Was she truly excluding him because it was sensible, or because she wanted to keep areas of her life to herself, as some kind of defence?

When Peter returned, he nodded soberly at her. So that was that. He had felt as she had. It was a done deal, but she was profoundly depressed at the thought. They would have to investigate what lay behind this. Perhaps it was nothing, perhaps only the remaining sadness of a tragic love story, and not the business of Marsh & Daughter. No unsolved murder, no injustice crying out to be avenged. In any case, why was she worried? Such investigations were their livelihood, so her unwillingness to face this one was weird.

'Odd place,' Peter said cheerfully to them both as they returned to the hotel. 'Did you see those large rocks in between the bluebells? Strange, don't you think? We're hardly in mountainous countryside here, so how do great lumps of Kentish ragstone come to be there? They must have been specially brought in, probably for a rockery garden at some time, and left derelict till the bluebells took over.'

This was a neutral subject, but even so Georgia was glad to be back inside the hotel. Peter disregarded the restaurant and made straight for the disabled entrance and then the bar. Of course, she realized, that's where he guessed 362 Squadron would now be. He had something in mind, which was fine by her, provided it didn't involve that dell.

Once inside the hotel, she went in search of the ladies' toilet before joining them in the bar, and soon found herself in the basement. This must have been where the kitchens were when the house was first built, but now it was home to conference rooms and toilets. The latter were beautifully appointed. The smell of fresh potpourri reached her, and the room was well lit. Yet it *felt* dark, and she came out of the cubicle distinctly eager to leave, glad of the whirl of the hand drier as distraction. It wasn't a return of the panic she had felt in the dell, but even so she was glad to reach the corridor again.

She found the squadron group ensconced in armchairs round a table in the corner of the bar. Peter was just sallying up to them with murmurs of great surprise at meeting them again. He continued with a flattering mention of the Magee poem, then his interest in the Second World War, and his own memories of Farnborough air shows in his youth. Of course he was too young, he said deprecatingly, to recall the war himself, but perhaps he could buy them a drink?

It appeared he could. Once drinks were distributed and introductions made, Peter embarked on a description of his father's RAF career in Burma – little of it true, from what Georgia could recall, but at least the ground was softened to the extent that she and Luke felt able to join them. Nevertheless, there was very much a 'them and us' atmosphere.

'Interesting hotel this,' Peter observed casually.

A wheezing laugh from the life and soul of the party, who had been introduced to them as Harry Williams, though apparently addressed by his mates as Porgie. Probably from Georgie-Porgie, who 'kissed the girls and made them cry' in the nursery rhyme.

'Thanks to Matt here,' Harry said. 'He used to own it.'

Peter was suitably impressed. 'Fine place.'

Matt turned out to be the thin man who had proposed the toast, he of the bewildered expression.

'Bought it for a song from the previous owners after the war, didn't you, Matt?' Harry continued, and Matt at last had to reply. Not through unwillingness, Georgia thought, more from a disinclination for the limelight.

'I ran it until fairly recently, then Andrew took over,' he half whispered.

'His son,' Harry explained helpfully. 'Sold out three years ago, then this chain took over. There's a manager here now.'

'Were you all at West Malling together?' Georgia asked brightly as conversation languished.

'For a time,' the academic one answered. His name proved to be Jan Molkar, and he had a slight accent that she couldn't immediately identify. Dutch, perhaps? Again no one added anything.

'Was this a hotel then?' Luke helped out.

'Of a kind,' the one called Daz replied. That must be a nickname, she thought, for he'd been introduced as the Reverend Bill Dane. No dog collar now. It was he who had read the Magee poem, and still seemed the liveliest of the five.

'It was our officers' mess,' he continued, 'and we bunked down here too. It was requisitioned at the outbreak of war, like the Manor House further up the road towards Malling. How the old order changeth. Its grounds are a country park now, and the building's being turned into flats. 26 Army Co-operation Squadron had bagged that in 1940, and there was no room for us when we flew in, so here we are.'

'Some way from the airfield, isn't it?' Luke asked.

'Aye, that was the point,' he of the sketchbook answered, Bob McNee. The name as well as his soft accent spoke of his birthplace. Georgia put him down as an obvious local councillor type, since every bit of him gave the impression of steadiness and reliability.

'The airfields got smashed up regularly in the Battle of Britain,' Bob continued. 'Bad enough losing them without losing the precious pilots too. Waste of all that training.'

'You must have known the area well,' she said. An inane comment but it seemed to be up to them to keep the conversation going. She would have suspected they wanted to get rid of them, but she decided it wasn't that. Their body language was friendly enough but there was some kind of tension there that she didn't understand.

'Aye.'

'And you're all that's left of the squadron?' she persevered.

'Not quite. We're . . .' Harry looked at the others. 'We're the Battle of Britain group. The whole squadron gets together at air shows and once a year in London.'

'Were you all in the same squadron after the battle?'

A pause. 'Gradually we all went our different ways. That was routine. Promotions, injuries, war going in new directions – any number of reasons why we split up.'

Try as she might, Georgia found herself thinking of that dell again. Here be dragons, returning fire with fire. That was an odd phrase for her, not one she normally used. It was almost as if she were thinking . . . She put a brake on her thoughts. She was here. She was listening to these former pilots and that was that.

'We had a bar in the basement,' Jan said. 'We called it the Hell's Bells Club, Angels all day . . .' Seeing her blank look, he explained in his careful English, 'That is the codeword for height in thousands of feet. And so we were devils by night.'

Perhaps all the group had needed was this push, for the ice suddenly broke, and the men broke into wavery song.

> The bells of hell go ting-a-ling-a-ling
> For you but not for me . . .

'And that, dear lady,' Harry concluded, 'is why the Luftwaffe called Kent Hell's Corner. News of our dark and daring doings in the Hell's Bells Club travelled fast. I joke, of course,' he added hastily, as the others' attention fixed on him, as though he had stepped outside his script. 'Kent got that name because of the hot reception our boys gave the Luftwaffe during the battle.'

Talk turned smoothly to the battle itself and the moment passed.

The Hell's Bells Club, Georgia concluded, could account for how she had felt in the basement earlier on. From the Hell's Bells Club to ladies' loo seemed a sad come-down. But at least it was no worse. Her imagination had simply been running out of control.

'We'd better be going ourselves,' Luke said with evident relief, as the group eventually showed signs of moving. It was four o'clock by the time they had said their goodbyes and left, and Luke was obviously fretting that they would be late for their own appointment in Wickenham. 'The TV people said they'd be there at five.'

Not that the TV people would be interested in their presence, Georgia knew. It was Mary Beaumont they would be coming to interview, the excuse being the publication of Marsh & Daughter's latest book, about a murder in the village in 1929.

'So that explains it,' Peter said to her as Luke went to pay their bar bill. 'Of course there's an atmosphere here, with all the violence and sadness of the past. Think of what they went through in the skies by day, and needed to drown out at night with drink, if only to forget the gaps caused by those who hadn't returned.'

'It explains the basement, perhaps,' Georgia replied reluctantly, 'but not that dell.' If only it did.

'Perhaps there was a Nissen hut for the pilots there. Who knows?'

'Between two banks?'

'Perhaps a V1 doodlebug crashed there later. Hence the crater.'

'Yes,' Georgia said gratefully, clutching this escape route. Of course. She remembered that there had been a similar tragedy on the borders of Charing Heath and Lenham which had wiped out a whole hutful of Royal Engineers. Perhaps there had been such an incident here, which, terrible though it would have been, would not be calling out for Marsh & Daughter to investigate. There would be nothing for them to find. Nothing to mourn, save the loss of a generation of young men who played with death, not football, and gambled with their lives, not slot machines. Men who drank to drown fear, not boredom, and who loved because there might be no tomorrow.

'Wait for me,' Peter said as Luke returned. He headed his chair after the disappearing barman, either for directions to the disabled loo or for some ulterior motive. Georgia hoped the former. She wanted to get out of this place and the thought of Peter sniffing the scent of a story only rekindled her own barely suppressed doubts. Peter was back after about five minutes, during which Luke had fumed about being late. He was in publisher mode now, with the smell of publicity in his nostrils, so Georgia sympathised. On his return, Peter had lost his temporary mask of frailty, however, and looked more like the ex-cop he was.

'Well, well.' He looked very smug, even for Peter.

'Did he tell you what you wanted to know?' Georgia asked politely.

'I didn't know what I wanted to know. But, thank you, yes.'

'Ancient retainer tells all,' Luke remarked. The barman must have been at least twenty-five.

'He came here after the new management took over,' Peter said. 'Didn't know anything about 362 Squadron or the hotel being requisitioned in World War Two.'

'So what *did* he know?'

Peter produced the rabbit he'd been carefully keeping in his hat. 'That there was an unsolved murder here in the 1970s.'

'Whose?' asked Luke.

'Where?' demanded Georgia simultaneously, thrown back

into turmoil. She had a terrible feeling that she knew the answer.

'Neither of these facts was known to my informant.'

'Nothing more?'

'Yes. He believes the victim had something to do with the hotel itself.'

'Staff?'

'Perhaps, but his use of words – which he could not explain when questioned – implied a somewhat closer relationship, the owners perhaps. Oh, and by the way . . .'

'Yes?' Georgia asked sharply when he broke off.

'He said he thought the murder happened somewhere in the grounds.'

With Woodring Manor Hotel on her mind, it seemed strange to Georgia to see Wickenham again half an hour later. She liked the look of it now, although perhaps it was a subjective judgement to imagine that the shadows hanging over it had now vanished. Perhaps it had always been like this, yet she and Peter had carried the same mental image of Wickenham as an unhappy village for ten years before its cause rose to the surface with the discovery of a skeleton.

Suppose in ten years' time the dell at Woodring Manor returned to haunt them? No Spitfires, no returning fire with fire, but perhaps a dragon in the shape of an unsolved murder. Ten years? Somehow she felt they wouldn't have to wait that long.

Two

The sounds of altercation reached Georgia's ears even before she had opened her father's front door. It was only the familiar argument of whether work or lunch came first – an argument that Margaret, his indispensable part-time shadow, rarely lost.

'Georgia, thank heavens!' came the cry. 'Kindly tell Margaret,' whose ears were presumably closed, 'that sandwiches can wait.'

'Not toasted ones,' Margaret said equably. Margaret came daily, her hours being a movable feast depending on who needed her most, Peter or her ailing husband. When Margaret found time for herself was one of those great mysteries of life. She had been a doctor's receptionist and had therefore had ample experience with stubborn patients. Peter of course did not see himself in that category. He saw it as an equal partnership between them – led by him.

'Margaret's right,' Georgia said. 'Anyway, I'm hungry, if I'm included.'

'You have no soul,' Peter said fiercely.

'And you no stamina,' Margaret rejoined. 'Have one of these, Georgia, and I'll make some more,' she said as she passed en route to the kitchen. Georgia advanced on both father and sandwiches.

'What's so urgent?' she asked.

'The case.' Peter condescended to pick up a square of toasted cheese and half a tomato.

'Case?' she asked guardedly, suspecting where this was

17

going. She and her father had adjoining terraced cottages in Haden Shaw's main street, and she had therefore been aware that Peter had been suspiciously quiet for several days. 'Nothing becomes a case until there's something to investigate.'

'Unsolved murder. That's enough, surely. And, Georgia, I'm sure I know now who the victim at Woodring Manor was.'

She had fully expected he would have despatched her forthwith to the Maidstone reference library to check the local newspapers for the whole of the 1970s, and had been surprised to receive no such summons. However, it was too much to hope that he'd have forgotten. Despite herself, her own curiosity was roused. A quarrel between staff? A guest at the hotel? A lovers' tiff? An unsolved murder was somewhat harder to track down than a solved one, which would have an ensuing trial, but Peter, it seemed, had already done so.

'It was fully covered in *The Times*,' he said.

Was it indeed? That must mean there was quite a story attached. Her curiosity grew. 'Who was it?'

'Patrick Fairfax.' Peter sat back complacently, obviously awaiting her cry 'of course'.

'*Who?*'

Peter sighed. 'I suppose it's my age. Growing up in the Fifties, I had an overdose of the derring-do of Spitfire pilots.'

A jolt ran through her. 'Spitfires?' she asked guardedly. Five shadowy elderly men marched through her mind.

'Correct. Patrick Fairfax, DSO, DFC. Thought to have narrowly missed the VC. Flew hard, played hard during the war. Anonymous author of *This Life, This Death* in 1942, reprinted under his name countless times after the war. Popular in society. Found murdered one evening at Woodring Manor in 1975.'

'In May?' Each step led onwards to the unwelcome truth.

'Correct again, Georgia. Saturday the tenth. Shot after a reunion. I don't need to tell you which squadron.'

'Or which reunion. 362.' Now Peter had put him in context, she realized she *had* heard of Patrick Fairfax. Not quite in the Johnnie Johnson or Bader league, but up there. And she had even read *This Life, This Death*, years ago. It was a thoughtful and moving, even poetic, memoir of a Battle of Britain pilot, rivalling Richard Hillary's *The Last Enemy* in its time. 'Wasn't there a film?'

'*Shooting for the Stars*,' Margaret supplied helpfully as she shot in with more toasted sandwiches.

'That's it,' Peter said triumphantly as Margaret scooped up the empty dish and departed. 'The obituary mentioned it, but implied it was pretty feeble. Probably the cat's whiskers when it was made in the Fifties.'

Georgia trawled through her memory, since she had a liking for old films. She had been born well after the days of double feature programmes at the cinemas, but Peter had indoctrinated her into the satisfaction of the really bad B films, usually simply programme ballast for the A league.

'It was more of a romance than a war film, I think.' It was beginning to come back to her. 'Lovers parted by war. She was a WAAF. Any mention of that in the obituary?'

'No, but he had a wife and family by that time.'

As far as she could recall, the romance was doomed through one of those tragic twists of fate once so popular in dramas like Ivor Novello's *The Dancing Years*, and the Cary Grant film *An Affair to Remember*.

'I've found a picture of Fairfax in his heyday in one of Dad's old books,' Peter said. 'Look.' He found the photo and pushed the book over to her. It was a drawing in profile, not a photograph. Light-coloured hair, classical features, the subject looking not at the artist but out into an unknown future. A scarf at his neck – very much the fighter pilot. Put him in today's casual gear, however, and this face would be gracing many a country pub at weekends.

'Any clues on why the death was unsolved?'

'Not yet. Give me time.'

'Or on who the suspects were?' No prizes for guessing here. 'Any suspicion of suicide?'

'Pass on the latter. On the former, someone was taken in for questioning. Not named. A more delicate age.'

'Any hints on motive?'

'No. *The Times* has no more to say after the memorial service was covered. The top brass of the RAF attended that, plus half of London society, actors, actresses, aviation darlings, former pilots.'

'If the murder was after the reunion, they must have been questioned, so—'

'We have a way in, of a sort,' Peter finished for her.

'But what about the murder's alleged connection with the hotel?'

'Sorry, I forgot to tell you. Patrick Fairfax owned it together with Matthew Jones and a third partner.'

Her stomach seemed to be churning, and it wasn't the sandwiches' fault. She and Peter were getting perilously close to the point of no return from it becoming a Marsh & Daughter case, and *still* all her hackles were warning her to run like hell. 'His name didn't come up at the reunion last weekend.'

'How would we know? We weren't with them all the time.'

'You'd think with someone so famous in their ranks they would have done some name-dropping,' she continued obstinately. 'Especially since they were happy to tell us Matt Jones was the other owner.'

'You're making too much of it,' Peter said – reasonably, she admitted. 'Besides, the hotel wasn't Fairfax's sole concern, apparently. His obituary said he also ran something called the Wormshill Aviation Club, and that was his main love. The hotel only received a passing mention, so perhaps he was a sleeping partner. Maybe he put up the money and let Matthew Jones run it.'

20

'You're hooked, aren't you?' she asked in trepidation.

'I must admit I find it tempting. Such a high-profile case, unsolved – and that dell.'

'If that *was* where he was killed.'

He grinned at her. 'Let's find out.'

'I'm surprised you haven't done so already.'

'I would have done if *some* people –' He raised his voice meaningfully as they heard Margaret's footsteps in the passageway on her way home – 'hadn't insisted on interrupting me.' The bang of the front door was the culprit's only response.

Georgia scribbled her signature on the courier's clipboard, a procedure she'd carried out several times since last Wednesday, and took the parcel in to Peter. He seized on it eagerly, tearing at the sticky tape and paper like a child with a birthday present. Oh well, she'd probably do the same, Georgia conceded. It was merely the knowledge that this must be to do with Patrick Fairfax that still made her want to ignore it.

'Excellent,' Peter proclaimed, gazing with admiration at a scruffy second-hand jacketless book. She leaned over his shoulder to look at the title page. *Dancing the Skies: The Life of Wing Commander Patrick Fairfax, DSO, DFC* by Jack Hardcastle. Did that, she immediately wondered, explain the reading of the Magee poem at the reunion they had gatecrashed? It might well do. A code between the survivors to read the poem in Fairfax's honour rather than just toast the name. Although that, Georgia told herself firmly, is hypothesis ahead of the facts.

'Does it cover his death?' she asked.

'Probably. It was published in 1977. It's his life that might be more interesting, however, considering his murder remains unsolved. I had the devil's own job to get this. It's the only biography of him. *This Life, This Death*, because of the time it was first published with wartime restrictions, is short on hard fact. I read it yesterday.'

21

'Didn't he write a full biography later? I thought that was usual for pilots.'

'Not all. Some preferred to forget all about the war, rather than dredge up old memories.'

'Even if there's a distinguished career involved?' Georgia had been doing some internet research of her own, and Patrick Fairfax had had an interesting career after the Battle of Britain. An injury had called a temporary halt to operational flying, leading to a short spell of instructing – maybe that's when he wrote *This Life, This Death*. Then he took command of 348 Squadron at Tangmere; he was shot down over France while on a delightfully named Rhubarb sortie, evaded discovery successfully and returned to England from Gibraltar having crossed the Pyrenees. He became a wing commander up north, then joined the Air Ministry for D-Day planning. Post-war he ran the Wormshill Aviation Club on the North Downs near Sittingbourne, which provided not only social weekend flying, but attracted aerobatic displays and also mounted air shows.

'Success had its cost in the war. Writing about it afterwards might not have been easy,' Peter replied.

'Then why did he attend squadron reunions to chew it all over?'

Peter frowned while he thought this through. 'Reunions with shared memories can be just for that reason only. No need to speak. They all knew what happened. Anyway, for whatever reason, Fairfax didn't write another book.'

'So who is, or was, Jack Hardcastle?'

'He's an aviation historian. He wrote the squadron history *Silvered Wings* – yet another Magee quote, you see. That was published in the 1980s, and he's a string of other books to his name now. No more about 362 though. Still, these should keep us busy for a while for background material.'

'Us?' She felt a deep foreboding.

'Yes.' He eyed her keenly. 'You don't agree?'

'I didn't like that dell,' she stalled. 'I admit it's getting easier now that we know about Fairfax, but we still,' she reminded him, 'don't know for certain that the dell has anything to do with Fairfax's murder. All we know is that the body was found "in the grounds".'

'Ah. Did I tell you that Mike is looking in this afternoon?'

Mike was Peter's former sergeant during his time at Kent Police's Stour Area, and was now a highly rated DCI. He'd had a spell away with what had been the National Crime Squad, now the Serious Organised Crime Agency, and so they hadn't seen him for a while.

'Social visit?' Of course it wasn't. Peter was after what he described as co-operation and Mike called arm-twisting.

'Mike was in Downs Area before he came to Stour. Could be helpful.'

Mike always was, thank goodness, despite his protests at Peter's flagrant disregard of what was, and what was not, possible under protocol and police regulations. If he and Margaret united in protest, they could form an effective trade union in Peter's life.

Mike was almost as laidback as Luke. He had one of those poker faces that rarely moved without thought behind it. On the rare occasions she saw him with his wife Helen and young family he still seemed unbending, though far from unreceptive. The poker face was useful nowadays because he could bounce Peter's more outrageous requests back as implacably as a squash ball by the wall.

Mike duly arrived halfway through the afternoon, and drank his tea while Peter talked. 'I remember,' he said at last.

'You can't have been there in 1975, Mike,' Georgia said incredulously. 'You'd only have been a child.'

'Right, but the case was still around. It wasn't finally closed until around the time I joined in the Eighties, as a raw PC.'

Peter pounced. '*How* was it still around?'

Mike considered. 'Frustration that they had to close the file unsolved.'

'Is that because they knew who did it but couldn't get evidence?'

'Can't say. Too long ago. All I know is it set me reading up on the war stuff. I used to go up to the Malling airfield and imagine it as it was in the Battle of Britain. The scrambles, the Luftwaffe raids on the airfields, the politics going on at high level and the pilots like Fairfax at the sharp end of them. Fascinating stuff. It seemed too bad for Fairfax – even to me coming in at the tail end of the case – to have survived all the Luftwaffe threw at him only to meet his death by a sneaky murder years later. It made our failure to solve the case seem even worse.'

'You don't recall who the chief suspect was?'

'Nope.'

Peter snorted in disgust. 'You can do better than that, Mike.'

'No, I can't.' He paused. 'But I know a chap who can.'

'And he is?' Peter's eyes gleamed. This was, Georgia knew, what he had expected all along, and Mike knew it full well. No gratitude would be expressed, although to be fair it was understood between them.

'The investigating officer was DI Wilson. Died in harness in the nineties. His sergeant on the case was Chris Manners. Retired now, living down in Sussex somewhere. I can find out for you.'

Peter beamed. 'And the case files . . .?'

'You'll be lucky,' Mike said sourly. 'You'll need the usual channels for those and to have plenty of reason for asking me.'

They had none, of course. Not yet. Georgia caught herself. Not yet? To her horror, she realized that she had just acknowledged that this case was in their sights.

* * *

'Are you coming, Georgia?' Peter asked when Mike reported back with Manners' contact details and he had duly called him.

Georgia considered this. The fewer people at an interview the better, which is why she and Peter usually did them singly. In this case, however, she was undecided. As an ex-policeman himself, Peter might be better alone with him, and yet instinct told her she wanted to be there – if only to face her own reluctance over this case.

Christopher Manners lived in Burwash, near the Sussex/Kent border. The village's chief claim to fame, she remembered, was that Rudyard Kipling had lived just outside it at Bateman's, now a National Trust property. Having visited Bateman's, she knew the village and liked its wide main street lined with cottages. Picture postcard it might look, but this was a working village, not a dormitory. They found Christopher Manners' cottage in a side street, and she was slightly surprised, when he ushered them into his study, to see a bookcase full of Kipling's works. He hadn't seemed the Empire and Raj type when he greeted them. This was stupid of her, she realized. How could one tell a *type*? One only had stereotypes – in this case of a tall, upright, moustachioed, fierce-eyed throwback. Christopher Manners wasn't. He was mild-mannered, grey-haired, of medium height, distinctly tubby and completely unthreatening – as many a villain must have thought to his cost in the past. His eye was remarkably keen as he summed them up.

'Interesting man, Kipling,' Christopher commented, seeing Georgia's eyes straying to the bookcase. 'You think you've got him pigeon-holed as a stuffy old gent, and then you discover he loved fast cars and had to flee the US because of domestic trouble with his in-laws. Agatha Christie, please step forward.'

'Did you pigeon-hole Patrick Fairfax?' she asked, amused that he did his own stereotyping. What had he placed her as? A merry widow? Single-minded spinster? Dedicated divorcée?

'Had to. He was dead when I saw him. He more or less pigeon-holed himself anyway.'

'How?' Peter asked.

'There were so many people breathing over our shoulders because of his chums in high places that we had the impression he was heading up to St Peter for sainthood.'

'And was he? You must have talked to a lot of his colleagues and friends.'

'Universal verdict favourable. No stones left unturned. A few grubs crawled out, but nothing survived scrutiny.'

'No serious suspects?' Georgia asked. 'Or was it more a suggestion of a random death by stranger, for theft or drunken brawl or whatever?'

'What's your interest in it?' Christopher asked bluntly. 'It's for one of your books, I suppose. Well, good luck to you. I mean that. You should know well enough, Peter, that if the Kent Police couldn't track the villain down, there's not much hope you can do so now. I wish you could. I'd like a hand in nailing the bastard.'

'Ah. Any particular bastard?' Peter enquired.

Christopher grinned at being caught out. 'There was only one motive suggested, and only one person attached to it. Matthew Jones, co-owner of the hotel. We hauled him in and grilled him like a dodgy sardine. Got nowhere.'

'Was it a personal motive?' Georgia asked.

'Money. That can be personal enough. So far as I remember, the hotel had Fairfax's flair invested in it, but Jones' money, with some input from another investor. Fairfax was a nice chap, no doubt about that. Well liked, even by Jones. But he didn't handle cash too well. He was pouring his own money into his aviation club and lavishing free hospitality for its members at the hotel. Both businesses were going down the drain and Matt with it, from what we could gather. Fairfax more or less treated the hotel as a social centre for the club – free drinks, free meals, free beds. That tended to drive away regular custom and bingo – no trade

26

left. The debts had mounted to the point where the receiver was about to be brought in, and Jones wanted Fairfax out of it, as his only chance of running things his way. He was the anxious type – with reason.'

'Do anxious types see murder as a way out of their problems?' Peter asked.

'I wouldn't have thought so in this case, but there was some other evidence so far as I can recall. Wishy-washy alibi, trace evidence, all explainable but it mounted up. In the end we had to let him go. For all his being the anxious type, he was a pretty determined sort of fellow, and we still had our doubts. After all, he was the only one of them left at the hotel. The others had gone.'

Gone? Georgia's hopes began to rise. 'The others being those at the squadron reunion?' she asked.

'Right. The place had been crawling with pilots earlier, plus one or two of Fairfax's aviation club cronies, but they all left in the late afternoon, a couple of hours before Fairfax was shot.'

'Were you first on the scene?' Peter asked.

'I was. Came with a PC, and when we saw what we had, we summoned the whole caboodle.'

'Can you show me where the body was? I've made a plan of the garden.' Peter handed that and a biro to him.

'No problem.' Christopher glanced at it, and made a mark. Georgia was once more stiff with tension; she could guess all too well where it was. 'A sort of valley garden. A rockery of sorts. It was covered in bluebells – and blood by the time the body had joined it. Fairfax had a bullet in his chest.'

'Gun?'

'None found by the body. I've been thinking about this a lot since you rang, and I'm pretty sure it was a Webley. It seemed to have been Fairfax's own. A lot of them never got handed in after the war. He kept it in the hotel along with his uniform, medals and other bits and bobs from the other pilots. He made a sort of Battle of Britain corner down in the basement bar.'

So that was that. The bluebell valley and the Hell's Bells Club, both leading straight back to the death of Patrick Fairfax. No wonder that dell was crying out so loudly to them.

'Fairfax was genuinely popular,' Christopher continued. 'It wasn't just lip service paid to him after his death. We talked to everyone we could root out, and that was the unanimous verdict.'

'Who found the body?' Georgia forced herself to ask. Even though most of the pilots at least seemed to be ruled out, their phantom presence was still lurking in her mind.

'One of the waiters, I think, out for an illicit fag or shag – sorry, can't remember which.'

'I presume the other pilots at the reunion were among those you interviewed?' Peter said.

'Every man jack of them.'

'How many was that?'

'Half a dozen or so. Maybe more. We didn't dig out much.'

'Any woman trouble?' Peter asked.

'Fairfax seemed happily married with grown-up kids. If there was a floozy we never rooted her out, even though he had a reputation for being a ladies' man.'

'If the film about him was based on fact, there was a previous serious girlfriend in the war,' Georgia pointed out.

'Then she waited a hell of a long time to get her revenge if he dumped her.'

She laughed. 'Were the wives there?' She remembered Peter's comment.

'Strictly stag.' Christopher hesitated. 'Actually, having said that there was no whisper of a floozy, I have a vague memory of a suggestion he had a thing going with one of the other pilots' wives. There'd been some kind of a spat at the reunion, and it might have been over that. Sorry, can't remember.'

Something to check into anyway. She made a note.

'What about the shots?' Peter asked. 'Were they heard in the hotel?'

'It was a Saturday evening. There was pop music blaring out for the younger punters.'

'And no one wandering round the gardens?'

'Not that I recall. It was a chilly night. I remember shivering while we waited for the doc and photographers. I do recall thinking a remote rockery garden was an odd place to come except with one's nearest and dearest. You wouldn't walk into that place with an enemy. It was almost dark when the body was found, and it was reckoned Fairfax had been dead an hour or two, but even so the light wouldn't have been too good for a bracing pre-dinner walk.'

'Any chance of a peek at the case files?' Peter asked hopefully.

'They're probably still around, since it was a high-profile case.' Christopher grinned, obviously reading their thoughts exactly. 'They'll need new info first.'

'Georgia?' Luke looked up in surprise as she walked into his general office in South Malling. She had come straight from Burwash, and unsurprisingly found Luke in conference with Sally Hobhurst, his invaluable assistant.

'Sorry. I know you don't need authors poking their noses in.'

'Not if you want to know your sales figures.'

There were piles of books everywhere, in boxes straight from the printers, on shelves, on chairs. Luke's list consisted not just of Marsh & Daughter's true crime series, but of two others: one military, the other local history and guide books. Seeing the ordered disorder of Frost Books renewed her doubts about the practicalities of his moving further towards them in Haden Shaw as he had planned to do. Luke not only had his own comfortable home here, but ran his business complete with his staff of three, two women and a young man, each of whom seemed irreplaceable to her. Each had an area of responsibility but they could all pick up each other's jobs when needed. How could she encourage Luke to upset this skilful arrangement to move lock, stock and many barrels to be nearer to her and Peter?

'Does the name Jack Hardcastle mean anything to you?' she asked after he'd ushered her into his tiny snuggery of a private office.

'Should do. I publish him.'

'You're joking.'

'I never joke about business,' he replied with dignity.

'He wrote the 362 Squadron history.'

'Not for me. In 2001 he did a guide to the sites where the flying bombs fell during World War Two.'

'So you know where he lives?'

'Of course. I can't hand over his address, but I'll contact him for you.' He looked at her more closely. 'Have some tea. You look as if you need it. Did you miss lunch?'

'I had a bar snack.'

'Don't tell me. At Woodring Manor Hotel.'

'How did you guess?'

'By your white face. See any ghosts, did you?'

'Plenty. Someone walked over my grave.' She grimaced. 'That's a stupid phrase, isn't it? In fact it was me walking over Patrick Fairfax's.' She hadn't yet told Luke about Peter's discovery, and until they had reached a firm decision she didn't want to, so how come she was blurting out his name? She could have kicked herself.

'The Battle of Britain pilot?' he asked with interest. 'Don't tell me. That isn't the unsolved murder, is it?'

'Yes.' Nothing she could do now. 'But before you whip out a contract let me tell you it isn't certain yet that we'll do it as our next book. We need to get further along.'

He pulled out a drawer, selected a new contract form and

waved it in front of her face. 'Take it, take it now. Fill in your own figures.'

That made her laugh. 'Sorry. I shouldn't be talking to you about Marsh & Daughter's professional wrangles.'

'Wrangles? You two wouldn't know a real wrangle if you met one in the street. You're the only partnership I've run across that actually *works*.'

'So I thought.' Georgia felt highly gratified 'Until we met this case.'

'What's the problem?'

'If I knew it wouldn't be one. I just can't get a mental grip on it, even though everything that Peter is turning up – plus what we were told this morning by the investigating police sergeant at the time – suggests there should be something to investigate.' This was as far as she'd go. No mention of the dell. He might remember how it had affected her.

'Perhaps you're prejudiced,' Luke replied matter-of-factly. 'That valley put you off for some reason, so you can't see the case as a justifiable one to investigate. You want to know why not? It's not the case of Patrick Fairfax that's upsetting you; it's the background behind it. The Battle of Britain.'

'Perhaps that's it.' Stop right there, Luke, she thought. She wasn't ready to dig deeper.

He hesitated. 'It's not my field, but perhaps it's too broad for you.'

'What on earth do you mean?'

He put his arm round her. 'Normally you begin a case with an individual, don't you? At the most, with a family. That's your starting point: Ada Proctor, Fanny Star . . . That gives you the handle on the situation, which leads onwards into the broader field with your hand still on the tiller.'

'And so?' She felt the prickle of self-defence rising in case he should come too near the truth – whatever that might be – and she would have to acknowledge it.

'And so here you don't. Even if the same factor is present,

31

in that Patrick Fairfax was killed by someone who hated him – jealous wife, jealous husband, the usual suspects – you can't see that. You're seeing him through the squadron's eyes because that's how you first approached it. Those five old men and what they represent. You're trying to grapple with a huge canvas full of death, painted at a time when young men like Fairfax were being shot out of the sky daily on both sides. That was war – and because you've seen the squadron survivors gathered years later, heard about the Hell's Bells Club and Hell's Corner, you're seeing Fairfax's death through that perspective, even though his murder was thirty years later. Beside the enormity of the numbers of dead brought about by war, you can't reach through in your imagination to touch the core of Fairfax. One man, one corpse, beside the loss of so many.'

'Yes.' Yes, she thought dully. That could be it. In the basement of that hotel, in the dell, and because of those five men, the hotel reeked for her of the Second World War, not the 1970s. If she could clear her mind and see them as they had been thirty-five years after the Battle of Britain, the case would be clearer. It would be *possible*.

She put her arms around Luke and kissed him in gratitude.

'Georgia,' he said after a moment. 'I had this in the post today.' He picked up a leaflet from his desk. It was an estate agent's circular about an old property near Haden Shaw. She hardly took in what and where it was. Only what it meant. 'Shall we go for it?' he asked.

'Yes!'

Three

'This one's yours,' Peter had told her. 'You can drop me off at Woodring Manor Hotel, and I'll wait for you there.'

'Thank *you*,' Georgia muttered as she collected her laptop and notebooks. She supposed it was fair enough that she should be the one to tackle Jack Hardcastle, since it was she who was dragging her heels over Patrick Fairfax. She had read *This Life, This Death* and *Dancing the Skies* but she still felt dissatisfied. She needed to get a firmer grip on the man himself. She could tell that her father was already hooked. Even though he'd been living with this case for only two and a half weeks, computer files were ready for the off, source lists were organized, and his pride and joy – the Suspects Anonymous software created for them by her cousin Charlie Bone – was raring to go. Peter had already set up the 362 Squadron pilots as participants – somewhat prematurely in her view. Factual details of timings, movements and motives could all be fed in, with each participant, whose icons were jovially named the 'Burglar Bills', complete with striped jersey and bag of swag, ready to move at the touch of the mouse. It was an apparently frivolous tool for a serious purpose, and Georgia only hoped the day would produce good data for it.

Jack Hardcastle lived in Eynsford, a Kentish village in the Darenth valley. It was still, if one hunted it down amid the super highways, an attractive village set in rolling country-side. After an inadvertent detour to Brand's Hatch, a favourite haunt of Peter's despite his accident, she found Bramley House set back on the outskirts of the village, in the direction of Lullingstone Castle and the famous Roman villa. Roman villas had once been spread all along this valley and she contemplated the fact that beneath her feet somewhere, their whereabouts probably noted in some dusty Victorian file, they or their ruins still existed. Rather like the dell was the unwelcome follow-up to this thought. What secrets lay hidden there beneath its blue spring covering? And did that mean she was duty-bound to find out? If so, to whom? To the unknown, to Peter, to Luke – or to herself? She had a nasty feeling it was the latter.

She brought her thoughts firmly back to Patrick Fairfax. Talking to Jack Hardcastle might be the deciding factor as to whether they should continue with this case.

As she opened the gate she saw someone bending down weeding behind the bordering hedge. In gardening smock and corduroy trousers, Mrs Hardcastle – as presumably she was – stood up welcomingly as Georgia entered. She liked the look of this garden. It was already looking promising for the year ahead with early roses in flower, plenty of spring flowers, and no gnomes or classically undraped stone ladies. Instead beautifully carved wooden aircraft – a Spitfire and a Hurricane, as she could now recognize – flew either side of the door, both well secured she noted. There was a bench too, and no ordinary one. It was a huge seat shaped into two Spitfire cockpits (or so she guessed) side by side. She tried hard to admire it, but failed.

Mrs Hardcastle must have seen her gazing at it because she laughed. 'I learned to live with it long ago. I'm Susan Hardcastle, you must be Georgia Marsh.'

As she spoke the front door opened, and Jack himself came out to greet her.

'Come into the hangar,' he said genially. Fortunately this hangar resembled an orthodox study, with workmanlike computer, box files and books, books, *books*. Georgia felt she could relate to this room – and, she thought cautiously, to Jack. He was a well-built and hearty man and looked to be in his early sixties.

'Are you a World War Two specialist or a general aviation historian?' she asked as he waved her to an ancient leather armchair.

'Bury my heart at Wounded Knee as they say, or in my case in the two world wars. Unfortunately man rarely lives by only doing what he wants so I've a broader range by now. Tell me to scramble and I'm off any runway in search of a cheque.'

'But your heart flies with 362 Squadron?'

He considered this as Susan brought coffee in. 'Thanks, love. Yes and no, Georgia. Kent in World War Two would be more exact.'

'Hell's Corner itself. Isn't that what the Germans called it?'

'Hell for both sides,' he said. 'The RAF went through hell as well as the Germans. So did the civilian population here. Think of it. It not only had the Battle of Britain waged over its head, plus the problems and the threat of invasion, but it went through pretty well non-stop bombing after that, including a raid on Canterbury. Then it was hit by the doodle-bugs – the V1 flying bombs – and the V2 rockets. It was jolly good of the powers that be to deceive the Germans into shortening the range of the flying bombs, but they had to fall somewhere, so the south-east of London and Kent copped it instead. Some of them fell in the countryside with luck, but a lot more didn't. Ever seen a map of where they fell?'

'No.' She peered curiously at the framed map hung on the one wall not dedicated to bookshelves and books. It was thickly speckled with black dots indicating the sites.

'And this map doesn't even show all of Kent. It stops at Dartford. Further towards London they were falling like conkers in a high wind. The map would have been solid with black dots if it had stretched as far as the county border.'

'Were you in Kent during the war?'

'I'm not competing with Methuselah yet,' he grinned. 'I was a babe in arms when the flying bombs fell in 1944 and '45. My father was in the RAF, that's why I got interested.'

'He survived the war?' Georgia decided she liked Jack Hardcastle. Hearty men weren't usually her type, but he exuded a genuine warmth.

'Yes. Never talked about it. Not a word. That's what made me curious.' He paused. 'Just like you and Patrick Fairfax. Your father said on the phone that you were thinking of his murder as a subject for one of your books.'

'We're undecided,' she said truthfully. 'From the little we know at present, it could just be a blind alley, if for instance he was killed without reason by a passing maniac.'

'I don't think you need go up that road. The disappearance of the gun would rule that out.'

A sharp man too, Georgia realized.

'I've read a couple of your books,' he continued. 'I thought they were good. What is it about Fairfax that attracts you as a subject?'

Attracts? That was hardly the word, so far as she was concerned. She sought for an answer and remembered Mike's comment. 'The fact he did so much during the war only to die in an apparently senseless murder.'

'How much do you know about him?' He shot the question at her abruptly.

Was it an odd one? No, not in the circumstances, she decided. 'We've read your biography and squadron history, of course, together with *This Life, This Death*, plus what the internet turned up, which is quite a lot. We always cover the secondary sources first, before talking to friends and family, so that we already have a pretty good idea of the background and of whether we're going ahead.'

'And what decides that?'

She was being tested, so nothing but the truth was needed here. 'We never know until it happens. How do you decide what book to write next?'

He chuckled. 'When I see a hole in the market I can fill.'

'With us, it's probably something that shouts so loudly to us that we can't ignore it. I suppose that boils down to the same thing.' Was that true, she wondered. The dell was still shouting almost too loudly and yet she longed for a chance to ignore it.

'And how does Fairfax's death fit with that?'

'He narrowly missed the VC, he wrote a remarkable book and was clearly an outstanding personality.' She was trotting out the obvious, but what else was there at present? 'Would you agree with that? You must have known him to write his biography after his death.'

'I only met him a few times. I was an insurance agent until I took up writing full time. Covered his club and the hotel in fact.'

'You liked him?' She thought she sensed reservations here, but she must have been wrong because he answered immediately.

'Everyone liked Patrick. He was the happy-go-lucky sort. Gung-ho. Up boys and at 'em. Dashed into one battle with his section without a moment's doubt. He was a pain in the neck as a business partner for Matt Jones, but as a man of the air, first class.'

'Were you at the reunion the day he was killed?'

'No. That reunion's a closed shop, restricted to Woodring Manor pilots, who were there in the Battle of Britain. I go to the general squadron reunions in London. After all, important though it was, that battle was only a part of the air war. The squadron arrived in mid July and flew out at the end of October when 66 Squadron came in from Gravesend. There were another four and a half years of the war still to go then.'

So Luke had been right about its being *part* of a reunion.

'There must have been more survivors from the squadron than the five we met, who were Matt Jones, Bill Dane, Harry Williams, Jan Molkar and Robert McNee.' It was hard to think of the quintet individually. Jack's phrase 'Woodring Manor pilots' was an odd description, she thought, or perhaps she was seeing innuendoes where none existed.

'Plenty more, but not from the Battle of Britain. Between July and October the squadron lost fifteen, shot down or crashed. The CO, Arthur Cox, was one of them. He was killed towards the end of the battle in October.'

'I thought it ended on September fifteenth?'

'That was the watershed, and after that the enemy postponed the invasion *sine die* and decided to concentrate on bombing Britain into submission, so the fighters were then chiefly attacking bomber escorts. Some of the novice pilots only lasted a day during the battle. They'd arrive eager to blow the enemy to smithereens and be picked off like baby chicks by a fox. Others died later in the war. Of those who survived, some of them have obviously died since, and some wanted out the minute they were released from the force. You can understand that point of view.'

'Yes.' Peter's father had, and so apparently had Jack's.

'For instance, Alan Purcell has lived abroad since the war ended. Won't talk about it at all. No use asking him.'

'Was he a Woodring Manor pilot? What does that imply anyway? Just those who were accommodated there?'

She must have passed another test because he looked at her with keen interest. 'The unspoken subject, Georgia. Yes, Purcell was flying officer rank during the battle. Woodring Manor was for commissioned officers only. They'd usually been through the proper channels – public school, university, university training corps, etcetera – but there were non-commissioned pilots as well, those who had the ability but not the background. Where they drank at night and what medals they were awarded had nothing to do with achievement, but everything to do with rank. Some of the best pilots in the battle were sergeants – Don Kingaby of 92 Squadron for example.'

She had difficulty coping with this. 'You mean, officers and NCOs deliberately didn't mix in the evenings even though they flew during the day?'

'Not deliberately. The Blitzkrieg broke out in May, Dunkirk followed at the end of the month, and after that invasion was obviously imminent and that meant an air battle first. The Air Ministry decided no one below NCO rank should fly – so a lot of airmen got instant promotion to sergeant or warrant officer. Good news for them because their pay went up, but they still had their own mess. That system couldn't be changed overnight.'

'How many NCO pilots were there in 362 at the time?' It seemed an innocent question, even though it was a side alley so far as Patrick Fairfax's death in 1975 was concerned. Nevertheless she sensed Jack wasn't eager to answer. Could he too be class-orientated?

'Four,' he answered. 'None of them around the manor in 1975, of course.' A pause. 'What did you make of the Famous Five you met at Woodring? Are you thinking of them as potential murderers?' This too seemed a casual question, but by now she suspected Jack never asked anything without reason.

'Too early to say,' she said just as casually. 'They'd have been in their fifties in 1975, and at least it has to be considered. It seems unlikely, since they'd mostly left by the time of the murder. As to what I thought of them, Matthew Jones seems very vague now. Not Alzheimer's exactly, but distanced. Shut up in his own worries. Was he always like that?'

'No. He used to be as sharp as a needle. He was commander of A Flight from August onwards. A real mother hen looking after his lads. Took it hard when he lost one – which was often. Went on to command a squadron in Malta, which was no sinecure either. He ended the war as a wing commander, like Fairfax. Came out, went into the family business, raked up the cash to buy the hotel, which was going for a song after the war, and then made his mistake. Patrick Fairfax suggested he joined him and Matthew agreed. Bonhomie and big names were what Patrick did, and did it well. I don't see Matt as the sort to murder his way out of a difficulty though.'

'And Bill Dane? He seemed the liveliest of the five.'

'Right. DFC. Daz Dane they call him. Know why? Daz for Dazzle. He was the one with attitude, the snazzy scarves, the poise, the lovable eccentric, the squadron madcap. He was in A Flight, went on to become a brilliant Wingco, pushed himself too hard, burnt out early in '45. Took orders not long after the war. Married a bishop's daughter called Alice. Settled down to pastoral life in Suffolk.'

'Not capable of murder in 1975 then?'

'Who knows? He'd need a damned strong motive though, don't you think?'

Even though she was aware he was watching her closely, she agreed. After all, Daz Dane had chosen the path of peace. 'Harry Williams?'

'Porgie Williams. Also A Flight. An eye for the girls. Married a model after the war and I guess only he and his missus know whether the eye closed then or not. In the war he'd chase anything in a skirt with the same energy he put into shooting down the enemy during the day. He won a DFC too. Continued active operations till he crashed, hurt his back, and thereafter made life miserable for his superiors as an instructor. After the war he went into business, filed for bankruptcy, was bailed out by Matt and from then on ran a pub with great success. Can't see any reason he'd have wanted Patrick out of the way.'

'And Bob McNee?'

'The steady one. B Flight commander in the battle and much respected. Steady career upwards, stayed in RAF after the war, then came out with his pension and became a free-lance cartoonist. Again, unlikely to have been moved to murder.'

'And the last?'

'Jan Molkar's interesting. He was in B Flight though he generally flew with Blue Section, not like Patrick who led Red Section. He's a Flemish Belgian. His wife and child were caught in Rotterdam when the Blitzkrieg broke out, and were wiped out in the bombing. Jan made sure he didn't go down when Belgium fell to the Germans, got himself over here, and dedicated himself seriously to winning the war single-handed. He also got seriously drunk every evening, according to the others. Stayed in Britain after the war and became a history teacher. If he decided Patrick had to go for some reason, he's the most likely to have had the stomach for it. As for motive – no idea. He eventually married again. A jolly English lady called Rosemary.'

'In your biography you wrote that it was a complete mystery as to how Patrick Fairfax died, but I imagine you had your own ideas?'

'If the police couldn't discover who did it, how could I?' Jack answered with ease.

She wasn't going to let him off the hook. 'You must have heard the rumours at the time. You were interviewing them all for the biography not that long after he died, and you covered his death in it. There must be more that you didn't put into print. All the rumours and so forth.'

'They all said they had no idea about who could have done it,' he threw back at her sharply, then added, 'They would, of course.'

'Were they protecting Matthew Jones?'

'I don't know.' Jack must have read her expression correctly. 'I really don't, Georgia. The Famous Five were there on the day, together with two others who've since died. Any one of them might physically, even emotionally, have been able to shoot him. They'd all have known that

41

gun was there. But it was, and still is, a tight-knit circle. Unless you can break through the magic ring that binds them, you won't get any further, Georgia. And to break it you need at least an inkling of why Fairfax was killed.'

'Did *you* break through it?' She realized he was right. It explained why she thought of them as a group, a quintet, and not as five individuals. They moved as one, they thought as one.

'Let's say I've broken through the outer ring. No one gets through the inner one.' He spoke almost as if in challenge. And perhaps, she thought, that was working.

'You really don't have any suspicions? That's hard to believe.'

'Not that I could find then.'

'And now?' She picked up on his hesitation. 'I was told, for instance, that he might have been having an affair with one of the pilots' wives.'

'If so, I never heard it.' He played fair with her, even though he looked annoyed. 'Look, whatever I said wouldn't even be rumour, not even theories, only a question mark. You need to talk to his family.'

'I'd like to. Is his wife still alive?'

'I gather so. I'd have heard if not. Jean Fairfax was fiercely flanked by their kids, a son and a daughter, at the time of the murder. Not that she needed much protection; she's the formidable sort. The son went into the RAF too.'

'Didn't he want to write his father's biography?'

'No. He said his father had been about to write another book himself, and now he, the son, was too busy flying Harriers to take the job over. He gave me access to Patrick's own notes, though.'

'I presume that the family were out of it so far as causing his death is concerned, since Patrick was killed at Woodring Manor . . .'

'Yes. Far more likely to have been some row he had with someone at the aviation club or one of his many creditors.

Nothing came to light though, apart from poor Matt's possible motive. I didn't dig that deep, since Fairfax's death wasn't my main point of interest. I just followed the police line: unsolved.'

Curiously weak, she thought, since Jack didn't seem the sort to *follow* anyone. She decided to tackle her own inexplicable deep-rooted fear. 'Could the motive have been rooted in the wartime?'

'Everything's rooted in the past. Nothing's ever buried completely, Georgia. It lives on within.' He was definitely evasive now, and she had to force herself onwards.

'Such as his wartime affair with a WAAF, if the film is to be believed.'

He looked distinctly wary. '*Shooting for the Stars*. Yes, I saw it.'

'Did you find out if it was based on truth?'

'Don't think I'm hedging,' he replied promptly enough, 'but you have to understand that during the war pilots had to drink and play hard to get over what was happening to them. In the Battle of Britain they could be scrambled several times a day to fight swarms of Messerschmitts, not to mention the Heinkel and Dornier bombers. And coupled with that the airfields, including West Malling, were continually being bombed during August. They couldn't get the runways in working order again before the next lot of bombs arrived. Even if they did, once the aircraft were in the air they might not be able to get down again at their home field, and would have to land at any old strip they could. It was a hectic time. If I'd tried to track down every WAAF and barmaid who got kissed, the task would be endless. In the evening the pilots might go into Town Malling, that's what they called West Malling then, to the pubs or to other hotels around. Women weren't rare anywhere the pilots went. It's my belief that the WAAF in *Shooting for the Stars* was only a symbol to make the story realistic for the 1950s.'

Hedging was precisely what he was doing, and she wasn't going to let him off the hook. 'What about his actress girlfriend?'

'During the war?'

Still hedging. No doubt about it, Georgia thought. She'd soon squash that. 'You mentioned her in your biography.'

'It was merely a rumour.' He did not look happy.

'A rumour that must have had a name put to it.'

'Tell her, Jack,' Susan intervened calmly, as she came in to clear the empty cups.

Georgia laughed. He could hardly not speak after this.

'It was Sylvia Lee,' Jack growled.

'The musical comedy star of the Fifties?' Georgia blinked. Not just A.N.Other actress, but a major one. It made sense, she supposed. The glamour couple. The golden-haired Battle of Britain pilot and the young and beautiful actress.

'The same. Only a starlet in those days, of course.'

'Did you interview her for your biography?'

'I met her. It was hardly formal enough for an interview. She was long married by the 1970s. She told me the story was true in a way. She was briefly and very unseriously Fairfax's girlfriend for a week or two during the Battle of Britain. There was no great romance. She went back to London to do her bit when the Blitz came, and never saw him again. So I hardly think she would have come down to Malling to shoot him thirty-five years later.'

'I'm only interested in her as background,' Georgia said, puzzled that he was so defensive. 'You said yourself that the past is always with us, Jack.'

'I did. But it should be raked up only if it's relevant.'

This line was obviously going no further, at least at present, and she was all too thankful to return to 1975. 'Someone described Fairfax to me as a ladies' man. You wrote that he was happily married as soon as the war ended.'

Jack had a prompt reply for this. 'The word "happily" for Fairfax meant despite the occasional fling. Jean, his wife, rarely appeared at the aviation club, for instance, and with half of London and local society passing through it, the temptations must have been many.'

'But you said you hadn't heard any rumours,' she reminded him.

'About the pilots' wives,' he shot back at her.

She took a different tack. 'We know several members of the aviation club were at the hotel the day Patrick died, and they might have had more reason to kill him than old-standing friends – save for Matt Jones of course.'

'I'm not a private eye.' He was holding on to his temper with some difficulty, she realized. That was good. She would press him further.

'In the 1970s you were in your thirties, making your way as an aviation historian. I'm in my thirties now, and I know I'd have probed fully. The whole story is what one needs, whether one prints everything or not,' she said matter-of-factly.

She'd done it. He flushed with anger. 'There's *never* a whole story. Not one you can get at. The *whole* story is locked inside people's minds, deep in their memories. Not even their nearest and dearest can get it out of them unless they choose.'

'But you tried,' she said gently.

'Of course I did,' he snapped. 'And got bloody nowhere. For what it's worth, it's my belief it *was* someone at that air club. Patrick could rub someone up the wrong way without meaning to, especially husbands. What's more, he tended to leave business details to others, and that could well have led to someone seeing an opportunity to bump him off. I should look into that, if I were you.'

'Is the club still going?'

'Good grief, no. It closed down pronto after Fairfax's death. Bankrupt, and without him there was no goodwill to sell.'

'Is there anybody still around I could talk to?'

He shrugged. 'Matt might know.'

'He might be biased . . .'

'For God's sake, Georgia,' he exploded. 'Neither he nor any of the other 362 Squadron had any reason to *kill* Patrick Fairfax, no matter how annoying he was as a business partner. That group has met every year since 1975 in Fairfax's honour, for heaven's sake. You think they'd have done that if they'd loathed the man? They thought he was a good chap, despite his peccadilloes. And if you think you can find any dirt, good luck to you.'

'I have to try.' Puzzling, Georgia thought. He was still on the defensive – where the pilots were concerned – yet he wasn't naming *anyone* who belonged to that club.

He calmed down. 'Of course you do,' he said. 'So why don't you go to the squadron reunion in Tangmere next month? That's the aviation museum at the old airfield in Sussex. I'll spread the word that you'll be around. You'll find them all there, rain or shine, arthritis, Alzheimer's, bloody-mindedness, the lot. All nattering away, including one of the sergeant pilots if you're lucky. You can ask them about the aviation club. They all went there from time to time. You might not get anywhere though.'

'Won't they talk to me?'

'Oh they'll *talk*.' He paused. 'Certainly about Patrick Fairfax, since there might be another biography and even film on the cards.'

'You're writing another memoir of him?' Why on earth hadn't Jack mentioned this before?

'No. The film's being produced by a company called Fair Winds, which is writing its own script and reissuing *This Life, This Death* with a commentary. It's going to be big.'

'Don't you want to reissue your biography, updated perhaps?'

He looked tired. 'I've done what I can. If there's something I missed, too bad.'

Something missed? That was interesting. Was that just a

throwaway? 'Will you be at the reunion?' she asked as she rose to leave.

'I have to be. Not for Fairfax, but my other work. Always looking for those few holes in the market.' He made an attempt at being his jovial self again.

'I'll see you there then.'

He didn't comment. What he did say was: 'This might not be the best black hole for you to excavate, Georgia. You or your father. Take care.'

As Georgia's steps crunched over the gravel at Woodring Manor, she could see Peter through the bar window looking somewhat forlorn, she thought, while he waited for her. He must have heard her footsteps for he glanced out and waved. He seemed remarkably pleased to see her.

'Well?' he asked eagerly, once he had put a drink into her hand.

'I learned a lot, but came to no conclusion at all. Jack's OK, a few years older than you, reasonably straight. He began by palming me off with the party line, but was curiously ambivalent because he was both encouraging me to go to the squadron reunion at Tangmere in mid June while at the same time saying the pilots could have had nothing to do with it, and that it was the aviation club we needed. Whoever we meet at Tangmere might clue us in about it, even if they didn't talk about themselves. Altogether, a mixed message, since Jack also warned us to steer clear of the whole business.'

'Did he indeed?' Peter brightened up immediately. 'Let's go.'

'Both of us? It's out near Chichester.' That meant a two-to-three-hour drive to West Sussex.

'Why not? We can take your car and you'll be there to add the woman's touch if necessary.'

She cast him a scathing look. 'While you're applying your gentle ex-cop touch?'

'A draw,' he said amiably. 'Why do you think Hardcastle kept changing his attitude?'

She had the answer to this, or *her* answer at any rate. 'He seemed to be hinting that there might be something to discover, but he wanted no part of it.'

'Part of *what* precisely? Investigating Fairfax's death?'

'What else could he have meant?'

'There has to be *something* to find,' Peter muttered.

'Why?' And then she realized where they were, and why he was looking so bleak. 'Is this place is getting to you?'

'Yes,' he admitted. 'You can still hear those pilots rioting around here if you listen hard enough. Understand their emotions, their fear . . .'

'Let's have lunch,' she said quickly. At least that would take his mind off the past. The last thing she wanted was for Peter to make connections between Woodring Manor and the other unsolved mystery in their lives: her brother Rick's disappearance over ten years ago.

'OK. We can take a look at the old control tower afterwards. It won't be closed in, like this place.'

Her instant reaction was *no*. Why should they? It had nothing to do with 1975. She forced herself to agree, however.

As they turned off the West Malling road to the King's Hill development, Georgia saw that Peter was recovering fast. Lunch was the best weapon for fighting bleak feelings. The sun was just coming out too, but by the time she parked at the golf club at the top of the ridge, where the airfield had been, it had disappeared behind rain clouds again, and they decided to take shelter in the club bar. Peter's hope that this hillside would not be 'closed in' had taken a severe beating. Houses were springing up all around, and more were under construction, taking the development even further than their map showed. At least the clubhouse with its windows overlooking the course provided some idea of what the airfield had once been like. She worked out that where they were at present was roughly where one of the runways had been, and with the open downland before them it was possible to imagine the roar of Merlin engines taking off sixty-odd years ago.

Since the rain showed no sign of stopping, she decided she should walk over to the control tower alone, leaving Peter at their window table to await her return. 'Just behind those houses,' the helpful lady at the bar told her, and she set off. As she reached the first houses of the estate all sense of 1940 vanished. New names for new roads, new school, new pub – but suddenly there it was. The 1940s resurrected, despite the tall iron fencing all round the site. A dilapidated building with boarded-up windows and peeling paint. The control tower. She had discovered that this one had only been built in 1942, taking the place of the pre-war watch tower. Nevertheless it served its purpose, for here it was possible to imagine only too clearly what it had been like as the centre of a wartime airfield. There was no way to get closer to the building from this side, with danger notices glaring forbiddingly at her, so she worked her way round through the streets to the other side of what was now a muddy site covered with weeds. At least there was an open gate here, and in she went.

She wasn't alone. There were other people who appeared from the far side of the building as she approached. From the man's accent as he talked to his wife she could tell he was American and, from his bearing, an ex-serviceman.

'Did you serve here?' she asked politely, as they all stared at the forlorn building. This man would be too young to have served during the war, she estimated. He could only be in his sixties. It emerged that he had served here in the 1960s with 9 Fleet Air Support Squadron, flying Dakotas.

'That's how we met.' His wife was clearly eager to tell her story. 'I come from Town Malling. My parents wanted to lock me in my room when the Yanks arrived, and when they found out I'd taken up with Ed, they said I'd come to grief.'

'Instead she came to Arizona. Best flight I ever made,' her husband chimed in. 'Sure is sad to look at this place now. At least the Rose and Crown's still going in Malling.'

'That's where we met. We came back for Sally B though,' his wife explained.

The man laughed at Georgia's puzzled face. 'The Liberator used for the filming of a TV series.'

One more story, one more memory, still as vivid as when it had happened – as it must be to the 362 Squadron pilots, she imagined. To her they looked weary old men, but to themselves they were once again twenty-year-old men fighting a war for survival. Or was it the 1970s those five men thought about when they gathered now, she wondered as she walked back to the clubhouse. This former airfield belonged to a time far in the past by the time Fairfax was killed in 1975, and there was no logical reason for her and Peter to be here at all. Logically the reason for Fairfax's death would lie in the 1970s, so why had her father taken it into his head that they should not only revisit Woodring Manor Hotel, but also walk the ground that had once been West Malling airfield? If she were honest with herself, she too now felt the need to be here. And where *that* admission led, she decided not to contemplate.

By the time she reached the clubhouse again, Peter was as usual best mates with the bar staff, and insisted that they should also visit the country park just out of West Malling village. Its landscaped gardens would have been on the route walked by the 26 Squadron pilots on the way to their mess at the Manor House, which she realized must have been the eighteenth-century building she had seen when she had driven through West Malling to meet Peter.

The rain was falling more steadily now, and once in the parking area of the gardens, Peter elected to stay put. Manoeuvring his wheelchair along muddy paths in the rain was not his favourite pastime, he said. Georgia was tempted herself; this was a bleak place in the rain, though in sunshine it must be lovely. She refused to be defeated, however, so donned her anorak and hood and set off along the lakeside path to look at the manor perched on the hillside on the far side of the road. It told her nothing, though its former interior must have had the same atmosphere as Woodring. Not far away were the ruins of St Leonard's Tower and she made a quick detour to see it on the way back. In 1940, perhaps, Fairfax might have come this way to visit the 26 Squadron mess bar, and strolled in the grounds after flying finished for the day. She shivered. The tower reminded her of Lady Rosamund's Tower in Friday Street, scene of their previous case, and this place seemed to have much the same atmosphere, especially in this gloomy weather.

Were the ghosts of the past watching her as she walked back to the car? And was she disappointed or relieved that they seemed to be offering her no definite link?

Once back in Haden Shaw, Peter immediately logged on to Suspects Anonymous to record the information that Georgia had brought back from Jack Hardcastle. She watched him despondently, with the feeling that so far they were only circling round the case – if it could be called that – without any idea where the core lay, let alone any hope of reaching it.

'Sylvia Lee,' Peter murmured, as he opened a new file. 'Golden girl of the 1950s stage. Married Richard Vane, later Sir Richard Vane. She later made a skilful transformation into a straight actress and now plays very ancient ladies in TV cameo roles.'

'Jack said she was only a casual girlfriend of Fairfax for a week or two during the war, and mentioned nothing about her being around in the 1970s.'

'*Cherchez la femme.* We don't know what's relevant yet, and what isn't. Anyway, nothing about the Battle of Britain was casual,' Peter said firmly, clicking save on the file. 'They lived intensely, therefore they loved intensely. Each day could be their last so it had to be made to count for something. Would you make love to Luke *casually* in those circumstances?'

Or he to Elena, she wondered. Perhaps Peter had her in mind too. It had been well over ten years since her mother left them, but she knew the pain still clung to him. Just as the pain of Rick's unsolved disappearance in France while on a walking holiday still hurt.

'I agree,' she said, 'but the *femme* should be Jean Fairfax, not Sylvia Lee, much as I'd like to meet her. Jean Fairfax belongs to 1975, whereas Sylvia Lee is very much in the past. Fairfax's wife might give us a lead on which we could make a firm decision as to whether or not to continue.'

'No. We make it *now*.'

He was right, of course. No point putting it off. There was no way she could turn her back on this challenge. Nor should she even want to. Patrick Fairfax, for all his apparent feckless ways, had been dearly loved. Like Rick. It was this thought that decided her.

'Let's go for it,' she said. 'After all,' she laughed shakily, wondering what they were letting themselves in for, 'Luke said he'd give us a blank cheque.'

Four

M itchell House. Did that give a foretaste of what she would find when the door opened? Georgia now knew enough about Spitfires to recognize the name of its designer, R. J. Mitchell. This was surely no coincidence. On the outside it looked a typical London Victorian townhouse, solid brick, a gable, imposing steps to the front door flanked with columns, and a gravelled garden in front with ferns growing through the pebbles. She suspected the interior would be centred on the Second World War, and that it might be even harder to remember that she had come to discuss a case from the 1970s.

It had been a joint decision that the way forward was through meeting Jean Fairfax, and 'mighty ladies and doughty dowagers are your province,' Peter had said firmly.

Perhaps, but she was well aware that Peter disliked driving in London, and so even though this house was on the outskirts, in Putney, it was automatically ruled out for him. Now that she was here it was clear that in any case the flight of steps and Peter's wheelchair would not have seen eye to eye. Anyway, he had informed her airily, he had plenty to do on the phone and internet.

'Not to mention,' she had gently reminded him, 'the proofs of the Friday Street case.'

He had naturally brushed this aside. Hell's Corner held promise for the future, whereas the Friday Street now lay in the past.

The front door of Mitchell House opened and closed

again as the chain was removed, and a gorgon – surely not Jean Fairfax herself? – stood before her. No, this must be her Cerberus, Georgia decided. From her age – late fifties? – she assumed this was the daughter, Mary Fairfax. Tall, well-built, grey-haired, a no-nonsense Cerberus, although disposed to be friendly.

'Come in,' she boomed. 'Mother ready. All set? Car parked?'

'Train.' Georgia automatically adopted this staccato approach.

'Splendid. Coat?'

Georgia obediently handed over her jacket and umbrella, watched them hung on a sturdy Victorian hatstand, flourishing branches like a reindeer, and prepared to meet the queen of the establishment. To her surprise, Jean Fairfax sat in a comfortable armchair in a normal comfortable living room with not a sign of a Spitfire anywhere, nor even a Forties décor. Georgia noticed a few family photographs adorning the tops of bookshelves and the mantelpiece, and then concentrated on Jean Fairfax herself. She was a much smaller woman than Georgia had expected after meeting Cerberus, who had disappeared, presumably to serve coffee. A tray set with silver teaspoons, sugar pot and milk jug together with a platter of tempting petit four biscuits stood on a low table. Georgia had been offered countless varieties of coffee over the years, ranging from instant in mugs to best Columbian, but this one promised to be outstanding.

There was certainly power in this mighty lady. The blue eyes were still steely with curiosity, despite her years. She must have been an excellent social helpmeet for Patrick, quick to charm and quick, she guessed, to spot weaknesses. This didn't tally with Jack's comment that she didn't appear at the aviation club, however, so perhaps it was a quality that had only developed after her husband's death. She was dressed, Georgia saw approvingly, not in the modest colours usually deemed suitably for the elderly, but rose pink. It was an excellent choice, complementing her white hair, despite the fact that it suggested a fragility that Georgia was by no means sure existed, save perhaps physically.

'What makes you so interested in unsolved murders, Miss Marsh? Your own sad experience?'

This was a terrifying knockout blow for Georgia. How on earth could she cope with this? What could she mean other than Rick's disappearance, and yet how could this woman possibly know about Rick? Wild scenarios shot through her head as she sought for an answer.

She was saved by an apologetic Cerberus, who had reappeared. 'Mother! I warned you . . .' She turned to Georgia. 'My fault. Sorry.' She looked genuinely concerned. 'Friend of mine knows your mother well.'

Another cold hand closed over Georgia's heart. This was forbidden territory indeed. Elena talking about Rick? She struggled for control, to separate past from present, private life from career. With a supreme effort she managed to reply: 'Don't worry. We seem to be fellow travellers. My family has a disappearance. Yours has your unsolved murder. How do you feel about that being reopened, if my father and I write a book?'

The reply from Jean surprised her. 'I see it not only as my duty, Miss Marsh, but I welcome it. Though what you could hope to find after all this time must surely be very little. Nevertheless, such a book would keep my husband's memory polished, and that is my only concern.'

Georgia nodded. In other words, there was no such thing as bad publicity.

'I am glad you understand, Miss Marsh,' Jean continued. 'Now that there are very few, if any, survivors from the First World War, the torch passes to those of us who survive from the Second. I was younger than Patrick, but it is through keeping his memory alive that I make my contribution to this.'

'Even though the memory of his death must still be so painful?' A steely lady indeed, Georgia thought.

'Yes. Tell me what happens if you find nothing to add to Patrick's case. Do you invent a scenario, thus turning it into semi-fact?'

Georgia kept her temper. 'No. My father and I make a decision as to whether the story is worth telling or not. If it has something to offer, we go ahead.'

'My husband's story, Miss Marsh, *does* have something to offer.'

Georgia debated whether to speak out now or leave it until it became relevant – *if* it did. Since Mrs Fairfax had no qualms about speaking out herself, she decided to risk it. 'There's also the question of what happens in the unlikely event that we discover something to your husband's discredit.' This was an important point, since it was out of the question that she and Peter could ever allow others to have any control over what they wrote, though many would dearly like it.

For a moment she thought she had blown it and was ready to depart forthwith as those keen eyes glared into hers. Then, once again, Jean Fairfax surprised her. 'Shall we go, Mary?'

For a moment Georgia thought they were walking out on her, but it proved to be a rhetorical question, as Cerberus Mary moved forward to help her mother walk out of the room with a throwaway, 'Mother first.'

'Of course,' Georgia murmured, now realizing that this was no loo visit, but included her. She decided that Jean Fairfax was a woman capable of anything, certainly of keeping the likes of Patrick Fairfax in order. As she walked to the door, his face, good-looking even in middle age, grinned out at her from a studio photograph, as if daring her to find out the truth.

The priority was explained by a stairlift. Wherever it was they were heading, Georgia was expected to follow. Cerberus ran up the double flight of stairs to the next floor first, with her mother following in the lift and Georgia bringing up a decorous rear. The lift was the superior kind that went round corners. On the next floor, Mrs Fairfax moved to another lift for another ascent, and so on. There were four storeys altogether, if one included the attic floor at which they eventually arrived. As Georgia made her way up the last flight in the lift's wake, she tried to suppress an irreverent thought of a mummified Patrick Fairfax lying in state up here. Fortunately he wasn't, although what she found was nearly as scary.

'Do please enter.' The two Fairfax ladies had waited by the door so that Georgia could get the full effect.

'Oh!'

Her gasp of shock was genuine. A six-foot-tall pilot with a mop of fair hair was running straight at her, goggles and Mae West in hand and clad in RAF uniform, Irvin jacket and flying boots. A second look made it obvious that this was a plaster replica of Patrick himself; his eyes fixed on her as though she were the Spitfire to which he was running. The face and figure were so well sculpted that its artist must have worked painstakingly from a photograph. It was full of energy and life, and Georgia was shaken.

'My Patrick,' said Jean softly. 'You will find nothing to his discredit, Miss Marsh. I can assure you of that.'

Having recovered her breath, Georgia looked around the attic room to find herself in what was half museum, half working study. Photographs, books, model aircraft, a blackboard with victories chalked on, like the famous Biggin Hill board at the White Hart pub in Brasted, which Georgia had seen in photographs. There was part of a tannoy system, a Forties gramophone, and wartime memorabilia everywhere. It was an Aladdin's cave for the aviation buff, and, Georgia imagined, for any child who came in here.

'This desk – ' Jean walked lovingly over to it – 'is where Patrick used to write in later years. I sometimes allow research students the privilege of sitting here.'

'Notes for his memoirs?' Georgia remembered what Jack had said about the son allowing access to Patrick's notes.

'Partly, but he wrote far more about others. He was a modest man.'

Was that a line shoot, Georgia wondered? Patrick Fairfax did not strike her as particularly modest, but how could one tell just from photographs? Behind the desk was a display of different editions of *This Life, This Death* together with a framed copy of the Yeats poem from which its title was taken: 'An Irish Airman Foresees his Death'. There must have been something of the poet in Fairfax to have written this book, which was a testament to his fellow pilots, both living and dead, a paean to the beauty of the skies and an execration of the blazing guns that destroyed it.

She leafed through one of the scrapbook albums, and was rewarded by finding a photograph captioned 'Patrick with Sylvia Lee'. That was interesting, since the wording implied it was Jean's caption, not her husband's, which in turn meant this scrapbook was probably put together after his death. Yet the photograph was clearly a wartime one.

The photo was an outside shot of the couple, arms round each other, in a garden. Then, as she looked more closely, she shivered. It wasn't just *a* garden but *the* garden at Woodring Manor. She couldn't be absolutely certain, but the lake looked familiar, as did the trees and path beyond it that led to the dell. They made a handsome couple, she with Veronica Lake shoulder-length blonde hair, he with his mop of hair, his arm firmly round her. It showed a remarkable objectivity in Jean Fairfax, Georgia thought, to include a picture of a former girlfriend in the scrapbook.

She became aware that there was music playing in the background. Wartime songs. 'We'll Meet Again', naturally, 'The White Cliffs of Dover', 'Run Rabbit Run', and then snippets from the Tommy Handley radio comedy ITMA, and, bleakly, an air-raid siren's warning. It was an eerie background as Georgia moved on to look at Patrick's uniform and medals, the DSO and the DFC with its bar across the riband.

'Of course Patrick should have been awarded the VC,' Jean said briskly. 'There was only one awarded to a Fighter Command pilot during the Second World War, and that was to James Nicolson. But for the frantic tempo of those few weeks, which prevented due note being taken of individual heroic efforts, there would have been two. Patrick's. You have heard of Eagle Day, of course?'

Georgia had, thanks to her swotting-up. 'The day the Luftwaffe made its all-out effort to destroy all airfields in Kent and the rest of south-east England.'

'Correct. That was August thirteenth. West Malling was thankfully spared that day, but not thereafter. On the fifteenth the field was attacked having been mistaken for Biggin Hill; the next day it was targeted again with both the airfield and aircraft being hit, and on the eighteenth more aircraft were destroyed, yet again on the twenty-eighth, and several times during September.'

'You've become a historian yourself,' Georgia said admiringly, hoping her memory was as good when she was Jean Fairfax's age. She received no thanks.

'Naturally,' Jean replied coolly. 'It is necessary for Patrick's sake. On August sixteenth a large force of Dornier bombers appeared with no effective fighter intervention. The airfield was still under repair from the previous day and a further eighty bombs were dropped. The squadron had already lost several valuable aircraft, both Spitfires and Lysanders, which had been caught on the ground. Patrick was not going to allow any more. The squadron was not officially scrambled by Group HQ, but Patrick rallied his fellow pilots to get their Spitfires airborne in order that they should not be lost to bombing. When all the Spitfires save one were in the air, he saw the remaining pilot was immobile, frozen with fear at the bombs exploding all round. He rushed out to the aircraft, pulled the pilot out, saw him to safety, with bombs still exploding, then ran back to take the aircraft up himself as another wave came in. In another incident on July twentieth, in the middle of a melee with Messerschmitts, Red Section was separated by cloud. As it thinned Patrick, the section leader, realized that the enemy aircraft were homing in on this same pilot, who was a sitting duck, and not even firing. Patrick went to draw the hornets off his tail so that he could escape. Patrick managed to shoot down two of the German fighters, and winged another.'

'Remarkable.' Georgia meant it. 'Your husband was an ace, wasn't he? Which means he shot down more than five of the enemy?'

Georgia received another reproving look. 'The true figure can never be known. Four were actually credited to him, but there were many unconfirmed. In the thick of battle it was often the case that those who could confirm the loss of an enemy aircraft were themselves dead. Patrick tells me the true figure would have been twelve at least.'

Georgia murmured something appropriate to the stare fixing her so resolutely.

'However, that meant little to Patrick,' Jean continued. 'At the time that was his job. What mattered to him were the lives of his comrades whom he was able to save. It's difficult to imagine what our existence would have been like today if the fight with the Luftwaffe had failed and the invasion followed. We would probably have been robots in a two-power world – the German empire and the Japanese – with an impotent and isolated American continent. The Soviets and China might well have fallen, even America itself. Who knows? It would most certainly have meant a united states of Europe, although on a rather different model to that envisaged today.'

'How would Patrick have reacted if the invasion had followed?'

'He would have inspired resistance, as he always did. People like Patrick carry the flame.'

'This,' Georgia said sincerely, glancing round the display, 'is a remarkable . . .' She caught herself. Museum would be the wrong word to use to Jean. 'Tribute,' she finished.

'Too little. It can never reflect his worth,' Jean replied dismissively. 'I do what I can. It is for others to finish his story, such as you, Miss Marsh.'

'Is there material here about the Wormshill Aviation Club too?' She had been waiting for an opportunity to switch the focus to Fairfax's later career.

'Very little. I have one or two scrapbooks you are welcome to see later.'

'Thank you.' She would take the offer up.

'However, shall we return downstairs for the moment, so that you may ask me your questions?'

'They will concentrate on 1975, I'm afraid,' Georgia reminded her gently.

No need. 'Of course. However, you will forgive me if I rest for a few minutes. The frailties of age. Perhaps you would take coffee with my daughter while I do so.'

'Your mother is remarkable,' Georgia said politely once established with Mary and coffee in the drawing room. (The coffee not as good as the array of silver and petit fours had promised.) 'Do you live with her?'

'Yes and no. I moved in after my son married. I'm on the third floor. One needs space.'

'And your brother is nearby? He was in the RAF too, wasn't he?'

'Other side of London. He too needs space. Though men –' she shot an amused look at Georgia – 'never see that. They do what they, or their wives, wish. It's the daughters who are called upon, especially divorced ones, such as me.'

'Yes,' Georgia agreed.

Her face must have given her away, for Mary quickly

61

apologized. 'Forgotten about your brother. Second time I've put my foot in it.'

'Rick disappeared over ten years ago,' Georgia replied. 'I ought to be able to speak normally about it. Especially – 'she forced herself – 'as my mother seems to.'

'I wouldn't be sure of that. Philippa, my talkative friend, is hardly the most tactful person. She's a ferret if she scents a story.'

Georgia laughed. 'Can you and your mother talk naturally about your father's death?'

'Took time. Easier for me to talk about it than my mother, of course. I was only in my twenties. Brother Roger was a young married man with two small children, and I was a giddy civil servant.'

'Ministry of Defence?'

'How did you guess? Dad's doing, of course.'

'Is that why your brother went into the RAF?' She had no hesitation in asking. After all, this was relevant to Patrick Fairfax. Two determined parents must have made this a hard family to be born into.

'Went through hard time. Not set on it, but did his best, a respectable one. Now that he's retired from the RAF, he's switched off aviation to Mother's disgust. Taken up ornithology, as he always wanted. It's left to the next generation to carry Mother's flame. It often skips one, doesn't it?'

It did. Her mother was an excellent needlewoman, a skill that had bypassed Georgia. If she ever had children . . . Don't go there, she warned herself. She might end up doing the right thing by Luke for the wrong reasons, as T.S. Eliot once put it.

'I gather you were speaking about Roger, Mary.' Jean Fairfax had reappeared in the room, and obviously had sharp hearing. 'A sad disappointment, Miss Marsh. Now please, do not hesitate to ask me anything you wish. I will try to answer objectively.'

Anything? Such as asking how she could speak about

her son in such terms to a stranger? 'We haven't seen the police files, Mrs Fairfax,' she began instead. 'But we have spoken to the investigating officer. Do you have any theories of your own as to what happened?'

'Of course. You would expect that, wouldn't you? You would also know that such opinions would be useless without proof.'

'Not necessarily. I'm used to picking out the proven from the unproven.'

'If you are telling me that I need not fear to speak out whether I have proof or not, you need not be concerned. I shall do so. Why not? It's been discussed with the police many times.'

'Do you think they did a good job or were you frustrated at the result?'

'They did what they could, in view of the fact that there was little hard evidence, or so I gathered. The gun – poor Patrick's own – was missing, and has never been found. The display cupboard where it was kept – *without* ammunition incidentally – was available to all who visited that downstairs bar. The new bar on the ground floor was already in use by 1975, but for reunions such as on that day the old bar remained open too. It was then referred to as the Cockpit rather than Hell's Bells.'

'Was the cupboard left open?'

'It was supposed to be locked, but the key was on top of the cupboard, a fact known to most regulars, I imagine.'

'But not to a casual visitor to the hotel.'

'And useless anyway, unless he had ammunition for a Webley revolver in his pocket.'

'One theory might be,' Georgia pointed out, impressed by Jean Fairfax's quick mind, 'that your husband could have loaded it for his own purposes only to have it turned against him.' She held her breath, waiting for an explosion.

It didn't come. 'That is possible,' Jean conceded, 'but unlikely. My husband was not in fear of his life to my knowledge, nor did he have any reason to shoot anyone else. He had seen too much killing during the war to turn to that method of solving a problem.'

'I met five of the seven other pilots who were present that day, although not to talk to at length. Matthew Jones seems to have been the only police suspect, and he was one of the five.'

'A so-called business partner of my husband's. Jealous of course.'

Georgia was startled. 'Of what?'

Jean sighed. 'Everyone will tell you that Patrick was driving Matthew into bankruptcy.'

'That wasn't true?'

'It was true that the hotel was failing, but not that it was Patrick's fault. Matthew Jones was a poor businessman. No vision. He refused to let Patrick promote the hotel in a way that would attract a younger generation. Consequently the hotel remained firmly stuck in the 1950s.'

'As a memorial to what they went through in the war?'

'No. One could understand that. It came about through Mr Jones' lack of expertise in applying improvements. It was a mishmash of dull post-war furniture set against hideous wallpaper. The food was even duller: traditional English at its worst, such as prawn cocktail with tomato mixed with commercial salad cream, tough roast beef and disgusting trifle. By the 1970s customers required something rather better. The only people brave enough to stay there were those seeking a quiet refuge where they didn't have to speak to anyone and could read the newspapers in an armchair all day long. Occasionally one or two might venture into the conservatory to gaze out upon a rose bed. That would be the height of adventure for Matthew Jones' ideal customer.'

Georgia laughed, as she hoped she was meant to. 'But that would be no reason for killing your husband,' she pointed out.

'That, Miss Marsh, is for you to discover. Is there not a

natural tendency to blame one's own failure on a more successful business rival? Particularly when that rival is as popular as was my husband.'

'Perhaps.' It still didn't seem likely to Georgia.

'Patrick's aviation club had many members of substance. He told me he had persuaded some to put money into the hotel to bail it out of its difficulties, and wished to entertain them at the hotel to show them its potential. Matthew refused to permit free hospitality, and on the last occasion Patrick had done this Matthew had the nerve to present him with the bill. On the day of his death he threatened to do the same again regardless of the fact that these were potential investors. I gather he was later extremely rude to them, with the result that Patrick was upset, and the investors left.'

'Do you know who they were?'

'Lord Standing, as he then was, was one, there was some industrialist, and Sir Richard Vane—'

'Sylvia's Lee's husband?' Georgia interrupted. Her mind began to spin with possibilities.

'You have done your homework well, Georgia. She was briefly my husband's girlfriend during the war, long before he knew me, of course. She retained an affection for him, however, and her husband took flying lessons, then flew with the club. She never came herself, to my knowledge.'

'I noticed her photograph in a scrapbook.'

'Yes. She was a part of Patrick's life, albeit a small one, and it seemed fair to include it in the Fairfax Memorial Trust.'

So that was its name. 'Did anyone else seem to have a motive? The club itself was in difficulties, wasn't it?'

'Who claims that?' Jean whipped back. 'I suppose,' she continued tartly when Georgia did not reply, 'you never reveal your sources. Let me assume therefore that it was Jack Hardcastle.'

'It wasn't in his biography.' Jack had told her, of course, but diplomacy was necessary here.

'Of course not. It was not true. The club was *not* failing.

65

My husband told me he was about to sign a new lease with the MOD. I'm afraid that over the years speculation tends to become fact. Doubtless you have run into this before.'

'I have, but it is usually possible to explore deeply enough to reach the truth, or what one can satisfy oneself to be the truth having investigated all sources. After all –' Georgia decided to deflect the conversation, since detours could provide a useful breathing space – 'people now believe that they *know* the truth about Richard III and the princes in the tower, despite Shakespeare's best efforts to pervert the course of justice – if he did.'

Cerberus growled. 'Nonsense to blame Shakespeare,' Mary said. 'Followed the historical line of the day, just as we do now.'

'As presented by the so-called historian Holinshed on whose work Shakespeare based his,' her mother rejoined. 'Both writing posthumously and in the age of Elizabeth, who would not wish to see her grandfather indicted for murder, and thus they put the blame on Richard.'

'All circumstantial evidence,' Georgia commented lightly. Time to return to Patrick Fairfax now that she had a clearer playing field. 'I need to get some idea of the people who belonged to the aviation club. Anyone who had a grudge against him, for example. Even the most popular of figures has a disagreement with someone, sometime. It's a consequence of having a high profile.'

'I am aware of that,' Jean rejoined stiffly. 'You need look no further than Mr Stock.'

'Oh, Mother, *no!*' Cerberus interrupted wearily.

'I have no idea why you feel I am speaking out of turn, Mary. Miss Marsh has reassured me that she investigates smoke and fire separately.'

'Who is or was Mr Stock?' Georgia asked politely.

'Paul Stock was the manager at the aviation club. He accused my husband of wasting money. In fact it was he who had his hand in the till.'

'Smoke or fire?' Georgia asked with interest.

The gimlet eye fixed on her, although the sweet smile was still in place. 'Fire, Miss Marsh, undoubtedly.'

'But why would he want to go so far as to *kill* your husband?'

'Because Patrick had discovered the truth. It is obvious enough.'

'The police . . .'

'Mr Stock was a creative accountant. There was no hard proof.'

'Was?' Georgia decided not to enquire whether in that case there would have been need for murder.

'I spoke incorrectly. He is still alive, although I trust no longer in charge of others' money.'

This was one line to be followed up, and she would do so, even though it was puzzling that if such an obvious motive existed that Christopher Manners had not mentioned it. There was another interesting line, however. 'No one else had clashed with him?' How else could she gently suggest rumours of affairs? 'The police heard there was some kind of quarrel that afternoon.' She expected to be slapped down, and was surprised when Jean answered immediately.

'No doubt over Bill Dane's wife, Alice. Patrick had told me about it himself some time before. A common little thing, for all Bill made great play of her being a bishop's daughter. Dane had the notion that Patrick's affair with her had been serious.'

Mary again stepped in. 'Emphasis on serious, Georgia. Dad was not entirely faithful to my mother, but there was no *serious* affair. Good-looking man was Dad, and women tended to throw themselves at him.'

'And usually they missed,' Jean added tartly. 'I met Mrs Dane once. She was one of those who threw herself and was briefly caught. One would have thought to look at her that butter wouldn't melt in her mouth, but I assure you it did. It not only melted but sizzled. It was some time ago in any case.'

Georgia was puzzled. 'Then surely it would have provided no motive?'

'I'm afraid Patrick was sometimes rather naughty. He liked to stir things up. I was later told that he had done so that afternoon.'

'You may think, Georgia,' Mary said bluntly, 'that Dad wasn't the paragon that he's been painted. He was. Today's media plays hero-bashing by revealing flaws, but some reputations remain intact. We don't think the less of Kennedy as president because of his sexual flings. Chip away at my father's reputation all you like, but it won't make a dent.'

'How was the doughty dowager?' Peter looked up eagerly as Georgia came into his office, after a restorative tea break with Luke on her way home. She had spent an hour in the Fairfax museum with the Wormshill Aviation Club scrapbooks, compiling a list of the members from around the time of his death on her laptop, together with other snippets of interest. When she emerged into the fresh air again, she had drunk it in with relief. London – even Putney – was no place to greet the arrival of June, particularly immured in a room so claustrophobically dedicated to the past.

'Overwhelming, but I rose again.' She decided not to tell him the odd thing that had happened as she turned to walk down the hill to the tube station. Ten to one she was imagining things. No one could really have been watching her, save perhaps Cerberus from an upstairs window, and yet she had felt under scrutiny all the way down Putney Hill. She had even succumbed and turned round once, but there was no one but a teenager in the distance, a postman turning into a drive and a couple of students wrapped in each other's arms. The prickles on her back had vanished as she got further from the house, and she had forgotten them, until her thoughts had been redirected to Putney on her return.

Obediently she related the results of her visit, together
with the list of aviation club members, so far as she had
been able to gather from the scrapbooks. 'Patrick Fairfax
seems to have had three particular cronies at the club,
judging by the frequency in which they appear in snap-
shots. One was Lord Standing—'

'Now a duke,' Peter interrupted.

'Another was Vincent Blake, a local business tycoon.
And the last –' she paused impressively – 'was Sir Richard
Vane, Sylvia Lee's husband. Interesting, but no evidence
that she ever came to the club herself.'

Peter was looking as alert as a March hare, ears metaphorically pricked up. 'Now there's a coincidence,' he observed.

'There was also,' Georgia added, 'an alleged crooked
manager, Paul Stock.'

'Ah, I wonder if Mike could find out . . .'

'Don't go there.'

'Very well. I had another chat with Manners about forensic
evidence. He's been curious enough to ask around, and no,
he doesn't have the file. That's strictly tucked away awaiting
proof that it's not idle interest on our part. There was a
consensus however that the gun was never traced, nor was
the one decent footprint. The cartridge was consistent with
the Webley missing from the hotel. There were thought to
be various other items of evidence and lines of enquiry,
including your Mrs Dane, incidentally, but everything
petered out.'

'No mention of this Paul Stock?'

'Yes, that's why I recognized the name.' Peter consulted
his notes. 'No dice. He's mentioned as having been present,
that's all.'

'Not a suspect?'

'Apparently not. Anyway, Manners reports that Fairfax
wasn't shot from point-blank range, but beyond that it
wasn't possible to tell. The footprints suggested about seven
feet. Various people said they heard what they thought to

be a shot, but not loud enough to investigate. The disco was starting up and Fairfax seems to have had the grounds to himself. And another thing—'

'What about blood spots?' Georgia interrupted. 'He'd surely have checked to make sure Fairfax was dead.'

'He could have discarded his outer clothes, particularly if he thought it out in advance. The hotel wastebins and grounds were searched, of course. Nothing found. Quite a few were tested for residue on their hands, without success, including Matt Jones and the waiter who found the body.'

'Gloves?'

'A possibility. No evidence.'

'So it's probable the killer didn't go back to the hotel.'

'Why should he? Even if he was one of our Magnificent Seven the party had broken up long since. Remember that it's seven because Tom Armstrong and Nat Dodds were there.'

'Yes. The two who've since died.'

There was a peremptory knock at the door, and Georgia went to answer it since Margaret had left for the day. She fully expected yet another smiling would-be persuader from a gas or electricity company, but she had a pleasant surprise.

'Charlie!' she cried in delight.

'Hi.' Her cousin gave his familiar grin, the mop of black hair as untidy as ever, as he stepped inside, presenting her ceremoniously with a sticky paper bag.

'What on earth are you doing here?' she asked.

'I brought you some buns for tea.'

'Excellent.' By buns Charlie usually meant éclairs, for which he had a sweet tooth – particularly the soggy ones at which his mother Gwen excelled. He had solved countless problems, he claimed, while her particular mix of mushy choux pastry, chocolate and cream melted in his mouth.

'Tea in the garden?' he suggested hopefully as she led him into Peter's office. 'Got something to tell you.'

'By all means,' Peter roared belligerently. 'After you've

checked out Suspects Anonymous. This monster has gone to sleep.'

'Eclairs first.' Charlie marched past Peter towards the conservatory and garden.

'Done,' said Georgia thankfully. It was ages since they had seen Charlie, since he was London-based, living in a flat in Clapham. Gwen's longing for grandchildren looked doomed to despair so far as Charlie was concerned. Ladies appeared and disappeared, chiefly because he was wedded happily to a single life and his work on computer software. He surveyed the garden before them, and threw himself down happily on to an old-fashioned deckchair that Peter insisted on keeping as a souvenir. Georgia was never sure of what.

'Eclairs ahoy!' Peter made his appearance, shooting his wheelchair skilfully down the ramp from the conservatory to the lawn.

'Not so excellent for waistlines.' Georgia departed inside to make tea and Charlie ambled after her.

'Luke's a man to appreciate a fine body on a woman,' Charlie teased her.

'What,' she asked to distract him from this subject, 'are you doing down here? You didn't come all this way to deliver buns.'

'I was in Canterbury on a job. Wanted to tell you about my neighbour's aunt.'

'Don't tell me she has a wonderful story for a book.'

'Just you wait.' He grinned and waited till they were outside again with the tea. Then his attention was distracted by an old Victorian chimney pot. 'What do you keep in there?'

'Slugs. Now tell us me about this aunt of yours, Charlie.'

'In my young day,' Peter observed, '*Charley's Aunt* was a much loved farce.'

'Today she could be the answer to your dreams.'

'Convince us,' Georgia said. This sounded good but things often did with Charlie.

'She's a widow who lives in Essex,' he proclaimed.

'So far so good,' Peter retorted caustically.

'Her husband was one Thomas Armstrong.'

'Not Thomas Armstrong of 362 Squadron?' Georgia cried with mixed feelings. Back to 1940 *again.*

'The very same.'

'He's a Burglar Bill suspect, Charlie.'

'Well, Burglar Bill's missus came to visit her nephew, my nerdish neighbour. I met her, made the same deduction as you, when she mentioned the RAF, and told her about Suspects Anonymous and your current case.'

'Charlie,' Georgia said warningly.

'Not much.' He flashed her a grin. 'Anyway, she never knew the Woodring gang well, because she only married her Tom in the 1950s.'

'Is "gang" her husband's name for them or hers? Did he go to the reunions regularly?' Peter demanded.

'Yes, he did, but she said he didn't seem to enjoy the Woodring Manor ones; he preferred the general reunions.'

'Why was that? Because of Patrick's death?' Georgia asked, curious despite herself.

'No idea. She did say he was a Fairfax fan and was stunned at the death. Couldn't believe it. She remembered the news coming through. Tom had apparently left the hotel in the late afternoon, and the next thing was a phone call from Bill Dane in the middle of the night followed by the entire Essex and Kent police forces the next day.'

'Did she remember anything her husband had told her that was unusual about the day? They must have hashed it over time and time again. Any idea who did it?' Her questions bubbled out.

'Something about a spat over Fairfax writing memoirs, that's all. Some were against it, like Tom, and some like Patrick were for it, even though he was a bit lukewarm. He told them it was being pushed upon him and he wasn't really that keen.'

'That's not what Jean Fairfax said. She said the spat was about an affair that Patrick had with Alice Dane.'

'Maybe. Can't help. Poor old Georgia. You can't get the staff nowadays. Have to make do with amateurs like me. This sainted aunt did natter on about some aviation club.'

'Charlie, you've been holding out on us. Speak!' she said. This was more like it.

'Nothing very juicy. Patrick made all the 362 pilots honorary members of it. Good for prestige he said, but her Tom felt he was being trotted out as an exhibit, although it quite amused him to go. You can ring Madeleine – that's her name – if you like. When she heard about your book, she sent me copies of a couple of photos. Arrived this morning.'

He whipped them out of his jeans pocket like rabbits from a hat, only rather more creased. One was a formal squadron photograph taken in 1940 and fully captioned; the other was of Woodring Manor. No doubt about that. It was captioned – presumably this too was copied by Madeleine from the original – 'May 10th 1975'. Now that was something. A group picture taken outside with Patrick in the middle with the seven other pilots, probably when they first arrived or during the lunch period before they repaired to the bar. Of the pilots she could just about make out the five she had met and Patrick himself was laughing at the camera. A few hours later he was dead. A standard reunion picture, but with a difference, she thought wryly. Why didn't Armstrong like attending it, she wondered.

'Any help?' Charlie asked curiously.

'About as much as Suspects Anonymous,' Peter informed him tartly.

'Excellent.' Charlie bit into his second éclair. Irony was always lost on him.

Five

It was hard to imagine this tucked-away place as an active wartime station, despite the fact that today Tangmere was hardly deserted. The car park was nearly full already, as people gathered for the reunion. The old airfield lying beyond the aviation museum's boundary was overgrown with rough grass; in the far distance, as in West Malling, the control tower stood as a lonely sentinel to its past and to the aircraft that once roared past it. Several veteran aircraft were lined up outside the museum and Georgia supposed there would probably be others inside, but their flying days were over – as were those of most of the pilots from 362 Squadron who would be here today. Although it was only ten thirty, there were already plenty of people about, but so far no one she had recognized. No surprise there, since the squadron had had a post-war life as well as its wartime role, and wives, perhaps children too, would be part of this reunion.

'Shall we go round the museum together to hunt down quarry, or shall we separate?'

Peter was abnormally quiet, and she had to ask this mundane question twice. Even then it took him several moments to reply.

'Play it by ear. Let's go.' He turned the chair round to return to the museum entrance. 'At least I'll be in good company.'

For a moment she didn't understand. Then she followed the direction of his eyes. Two wheelchair-bound visitors were making their way from car to entrance, one independent, the

74

other being pushed by a companion. That made it easy to follow Peter's thinking. Father in the RAF, Peter in wheel-chair. Career over. That's how he was, at least momentarily, viewing the situation. Fortunately she'd dealt with these rare lapses before.

'CID only stands for Clock In Daily.' She trotted out his own grumble when he'd be a DCI in Stour Area police. 'Today you're clocking.'

He cast her a scathing glance and shot past her towards the entrance. 'And DCI stands for Drink Coffee Instantly,' he threw back at her.

They'd left Haden Shaw at eight that morning, as soon as Peter could be ready, and whipped easily through an assortment of Kentish and Sussex lanes to avoid the worst of the rush hour. Coffee indeed was on the priority list, and they made straight for the cafeteria. Others had the same idea, for it was already full, but she secured two cups and perched on the arm of the wheelchair.

'Sit here, Georgia.'

A now familiar voice boomed at her as Jack Hardcastle rose to his feet. She hadn't recognized his back view. There was no sign of Susan, so this was obviously a working day, not a pleasure trip for him.

'Jack!' Georgia was glad to see him and introduced him to Peter. 'Tell us about what happens today, when we'll be welcome to join in the highlights and when we won't.'

'Easy. The Big Bunfight is over lunch. At midday coaches whisk them away to a local hostelry for speeches and formalities.'

'That's it?' she asked blankly. 'We only have till twelve o'clock and then we're turned into pumpkins?'

'No. They'll all be back for chit-chat and tea. Then comes a short service in the memorial garden to end the day. Only the service and lunch are closed. Otherwise you can barge in. They're expecting you.'

'Good.'

To Georgia's relief, Peter was beaming. He was over his doom-laden moment. These were natural enough, but there was always the risk that if they continued they would lead to one of his periodic 'turns', when the nightmare of Rick's disappearance would consume him, leaving him feverish and distraught, trapped in a black hole from which he had to claw his own way out.

'I'd like to meet that film man – Martin Heywood,' Georgia said. 'It will be interesting to see what line he proposes to take about Fairfax's death.'

'I'll look out for him,' Jack promised. 'The others you'll recognize, won't you? They all live in the south, so they hire a minibus to pick them all up.'

'Oh, and Paul Stock,' Georgia dropped in, apparently casually. 'Will he be here?'

Jack's face changed. 'That bastard? He'll be here, but I won't be looking out for him.'

Taken aback by the vehemence of his reply, she began to apologize but he shrugged it off. 'He and I go back a long way,' he added grimly.

'So that's why you didn't mention him when we met.' Georgia was intrigued. What was this all about?

'No need to. I knew you'd find out soon enough. I'd be only too pleased if you could pin Fairfax's murder on him, but I doubt if you will.'

'Mrs Fairfax seems to share your views.'

Jack gave a harrumph of laughter. 'I can guess what she said. Maybe she's right, but she would have had that straight from Patrick. No one could ever prove it now, so I doubt if Stock will shiver in his shoes if you start work on him.'

'Money seems a possible motive at least, if Fairfax was threatening to expose him, and presumably sack him for theft. If,' she added, 'that was the case.'

Jack hesitated, then moved to one side to let people through, and used it as an obvious excuse to leave. 'See what you make of him – and enjoy the show.'

Georgia watched his burly figure strolling back along the passageway towards the two large halls of the museum where the aircraft were kept. So the jury was out on Paul Stock. Did he fiddle the books, or didn't he? It was little enough to go on, but if one didn't pull the corks out of bottles one never got to the wine beneath.

There was plenty to see in the museum with one hall devoted to the Battle of Britain, another to D-Day, another to Tangmere's secret wartime activities, which involved dropping agents into France by Westland Lysanders at night. In the Battle of Britain room there was an enormous collection of memorabilia, centred on the lives of representative pilots. She couldn't see one devoted to Patrick Fairfax, though. Was that odd? No, she realized, because his battle had been spent not at Tangmere but at West Malling. He came here to command his next squadron, 348.

'James Nicolson,' Peter remarked as they reached the section devoted to him. 'Didn't you say he was the only Fighter Command VC of the war?'

'You should have heard Jean on the subject of Patrick Fairfax and his missed VC,' Georgia said wryly.

An elderly man standing at the next exhibit case shot a look at them. His face was wrinkled, his hair thinned, but his eyes, she saw, were sharp as buttons. 'These gongs were all a lottery in wartime,' he chirped. 'The lady's probably right. Story goes that Nicolson could never quite believe he was any more worthy of it than his mates, so he spent the rest of his war trying to deserve it. Killed in Burma flying mission after mission against the Japs.'

'I've heard a similar story about Charles Lightoller,' Peter commented.

'Who?' Georgia asked.

Their companion moved closer and answered for Peter. 'Second officer on the *Titanic*. The most senior officer to survive. Won a DSC in the First War. Lived in Dover, and when the Admiralty wanted to requisition his boat for

Dunkirk in the Second War, he insisted on taking it to Ramsgate to take over himself. I grew up nearby, and met him. He lived on till the 1950s, see? A great old sea salt, he was. I nearly volunteered for the Navy, but he said to me, "Eddie," he said, "your head's in the clouds, not in the waves." So the Air Force got me.'

Eddie? Georgia made a stab in the dark. 'You wouldn't by any chance be Eddie Stubbs of 362, would you?'

'I am the pilot of that name.' He gave her a mock bow.

'You're on this photograph.' She produced the squadron photograph that Charlie had given them, and he peered at it.

'That's me. Taken the day we flew in to Malling, that was. Standing between Pilot Officer Molkar and Sergeant Tanner.' He stared at the picture before handing it back to her.

'We met Mr Molkar at the Woodring Hotel reunion. Do you ever go to them?' It was worth asking even though she got the answer she expected.

'Not me. I was only a sergeant. We had our shindigs at the Rose and Crown in Town Malling instead. Didn't miss much, if you ask me. In fact we reckoned we had the best of it. Did our bit by day and escaped the spotlight by night.'

Time to hone in, she decided. 'We're interested in Patrick Fairfax's death.'

He nodded. 'I heard. Writing some kind of book, aren't you? You and that film chappie who's around here some-where. All of a sudden, it's nothing but Fairfax again. Like the old days.' He chuckled.

'We're approaching the story from a different angle,' Peter said mildly. 'We're looking into his unsolved death.'

'Can't help you over that. Shocking thing.' Eddie shook his head. 'Missed him at squadron reunions after he'd gone.'

'You did know him, though. You flew with him,' Georgia put in.

'Nah. The Spits were single-seater,' Eddie said with a straight face.

Georgia laughed, determined not to be put off. 'I meant you saw a lot of him during the battle.'

'Probably. Can't really say. Vic Parr was my mate. At dispersal you were too hyped up over what lay ahead to think about the others. There was a station dance once – amazing really when you think what was going on – and someone organized that for all pilot ranks. Good for morale, I suppose. Anyway, there was Fairfax, dancing with the prettiest girl in the room.'

'Was that Sylvia Lee?' A leap in the dark.

Eddie took his time. 'That's right. Perhaps she was nothing so special, but she seemed so then. A sort of angel come down to see us through. Or perhaps it's just the passing years have polished up her wings a bit.'

'Didn't you resent being in a different mess to the officers?' Peter asked.

'Nah. We were used to it. We were so chuffed when they put us up to sergeants and warrant officers, all because it didn't look good in the papers to have us erks flying their aeroplanes. Human nature never changes, does it?'

Peter agreed. 'Did you get on with Fairfax?'

Eddie shrugged. 'He came across as a decent enough chap. Always bought you a drink no matter your rank, if he met you in a pub. Not done, of course, but there you go. Anyway, we needed figureheads like him. Never forgot seeing him dance with that girl. Like they'd been specially picked out by God to show us the best He could do. Better than Astaire and that Ginger Rogers.'

'Did you stay in touch with Fairfax after the war?'

'Yeah. Used to go to that aviation club of his. He'd trot us out like trophies, free booze, free grub. "Call me Pat," he used to say. All pals together, only somehow you never forgot who was top dog, for all we were pals. Nice people you met there, though.'

'Did you know Paul Stock, the manager?'

'Certainly did. He's around here somewhere. Saw a lot

79

of him at the club – going through a bad time, he was, so I had quite a few chats with him.'

'The finances?' Georgia ventured.

Eddie regarded her steadily and chuckled. 'Wouldn't know.'

'Are any other sergeant pilots from this photograph likely to be here today?' she asked, realizing they would get no further with this line of questioning.

He took the photo back and squinted at it again. 'There were only the four of us. Look at us, grinning our heads off. We didn't know what we were in for then. I'm the only one of us left. Vic Parr passed away a year or two back. Still miss him. Lived in Margate, he did. Not a gong between the four of us. Tanner and Smith, being LMFs, didn't contribute to the war effort. They were mates – well, they would be. Smith's not in this photo. He joined us a day or two later. Vic and I reckoned we shot down a Messie or two each, but only one was ever confirmed. It went like that. Good job the beautiful game don't work on that principle.'

'LMF stands for lack of moral fibre?' Peter asked.

'That's it. There's always one or two who can't hack it. Today it's expected, but during the war they had to be made an example of, or they might infect the rest of us. It was only being so bloody confident that got us into the air day after day. That's where Fairfax was good.'

'What happened to LMFs?' Peter asked.

'They weren't shot, if that's what you mean. Not like the First War. In our day they were sent to a special camp before they pressed the panic button for the rest of us. Tanner died; he deserted once it all came out, and there was a rumour going round that he drowned to save his family the disgrace. Joe Smith got shunted off to a special camp, and later on I heard he'd died too. Things went too fast to care. Our mates were dying all around us through enemy fire and accidents. Other pilots came to fill the gaps, only to get shot down too. Never even knew their names, never had time to unpack their kit some of them. Only remembered these – ' he flicked the photograph in Georgia's hand – 'because they flew in with us. We were a team then. We didn't think much of the LMFs. Vic thought Tanner was OK, but he had no time at all for Smith, and we'd no sympathy for either of them. We all lived with fear. Plenty of it. Kept it down with adrenalin by day and drink by night. If we were lucky, a woman too. Mind you . . .' He paused, then said casually, 'Seen the replica Spit in the Marston Hall, have you? Let me show you.'

As Peter manoeuvred himself to Eddie's side, and she brought up the rear, Georgia wondered what Eddie had so nearly said before he had obviously decided enough was enough. The trouble was that in their line of work enough was *never* enough.

The Marston Hall was a hangar packed with aircraft both wartime and post-war, including the Hunter in which Neville Duke had broken the speed record during the 1950s. There was no mistaking the Spitfire though, even to her uneducated eye.

'Not the original, of course,' Eddie said regretfully. 'It's a replica made by the pilot's family in Norway as a memorial. This is a Mark II, but we were flying the dear old Mark Is. Only one surviving from the Battle of Britain now, and that's up at Coningsby. Look at this beauty though. Isn't she lovely?' He began to sing in a wavery voice. 'Remember that Stevie Wonder song from the Sixties, "Isn't she lovely?" Forget women and kids or whoever Stevie was bleating about. Look at this sweetheart. *Achtung Spitfeuer!* That's what the Germans used to shout out, and you can see why. You felt so much a part of her, it were like flying a woman . . .' He coughed in embarrassment, to Georgia's amusement. She let Peter take over again and soon he and Eddie were deep in technical discussions of heights, speeds and Merlin engines.

'They were just bringing those bulging-out canopies in during the battle so the taller pilots weren't so cramped.

81

Fairfax was one, always complaining there wasn't room. Didn't stop him shooting down Messies though. Fairfax was Uncle Arthur's blue-eyed boy. Promoted him to flight commander in October when Bob McNee was shunted upwards to a squadron command.'

'Arthur Cox?' Peter queried. 'The 362 commanding officer?'

'Right. Old Arthur was a lovely chap. Very straight. You could pull the wool over his eyes like a cashmere sweater, because he didn't realize not everyone marched to his tune. Upright he was. A real gentleman.'

'And did you pull any wool?'

'Nothing important. Siphoning off the odd bit of petrol, that sort of thing. No one wanted to let Arthur down. And then somebody *shot* him down. Good job we were rested shortly afterwards. Sent to Wales for a spell.'

'Eddie, greetings!'

They'd been joined by a newcomer, but Eddie didn't look as though he wished to return the welcome. The speaker looked out of place in this smartly dressed gathering in designer jeans and tee shirt. In his thirties, Georgia thought, and he had the lean and intense look of those with a single-track mind. His dark, intense eyes swivelled quickly to them.

'You must be Georgia and Peter Marsh. Martin Heywood,' he said abruptly, as he shot out a hand towards Peter. So this was the great film director, she thought with amusement. She could believe it. In his case the single-track mind would be focused on Patrick Fairfax. He was a good-looking man, and his eyes were fixed on them so intently that he could have been checking their make-up for the next scene under the lights.

'You're writing about Patrick Fairfax, aren't you?' he continued. 'We need to talk.'

Do we indeed, Georgia thought as Eddie took the opportunity to vanish. She could sympathize. She wasn't sure she would be on the same wavelength as Martin Heywood, even though he seemed genuine enough. 'I gather your next film is to be based on Patrick's war,' she began.

'The whole man,' he said with the enthusiasm of the zealot. 'I won't be exploring the reasons for his death, which I gather is your focus, only its tragic irony, having cheated death so often. Of course, that's why I see this – ' he looked around him – 'as the resolution of that paradox.'

Georgia did her best to contribute to this lofty conception. 'How do you approach a film about a hero of the Battle of Britain for today's audiences? They're used to such a different world, one which selects its own heroes but denies the existence of those of the past. Especially wartime figures.'

'Quite simply, my film – and my contribution to the new edition of *This Life, This Death* – will show the real man, just as the battle will be depicted in real terms, with all the nitty gritty of warfare; the cost in human terms set against the victory, the ultimate denial of the individual and his triumphant fight against such denial.'

Aware that Peter too had left her, Georgia fumed. She needed him to help her break through these sound bites and jargon. If, of course, there was anything on the other side once the breakthrough had been made.

'That sounds interesting,' she said enthusiastically. Make my day, she thought with resignation, tell me more.

He did. 'Because resolution of Patrick the man is my aim, chronology won't be paramount. Scenes from the height of the battle might be juxtaposed with the genial host of the aviation club, or the raw kid at university. Remember the famous Oxford Union debate that in no circumstances would the house fight for King and Country? The motion was passed, yet six years later they rushed to the colours. It's what happened in the months between joining the RAF and the Battle of Britain that interests me. What changed Fairfax from being a playboy student and rowing blue at university to the daredevil but dedicated pilot he became? Is it the individual or was Fairfax symbolic of a sea change in all these young men?'

'Not all of them,' she said sharply, determined to cut through the rhetoric. 'Some didn't make it. What about the LMFs? There were a couple in 362, one of whom apparently committed suicide later. Will you be exploring their stories too?'

She had succeeded in stalling him. He looked far from pleased. 'Those kids that didn't make the grade serve to set in context those that did.'

Glib words. 'You're exploring Fairfax's death.' She pursued her advantage. 'Why not theirs? The LMFs would make a good counterpoint.'

He looked at her strangely – as well he might, she supposed, since she had no idea where she was going with this argument. 'Fairfax was my focal point. As his death is yours. Nevertheless you no doubt will continue asking questions about the Battle of Britain, just as I will about his later life. Have you any grounds, incidentally, for suspecting the reason for Fairfax's murder stemmed from his past?'

This man was not just a head in the air, Georgia realized. It was time for her to adopt an innocent and earnest approach. 'We first became interested through meeting the surviving pilots at Woodring Manor Hotel, which meant that we met his story through the past. Both the murder and his Battle of Britain career were connected to the hotel. One must,' she finished earnestly, 'as you say, see the whole man.'

'And to think that five of these guys are here today,' he murmured. 'Including Daz Dane. Ah!' A conspiratorial look. 'I see by your expression that you've heard about his quarrel with Patrick. I can't think what possessed Fairfax. Such a dull woman.'

'Dull or not, it threw an interesting light on Fairfax.'

'Of course,' Martin continued earnestly, 'this isn't my point of interest, but I'd put my money on the cause of Patrick's death lying elsewhere.'

'And where would that be?' She was surprised at his comment, since she would have thought that dark tale of hidden passion would suit Martin Heywood's film excellently.

'In sordid money, of course. The hotel and the aviation club. The answer must lie between those two. Patrick was determined to save that club, as you know, which is why he invited his friends along to that reunion. Or, to be exact, to the open bar afterwards. Patrick was a generous man.'

'I gather to no purpose, however. Matt Jones wasn't interested, he just wanted Patrick out. Were all the club members there that day willing to put money in?'

He looked vague. 'Jack will know, I expect, even if Matt won't tell you. Did he tell you Paul Stock was there as well?'

'No,' she said truthfully. "The bastard" Jack had called him, she remembered. 'The manager with his alleged hand in the till?'

'It's not the hand in the till that Jack disapproves of,' Martin replied matter-of-factly. 'It's the pass he made at his wife while Jack was researching the biography.'

Susan? Georgia struggled to see the contented gardener of Eynsford in sexual terms. No wonder Jack hadn't expanded on the subject of Paul Stock.

'Paul, I understand, was quite proud of it,' Martin continued, 'but it was almost pistols at dawn when Jack found out. Still seems to feel pretty strongly about poor old Paul.'

'What was he doing at the hotel on the day Patrick died?' This was the salient point.

'I don't know. I only found out by chance that he was there. You can ask him,' Martin said casually. 'He's around here somewhere.'

He was. When she disentangled herself from Martin's company, she went in search of Peter, who was sitting by one of the outside tables of the café. He wasn't alone.

'Georgia, meet Paul Stock. Paul, my daughter, Georgia.'

Blinking at the coincidence of his not only being here, but chatting happily to her father, she felt guilt written all over her face because of what she'd been hearing about him. Having expected a full stage villain twirling black moustachios, the real Paul Stock – a man in his mid-sixties of medium height and thinning hair – disconcerted her, especially since he was holding out a welcoming hand to her as he rose to his feet. He insisted on fetching her a coffee, and Peter grinned as they were briefly left alone.

'Stop looking so smug,' Georgia said firmly. 'What's been happening?'

'You arrived at a most timely point. Our new friend Paul has just begun to tell me about the day of Fairfax's death, at which he was present.'

'So I've just been told. I presume not at the actual murder though?'

'I'm afraid not,' Paul said apologetically, returning with her coffee. 'I went there in the afternoon at Patrick's suggestion with some of the members. We were interviewed by the police later, though apart from myself and Matt everyone had left by the time Patrick was killed.'

Why hadn't Christopher Manners mentioned his name if he was still in the hotel at the time of his death? Presumably because he hadn't remained in his memory as a vital witness, Georgia reasoned.

'I gather there were three members of the club with you.'

'Right. John Standing, in those days a keen aviator, Richard Vane, and Vinny Blake. We got there after lunch and walked into a difficult atmosphere.'

'About an affair Patrick Fairfax had had?'

He looked surprised, almost shifty, she thought. 'Not when I was there. They were arguing over the pros and cons of memoirs, but there might have been earlier discord. No matter, since everyone had disappeared by five thirty or so, pilots and club members. I thought Patrick had gone back to the club, but obviously he hadn't. I went to talk to Matt in his office about the hotel and club finances, left him about seven, went to find Patrick and failed.'

'Wasn't he at the discussions you had with Matt?'

'He wasn't intended to be. Not at first. At that stage he would only have been a hindrance,' Paul said wryly. 'We proposed to approach him after we'd decided what, if anything, could be done. Unfortunately Patrick realized what was going on, and brought in the club members to make their offer. Matt sent them all politely packing, but Patrick burst in again later after he'd downed a few more drinks to tell Matt – and me – what he thought of us as a result. We had to escort him out, then wound up our by now pretty pointless discussions. I went to find Patrick – and failed, as I said.'

He was being frank, Georgia thought, considering that he might have a motive for murder. Was that a point in his favour, or a pre-emptive step to ward off trouble if, as she presumed, he had made a statement to this effect at the time?

'And then the club went bankrupt.'

'Yes. I'm sorry to say his death settled matters. He wasn't the sole owner, in fact. I had money in the business, and so did some other members, but there was no way it could carry on without Patrick as figurehead. Bankruptcy was the only course, since no one would buy it with all those debts. Matt was in a different position; without Patrick he had a chance to run the hotel more efficiently. He wasn't so dependent on having a figurehead. As for the hotel, Matt owned fifty-one per cent, but Patrick's estate would still have had a significant say in the matter had there not been a third partner reducing the estate's claim to a minor one. It could be out-voted, and Matt later bought the estate out – hardly an expensive proposition.'

'Who was the third partner?'

Paul looked embarrassed. 'I'd rather not say.'

'It would be on public record somewhere,' Peter pointed out.

'It would mislead you,' Paul said firmly. 'You'd think it relevant, but it's not.'

'We're trained not to chase trails for their own sake,' Peter persisted pleasantly.

Paul looked undecided and Georgia held her breath. 'It was Mrs Dane,' he said at last, looking at them defiantly. 'And yes, she was at the discussions too. But it has, you must be assured, no relevance.'

'Thank you,' was all Peter said.

Inside, he must be purring with pleasure, Georgia knew. And with good reason. Affair or not, by 1975 at least, Mrs Dane was on Matt's side, not Patrick's.'Why hadn't she helped Matt curb Patrick's excesses?'

'Have you ever been involved in a small company, Georgia?'

'Only ours,' she admitted.

'Personalities can count for as much as shares. The most difficult thing in the world is to pull the plug on a co-partner or director whom you personally *like*. It's not something you tackle easily, particularly when they are – as Patrick was – the public persona of the hotel.'

'And is this what went wrong with the club too?'

'Yes, though he was the major shareholder in that case. It got into debt – not, as many still believe, because I'd been fiddling the books.' He glanced at them, but neither of them commented. 'The position came about because of high maintenance and insurance costs, purchase of inadequate aircraft and cost of repairs, too few members bringing in money and too many taking it out through scrounging off Patrick's good nature – if that is the correct term. My relations with him were extremely strained towards the end.'

This had the ring of truth. On the other hand, Georgia said to Peter after Paul had left them, 'Hamlet might well have said the same of Claudius.' One could indeed smile and smile and be a villain. The finger pointing at Mrs Dane could have been deliberately produced. Jack couldn't stand him, and he was allegedly a thief. Where lay the truth?

* * *

At twelve o'clock they watched the two coach loads duly leave with the squadron personnel and its companions on board. It was interesting to see that even here the five pilots of Woodring Manor kept more or less together, although on this occasion they had their womenfolk with them. The band of brothers, she thought. There they go, bonded by the past, which served to give them a quality of detachment even though they were laughing and joking with those around them. There was no sign of Eddie, though.

Peter had elected to get away from Tangmere for a while in favour of a country pub for lunch, and they duly found that the Anglesey Arms a few miles away provided a welcome breathing space, especially on a warm June day.

'Not a bad morning's haul,' she said cheerfully. 'Jack Hardcastle, Paul Stock, Martin Heywood, and Eddie Stubbs. Have you spoken to any of the Woodring Manor mob yet?'

'I made a managerial decision in the absence of my business partner to leave that till this afternoon. They will have had their fill of talking to each other by then, and be mellowed with liquor.'

'They'll probably be asleep.'

'They won't. They're too tough. This is one of the great moments of the year for them.'

'Is it always held at Tangmere?'

'No. Jack said it could be Brenzett, Duxford, anywhere. Tangmere is popular because so many of the squadron flew here after Battle of Britain days.' Peter paused. 'What did you make of Heywood?'

'Plays the role of Great Artistic Director, but passionately involved in what he's doing. His aim, he says, is to show what the battle and Fairfax were *really* like.'

'Impossible.'

'Why? I don't necessarily disagree but it might be *possible*, with the caveat that it would only be one man's interpretation.'

'How can anyone be sure that what's represented is real to 1940 and not just to the twenty-first century?'

Georgia fell on this with as much enthusiasm as on her ham salad and chips. 'One can't. There has to be some accommodation in order that the latter can be appreciated by the former.'

'So nothing Martin Heywood tells us is irrelevant.'

'You're wrong.' Georgia looked at him. 'We're dealing with 1975, not 1940.'

Peter looked appalled. 'You're *right*. Why do I keep thinking about the Battle of Britain?'

When they returned to the museum, they decided to remain in the garden where they could see the cars and coaches pulling up. No way were they going to let those pilots escape them. It was Jack Hardcastle who strolled up first, however, for there was no sign yet of the coaches.

'I met Martin Heywood,' she began cautiously as he sat down at Peter's encouraging wave of the hand.

'Runs on monorail only. Closed to all other traffic,' Jack said dismissively. 'Take no notice of anything he says; follow your own noses.'

'Good advice,' Peter said heartily. 'Especially where Fairfax is concerned, eh?'

Jack didn't smile. 'Yes.'

'We met Eddie Stubbs too,' Georgia persevered tentatively. She sensed that somewhere they were going wrong, or not picking something up. 'He says he's the only sergeant pilot of 362 left. The others on this photo – ' she produced it again – 'are no longer alive. What about the other officers?'

Jack took it readily – almost too readily, she thought. 'Armstrong and Dodds are dead, as you know. Alan Purcell is in France and out of the picture. Ken Lyle was killed later in the battle. This one, the A Flight Commander when the squadron flew in to Malling, was killed, and Matt Jones took over. The Adjutant died in the sixties, and Spy, the intelligence officer, not long after the war. The CO copped it in October 1940. Why so interested? This isn't to do with 1975.'

'Too much information never hurts,' Peter said blandly. 'Doesn't Alan Purcell ever turn up in England?'

'France suits Alan better.'

'Sounds as if he talked to you at least,' Georgia said – she hoped lightly. The use of 'Alan' hadn't escaped her. There was definitely something here they weren't getting – and Jack would see that they didn't, she suspected. 'When you wrote the biography perhaps?'

A silence, then: 'Alan was in B Flight. Flew in Blue Section normally, number two to McNee. Known as the Cherub because of his youthful looks. He never talks about the battle or the squadron. I got my information from other sources.'

'Of course.'

Jack capitulated, and grinned. 'Not another word, but I gather it's a nice house he's got out there.'

'No one else knows that?'

'You bet your sweet life they don't. And nor do you. Understand?' Jack was clearly in earnest. This was no light matter. 'And since he wasn't present in 1975 there's nothing for you so far as he's concerned.'

'He was part of Fairfax's past.'

'I doubt if Heywood would agree.'

Why not, Georgia wondered.

Jack must have seen her puzzled look, because he added, 'Heywood's interested only in Fairfax. Don't forget that, Georgia.'

Did he mean that Heywood was officer-obsessed? That would fit with his focus on Fairfax and his lack of take on sergeant pilots. But what stance would his film take? For all his posturing Heywood might prove to be anti-Fairfax, rather than pro him. His stated aim of the 'real' man could work both ways.

Before she could tackle Jack on what he meant, however,

he pointed towards the forecourt where the coaches were just pulling in. 'Here come the troupers.'

The occupants of the coaches were descending rapidly or slowly according to age, women in bright colours, men in the occasional RAF blue uniform, now and then a familiar face. She saw Bob McNee limping towards the garden, and Matt Jones, shuffling on two sticks guarded by two women. Harry Williams also had two sticks, while Bill Dane and Jan Molkar were walking slowly but unaided behind. Well over sixty years ago, these young pilots had jumped down from the station brakes taking them to and from Town Malling and their messes. Time was an odd thing, she thought not for the first time. Suppose there were parallel universes side by side and that one only had to press a computer button or make a wish and the walls between them would dissolve. She could imagine this now. To each other they were in the world of 1940, divided only by time from everyone else here.

Whom to tackle first? Peter was still talking to Jack, who nodded, and walked over to Matt Jones.

'Gentleman's offering you a cup of tea, Matt,' she heard him say jovially. 'That'll chase the whisky down nicely.'

Matt looked over and smiled, turning his sticks and then his steps towards them, flanked by the two women – wife and daughter presumably. He sat down at their table with a sigh as the women and Jack went off to order tea.

'Do you feel up to talking about what happened at the 1975 reunion?' Georgia asked gently. 'We realize it must be a sad memory for you.'

His unfocused eyes wandered over her. 'Why shouldn't I?'

There was no answer to that. 'I met Mr Stock this morning, and he told me you talked about business with Mrs Dane after the other pilots left the hotel.' She'd mishandled it, leapt in too deep, too soon. There was no response or any sign that he had heard her.

'The hotel,' Peter prompted. 'You ran the hotel, and it was in financial trouble.'

92

Suddenly Matt was quite clear. 'Patrick of course,' he snapped. 'He would do it. Fancy bringing them to the reunion. No taste at all. That was *our* time. All four of them towering over me. Nothing comes of mixing business with pleasure. Wanted to put money into the hotel. I tried to tell them it was no use, they'd lose it all, but they wouldn't have it. Patrick was shouting the odds at them and me. Then he was dead.'

'Did Patrick return later?' If Paul Stock was right, this was an important point because it could only have been shortly before he died, and it occurred to her it might account for the trace evidence the police found.

There was no answer, and Matt Jones continued to drink his tea.

'Do you remember the police coming?' she tried again.

'Yes,' he said doubtfully. 'Stomping all over my office. Talked to everyone. Staff, restaurant customers, even the kids in the discos. Fat lot of good it did them.'

'Your RAF friends had all left by the time Patrick was killed, and Mr Stock told me that the aviation club members had too. Could anyone have stayed on without your knowing?'

He looked at her as though she were simple-minded, and amused she saw a glimpse of the masterful flight commander of the past. 'Can't be everywhere. Lots of rooms in that hotel. Car park too. Didn't check that. Why should I? Not a blasted traffic warden.'

'Was there a car park attendant?' Could one of the group have stayed there unnoticed?

'Couldn't afford one. Bad enough getting staff as it was.'

This was hopeless. They were getting nowhere. 'Who were your staff then? Would there still be a list?' If only they could get at those police files.

'My dear young lady,' he explained patiently, back in flight commander mode, 'today it would be immigrant labour. In the Seventies, it would have been immigrants, students, other seasonal labour. Some of our staff were regulars, but the

93

chambermaids, waiters and bar staff came and went. I hardly knew their faces let alone their names.'

A different tack. 'The party hadn't gone well that day, had it?' Peter asked casually. 'You'd had a bit of a row.'

'Had we?' He smiled politely with tired eyes. 'I really don't remember.'

They were grasping at will o' the wisp shadows. 'There had been a quarrel,' Georgia said. She took a risk. 'Was it because Bill's wife was your partner in the hotel?' Nothing in response. Talk about leading the witness, she thought in despair.

He flushed red. 'Very naughty of Patrick, inviting outsiders.'

She gave up. Was this just the effects of age, or did the magic ring binding this quintet still hold firm? For perhaps the best of reasons, no one would remember anything about that day. Anything that would take Marsh & Daughter forward, that is.

After the museum had officially closed to the general public, the squadron drew together as they made their way to the memorial garden. The sun was getting lower, but it was still warm, as Georgia and Peter followed them, not to the main part of the garden where the squadron gathered round the memorial to the fallen, but to one of the smaller areas devoted to small plaques commemorating individual loved ones. Here they could watch without intruding, together with the carers, wives and children. Not that anyone would notice their presence. The former pilots were gathered round, as again Bill Dane recited from 'High Flight'. A blue-clad officer in his late thirties – the current CO perhaps – read out the roll of those in 362 Squadron who had died either during the Second World War or after it in the course of duty. The list seemed endless. Two names struck her: Joseph Smith and Oliver Tanner, the two LMF sergeant pilots. What did that indicate? Acceptance of frailties? Forgiveness?

Patrick Fairfax's name was not on the roll, which surprised

her until she remembered that he had not died in service. And yet to her he seemed here, a dancing, laughing presence, defying them to find the truth.

As if reading her mind, as the ceremony ended she realized that the five pilots were coming towards them, and only belatedly did she realize that she and Peter were blocking some of the individual memorials – and one of them must be to Fairfax. Hastily, they moved aside. Bill Dane led the quintet, and glanced over to them as he did so. He seemed to be looking at her closely, but whether in challenge or appeal, she was not sure. Perhaps it was just a flight of fancy because when they finished the ceremony, he beckoned to them to join the quintet.

'Mr Hardcastle tells us you want to write a book about Patrick's death,' he said quite normally.

'That's so,' Peter answered. 'It won't conflict with either the film or his new edition of *This Life, This Death*, if that's what worries you.'

'Worries?' Harry Williams answered, his voice still deep and confident. 'I should think not. We're all for it. Good old Patrick deserves it.'

'Anything we can do to help, we shall,' Bill added. 'The only worry we have is that Patrick's murder will remain unsolved. We want the case reopened officially. Can you do that?'

'If we produce a credible case,' Peter told him.

'The police did not succeed,' Bob McNee reminded them in his soft Scottish accent. Georgia had been aware that he had been watching them carefully. 'If there's unfinished business, it's better we know.'

Georgia was too dumbfounded to speak as contact details were exchanged. Why had she assumed that the quintet would decide as a whole not to assist? Did that mean that they were sure none of them were involved? Or, it occurred to her, did it mean the opposite? They might wish to monitor what the Marshes were up to.

'We thank you.' Jan Molkar made a quaint bow. 'It is most fitting that we have met you again.'

'We shall do our best,' Peter promised gravely. 'Tell me, do you feel that the reason for Patrick's death stems from 1975, or . . .' He looked from one to the other.

'Or?' Bill Dane picked up evenly. 'What were you going to say, Mr Marsh?'

'From his earlier life. From the war perhaps.'

Georgia saw amazement on their faces, even on Matt's, but it was followed by something else that she could not define.

'How could that be?' Bill asked.

'Are you asking whether one of us fired the shot?' Bob McNee laughed. 'I think you'll be a wee while proving that.'

'I should leave us out, old man,' Harry joked. 'Plenty of folk Patrick rubbed up the wrong way in the course of his life, creditors, husbands . . .'

He stopped as his friends looked at him. Including Bill Dane. 'Only joking,' he continued hastily. 'Poor old Patrick.'

That night Georgia slept badly. Images of the five pilots descending one by one from the coach grew more and more vivid. As black silhouettes following one behind the other the steadily advancing line began to turn from weirdness to nightmare, as she and Peter looked on. Then the line stopped, and at a sign from one she half recognized as Bill Dane they turned direction to walk slowly, inexorably, towards them, grinning not in welcome but menace. Peter retreated, but the line came on. And on. Chuckles now. Leers. Whispers. Implacably advancing on them. Finally she and Peter could retreat no more. His wheelchair stuck and she was power-less to intervene. Bill Dane leant over the wheelchair, stick outstretched. A hoarse whisper reached her.

'We only want to help you.'

As the stick crashed down, she woke up sweating.

Six

S he was still shaken the next morning, and her mood was not lightened by finding Peter already at his desk. On Sundays this was officially forbidden except in emergencies, and she took herself into the garden for the rest of the day since she'd be seeing Luke tomorrow. Weeding provided a clearer perspective, and when on Monday she found Peter in exactly the same place she felt better able to cope.

'This case is like a football match,' Peter said gloomily. 'A foul's called and the team's ready to kick off again, but in our case, who blows the whistle?'

'Elucidate, O great Plato.'

'We have a clear path forward if we agree that the Fearful Five genuinely want us to find the truth, but suppose only four of them do?'

She saw his point. One of the group might have been Fairfax's murderer, unsuspected by the others. She peered over his shoulder at the playing area on the Suspects Anonymous screen. It was blank, with Burglar Bills and Bettys waiting for the off.

'Suppose the pilots just throw us sticks to run after and bring back to them wagging our tails, while all the time the *real* business is going on between them.'

'I don't follow that. If they are genuine about helping us, any other *real* business, as you put it, can have nothing to do with the case.'

'Or they believe it doesn't,' Peter pointed out.

'You're right.' Georgia's optimism was rapidly vanishing.
'Such sweet words.'

'That could have been the police's problem in 1975.'

'With hindsight we do better.'

'Not always,' Georgia said fairly. 'Remember that woman
who claimed her sweetheart had been murdered for knowing
too much about the Falklands War. Turned out to be a total
fantasist, as Mike had warned us, and —'

'Yes, yes,' Peter cut her off impatiently. 'But that was
then. This is now, and there's still a gate through somewhere, I know it. It could be Sylvia Lee.'

'Only if we think the 1940s are the key to what happened
in 1975. And we haven't a shred of evidence to suggest
that. There's far more on the aviation club members.'

'Sylvia's husband was one of the people present in 1975.
He's no longer alive, but she is. Why don't you pop up and
see her – just in case?' he added placatingly.

'But *why*?' she wailed. 'I have to have a reason.'

'Background,' Peter said firmly. 'Make an appointment
for next week. How do you fancy tackling Bill Dane right
away?'

Georgia considered this. 'Yes.' Instinct told her this might
not achieve anything either, but she couldn't justify it. It
might still be the thought of the nightmarish stick crashing
down.

'Good. Now, this house you're going to see with Luke.
Is he serious about it?'

'It's his second look. He's never got that far before or
invited my opinion before.'

The butterflies fluttered in her stomach. How ridiculous of me, she thought. A step too far, her cautious side
said; a step in the right direction replied her rational self.
But suppose his living so close brought a different perspective? Changed things? Ah, but suppose doing nothing
proved a signal for Luke to drift out of her life. He'd been
generous, he was taking the first step, whereas it should

have been her. She should signal acknowledgement of that fact.

Peter's eyes gleamed. 'I'll treat you both to lunch in the White Lion afterwards to celebrate.'

'He's unlikely to have contracted and completed the sale by then,' she quipped blithely.

'Georgia, do try.'

This was the only direct piece of advice her father had ever given her, she realized with surprise, as she unlocked her Alpha Romeo. On a good day the distance to Medlars, the house Luke had his eye on, might be walkable. Then she realized the way her thoughts were moving and laughed at herself. A small part of her must think this was a done deal. Two lovers strolling hand in hand along a country lane made an idyllic picture – even if it did mean their leaping into the hedgerows every so often when a car swept by.

Medlars was on the road to Old Wives Lees, a name which Luke had deemed propitious. She had retorted that the postal address of the house was still Haden Shaw. In fact it was in a tiny hamlet called Cot Street, which had a lane direct to the Canterbury Road. For a business such as Luke's this was a plus, even though his main distribution was carried out by a firm in Folkestone.

She was surprised to find her heart beating very loudly as she turned into the Old Wives Lees road. This wasn't one that she normally used, and so she didn't know precisely where Medlars was. First of all she saw a For Sale sign, then the white gates Luke had described. They were open, but she paused for a moment before driving in. She needed to get this important first impression. It was an old Wealden House, not from the look of it in good repair, but comfortable in its skin, as the French would say.

She could see immediately what attracted Luke. There was an old oast with a barn attached on the left of the large forecourt in front of the house. The barn was pretty dismal-looking with black painted clapboards, and the oast must be the only one in Kent with chipped, worn paint, but they could do something about that. *They?* She felt a sudden stab of panic. Was it going to be difficult to think in terms of he and she if Luke moved in here, only of some amorphous blob called 'they'? She'd done blobs with her ex-husband, Zac. Never again.

She disciplined herself into sense and advanced into the forecourt. It was gravelled with trees and shrubs on the side facing the oast, all in need of a prune. It looked welcoming – and expensive, despite its dilapidation. Oasts didn't come cheap, particularly with Wealden houses guarding them. Luke would be making a big commitment. *Stop making reservations*, she told the butterflies, which were beginning a dance of victory.

To her pleasure, Luke was already there, his car parked by the oast, and he was lolling against it eyeing the house speculatively. He already looked as though he belonged there. The moment her car crunched on the gravel, he looked round and strolled towards her as she parked next to him.

'What do you think?' he asked her.

'Too good to be true,' she answered frankly.

'Possibly. Every deathwatch beetle in Kent might have been incubated here.'

'Can you afford it?'

'With a little help from a poor survey so that they'll accept an offer.'

'Plus a best-seller or two,' she joked. 'Does the barn have a business licence?' It seemed unlikely.

'You won't believe this, but yes. The owner's son was going to move in to use it as a regional office, but the firm went bust before he got going. Should be no problem over it. A publishing company should be considered a desirable presence. Let's hope so anyway.'

Yes, she thought with some surprise, let's hope.

It was obvious as soon as she stepped in the door that this should be Luke's home. He would fit into it like a comfortable old boot. The building itself had been extensively patched up over the years with Tudor red-brick walls at the rear of the house, and inside it had greatly changed from its original medieval layout. Not, thankfully, by a 1960s modernizer, as in other houses she'd seen. The changes here had been to larger rooms and a decent-sized kitchen. The passage could still be traced back to its medieval ancestry, however.

The oast barn had been half fitted out as an office, then abandoned. 'Potential,' the owner said genially as they looked at the piles of planks and paint left awaiting the realization of this dream. Luke agreed wholeheartedly. His office could be in the oast and storage and open plan offices fit into the barn.

'More light,' she heard him murmur to himself. 'They'll need more light.'

'They?' She hadn't dared ask about his staff. One step at a time. Luke looked so relaxed and excited that she wasn't going to take risks.

'I can see Frost Books, here, can't you?' He glanced at her tentatively.

'Yes.' No doubt about that. She could. Could she see herself in the house – either as 'she' or 'they'? Honesty forced her to admit *yes*. Given time.

'Do you want to come on our next visit, Peter?' Luke said an hour later at the White Lion.

'Certainly,' Peter said promptly. 'I need to see our publisher won't be making a gigantic mistake. Are you going to make an offer?'

'Yes. The fellow's had a survey done already, which is a help. I've made an offer subject to my own survey anyway and my checking out the business licence. So it's full steam ahead. With Georgia's permission,' he added straight-faced.

'Full permission,' she said, firmly subduing a rebellious butterfly.

'How's the Fairfax book coming along?' Luke asked, once they had given their order. 'I brought you the cheque incidentally.' He fished in his sports jacket pocket and produced the envelope for Peter.

'Excellent. A splendid spur to our investigation.' Peter took it from him.

'No doubt. How's it going though?'

Georgia did not dare look at her father as Peter replied: 'We are scuffling round the perimeter.' He beamed so confidently that one might have thought he'd announced he was on the last chapter.

'At least that's honest. Suppose there's nothing inside the circle? Not that I want the cheque back,' Luke said hastily.

'There will be something there,' Peter said, more confidently than Georgia felt. 'It's a question of finding the way in.'

'How can you be certain of that?' Luke asked curiously.

'We know,' Peter said, glancing at Georgia, 'that there *is* something to find out.'

Georgia kept silent. The dell shouted so loudly in her mind that she felt its presence must make itself felt to Luke too.

'But how?' Luke persisted.

'How do you know which of two books to publish and which to reject if they both seem publishable?' Georgia answered at last.

'Instinct.'

'Precisely.'

'I had an interesting talk with Mike while you were gallivanting at Medlars,' Peter said casually when they returned from lunch. 'Before you see Bill Dane, I thought we should have another go at seeing what was in their original statements.'

'Why didn't you tell me?' she cried.

'I *am* telling you. He's a good chap,' Peter said

condescendingly. 'He's already looked up the file on the Fairfax case. He rang me, not me him. Went over to Malling specially, so he said, but he might have been overstating the case.'

'Why? What made him go? Is it being officially reopened?'

'No. We've nothing to justify it yet, but Mike saw our dilemma. How can we produce a rabbit if we don't know what's in the hat with it? He believes in a flat playing field, does Mike.'

'Can we read them?'

'You're joking. As it is, he says we owe him.' Peter looked pained. 'Imagine that. After all I did for him.'

'We *do* owe him,' Georgia said scathingly. 'What's the gist of it?'

'He's emailed me the notes he took. I've forwarded them to you. One of the diners in the restaurant saw Patrick Fairfax leave the hotel to go into the gardens. He was alone.'

'Time?'

'Thought to be about seven o'clock.'

'What about the waiter who found the body?'

'Nothing of interest. He seems to have been thoroughly grilled and ruled out. Matt claimed to have been alone in his office until nearly eight, and didn't see Patrick after he'd been thrown out just before seven. Paul Stock did indeed say he went to find him in the downstairs bar but failed. So far nothing new on any of the pilots. Sir Richard Vane said he left the club a little earlier than the other aviation club members because he wasn't well. Plenty of staff said they saw Patrick that day. The other restaurant waiters, reception staff, bar staff, were all interviewed. The latter in particular. One barman saw him drinking in the bar – the upstairs one – after the others had left; another in the downstairs bar.'

'Alone?'

'No, with a woman. Probably Janet Freeman.'

'*Who?*'

'I thought that would get your attention. It seems this Mrs Fairfax was selective in which photographs she put in these scrapbooks – *and* with the truth. There were *four*, not three, aviation club members who went to the hotel that day. Janet Freeman also made a statement to the police.'

Georgia had been thinking. 'You don't mean the traveller? Writes or wrote books on women explorers?'

'I imagine the same one.'

'Now that is interesting.' The further 1940 receded, the better. 'What about the staff? Was it the sort of barman who if not still working there might be contactable?'

'Checked that. Their hotel staff records don't go back as far as the Seventies, but the maitre d' says that when he came to the hotel, the barman who'd been there for thirty years was just about to retire. The three barmen interviewed in 1975 were Jim Potter, Tony Wilson and Thomas Langley. The first two were casual labour, and Langley was the one who'd been there since the year dot.'

'Who was on duty that night?'

'All of them, I gather. The two bars were going full tilt and they alternated service. Langley remembered seeing Fairfax in the upstairs bar, and later Wilson saw him downstairs. He said Fairfax left at ten to seven and the lady a little later. She told him to tell Fairfax she'd be in the gardens. Which fits with the story of Fairfax's sighting at seven.'

'So Janet Freeman is on our list. What about Mrs Dane? Was she interviewed?'

'Yes. She stated that she was at the meeting with Matt Jones and Paul Stock, and confirms that Patrick stormed in with the potential investors and was promptly thrown out again. Nothing decisive happened in the meeting to provide a motive for murder, in her view. She left about six o'clock to meet her husband.'

'And what about the row between the pilots?'

'There's the interesting thing. Not mentioned. Three of them said that Patrick left them for ten minutes or so, and came back with Paul Stock. There'd clearly been words between them. It wasn't long afterwards that three aviation club members came in, followed by Janet Freeman a little later. I bet fur was ruffled over that.'

'Paul Stock didn't mention meeting Patrick outside.'

'Another one economical with facts?' Peter raised an eyebrow. 'Richard Vane told the police he left about five twenty p.m. and drove home immediately since he was feeling unwell. Evidence corroborated by his wife – so the police obviously were pretty thorough. She said he arrived home in London much earlier than expected, about six thirty, and his son Harvey confirmed that too.'

'That probably clears him then.'

Peter grunted. 'I suppose so. I'll put him and Sylvia Lee in as background evidence in Suspects Anonymous. Now, what about Mrs Dane, a shadowy figure if ever I saw one? A dull woman, so we're told, the little warm wife of the Fifties. Yet she was the third partner in the Matt Jones company, and by rumour Patrick Fairfax's lover – a sleeping partner twice over, albeit a transitory one where sex is concerned.'

'As was Sylvia Lee, yet you seem intent on my seeing her. It's a good job I like tying up loose ends.'

Peter had the last word. 'But avoiding the knot?'

Bill Dane lived at Coggeshall, a stunningly attractive Essex village with each cottage painted brightly in varying colours. All carefully planned, Bill told her. He radiated pleasure at seeing her, which half of her appreciated while the other half still remembered that stick and the grinning gargoyles of her nightmare. Nevertheless it seemed a good start. Inside the house was delightful, full of interesting objects, although it struck her as a widower's house. The only sign of his 'dull' wife was a large photograph of their wedding. Alice wore a New Look dress, with pinched-in waist and wide three-quarter-length skirt, dating it to between 1948 and 1950. She didn't look at all dull to Georgia.

No coffee, or even tea, in this household, even though it was early afternoon. 'How about a glass of something?' he asked her. She joined him in a glass of wine, which served to break any remaining ice, and duly admired the photograph.

'I understand your wife was a partner in the Woodring Manor Hotel?'

'Not an active role. She had great faith in Matt Jones.'

'But not in Patrick Fairfax?' Rather a gauntlet to lay down on her part, but he had promised to help them.

He smiled. 'Patrick was a wonderful person. We all loved him. But he was no businessman. His death was an enormous shock to us all. We still feel it, and that's why we decided to help you. We were perhaps too close to see much at the time.'

'Guarding what did not need guarding?' Where had *that* come from?

'Who judges that, Georgia, apart from God?'

'I'm afraid we have to.'

He regarded her thoughtfully. 'I see that. So where shall we begin?'

'Would your movements have varied from the statements you gave then, or can we take them as still valid?'

'Details corrected now might be suspect.'

'But you must have talked them over between yourselves?'

He answered almost too quickly. 'Obviously we did. There was no disagreement over what happened.'

It was time to push, Georgia decided. 'There was some kind of fracas with Patrick Fairfax that afternoon. Perhaps two blow-ups. One he had with Paul Stock outside and another disagreement between the eight of you. That's not in the statements, but we've been told two different stories.

That it was about writing memoirs, or that it was over a personal problem . . .'

'Over my wife,' he finished for her. 'I'm accustomed to that canard. No doubt you heard that she and Patrick had had an affair, and that Patrick taunted me at the meeting.'

'Yes,' she agreed gratefully.

'So now you wish to know if it was true. Let me tell you an old army joke I used to use in my sermons. A chestnut, no doubt, but worth boring you with. The commander leading a column of troops despatched a verbal message back through the men: Send reinforcements, we're going to advance. By the time the message had reached the rear of the column it had been transformed into: Send three and fourpence, we're going to a dance.'

She laughed. 'Peter and I are used to that problem, but I haven't heard it put so well before. That's what happened over your wife?'

'Whispers grow out of proportion and alter their direction. My wife came from a wealthy family. Patrick was keen to begin the aviation club, and Matt the hotel. Patrick spent a long time trying to persuade Alice to invest in the club but she chose the hotel, trusting Matt rather than Patrick where money was concerned. Patrick had escorted her to many events in the meanwhile, providing the basis for rumour. My wife had great beauty but it shone from within. Not Patrick's style for his casual amours.'

'But if the rumour was false why did Patrick apparently tell his wife it was true, and why did a row blow up on the day of his death?'

'It didn't.'

'Your wife was there . . .' she began doubtfully.

'Yes, but not in the bar. That was a stag do, or meant to be. In fact Janet Freeman joined us, which displeased my misogynistic friends. My wife did not so intrude. We had friends living nearby, whom she visited and then drove over to see Matt later. She left the meeting before Patrick burst

107

in for the second time, when only Matt and Paul were left. He had to be patiently persuaded not to throttle them both, I gather.'

'How did the rumour first get around about the affair?'

'I've no idea.'

She wasn't having that. 'You must have. You'd have been hopping mad if false rumours were going round, and certainly your wife would.'

'Bowled leg before wicket,' he chuckled. 'Very well. I suspect Patrick himself at least helped spread the rumour and then told his wife.'

She blinked in disbelief. 'Why?'

'Patrick had the gift of the gab. What better way of hiding an indiscretion than by confessing to another, particularly one that could be implied to have been in the past?'

'You mean there was a current one?'

'One never knew with Patrick. It could have been to deflect poor Jean from his monetary troubles. A hint of an affair with Alice could explain all too easily why he was getting flak over the hotel.'

'Yes,' she agreed. That made sense. 'So the argument in the bar on the day of his death was about memoirs?' This seemed odd to her.

'Correct. Some of us felt strongly that Patrick should not write such a book.'

'Why ever not?'

'After so long how could he see things clearly? One could look at one's logbook and read the brief notes made at the time. "Shot down Me 109, Ashford." But how could all the circumstances be recalled? Imagination, with the best will in the world, must always be helpfully hovering to help out. Suppose one forgets the horror of seeing one's comrades shot down in flames, and the equal horror of doing it oneself. Suppose one remembers only the face of God, the glory of the skies and not their darkness. The whole truth can never be recaptured.'

Fine words, but she was still puzzled. 'Why did Patrick want to write his memoirs in the 1970s when he had already published such a classic in *This Life, This Death*?'

'Family pressure, I seem to recall. The earlier book is naturally short on detail. You have no doubt seen how enthusiastic Jean still is to keep his flame alight. She supported, indeed suggested the biography of him, written by Jack Hardcastle. Now she is naturally eager to help with the film and revised new edition.'

'Who amongst you supported his writing a new book?'

'Dear Harry, Matt, and Fairfax himself were in favour. Tom, Jan, Bob McNee and myself opposed it. I can't recall what stance Nat took.'

'And that's fact,' Georgia asked lightly, 'not hindsight?'

He didn't take offence. 'It is fact. I know that because we continue to hold the same views. Helping a historian or biographer is one thing. Writing our own stories seems to me another. We couldn't stop Patrick writing his, but we could certainly make our opinions known. We did, and he didn't like it.'

'It doesn't seem to be mentioned in your statements.'

'Because, Georgia, animated discussion is hardly murder material. Do you really think one of us had a hidden secret and was so fearful of its being revealed in Patrick's memoirs that he killed him? If there was such a secret it would have emerged in Jack's biography. Killing Patrick would have achieved nothing. No. You must realize that we loved the man, Georgia.'

He spoke with conviction, and it made sense. 'Do you still talk about the day Patrick died amongst yourselves?' she asked him curiously.

'Mostly not. The link is there without its being spoken of. As it is with the Battle of Britain. Public perception of such reunions is that their purpose is to hash over old times. In practice they work out differently, especially as we meet regularly.'

'Why do you?' Georgia asked bluntly. 'Didn't the shock of his death tempt you to give them up?'

'I believe I see it as my duty to continue. I cannot speak for the others.'

'Duty towards whom? Patrick?' She found this so interesting that it was worth risking his annoyance by persisting.

The blue eyes held her steadily. 'Why do most of us send Christmas cards year after year to people we'd love to see again but probably never will? Time does not permit. We change. The Christmas cards are a sign that the past is still with us and that the future still bears hope. All this in one small gesture – yet some say it is pointless, too expensive. Nonsense.' He smiled. 'So, to answer your question, it's something that Bob, Harry, Jan, Matt and I need to do.'

'A memorial to Patrick?'

'To the dead, Georgia. Remember that.'

He was very serious now, and yet they were getting away from the point, even though Bill seemed to want to impress this strongly on her.

'Was the memoir discussion ended when Patrick left you and later returned with Paul Stock?'

He hesitated. 'I believe so. After that three members of the aviation club arrived, followed by Miss Freeman. It was not well received. We are a hospitable bunch, but we like our time alone. Your father was of course an exception,' he added politely.

'You were very gracious to him.' She wasn't going to be fobbed off. 'But animated discussion was over?'

Again he hesitated. 'Well, yes . . .'

'You said you'd help,' she reminded him, 'and making sense of all this is essential.'

He made a rueful face. 'It's a fair cop, Georgia. I was hoping to keep this out of it. The real row was between Patrick and Paul Stock. Patrick had gone outside – we didn't know why – and then they both came in very angry.'

'But why wasn't this in the statements?'

'We couldn't swear to something that took place out of our hearing. Anyway, it was well known that Patrick and Paul had a rocky relationship at that time. It had nothing to do with our reunion.'

'Then you can tell me. If it leads nowhere there's no problem,' she said instantly. She was getting somewhere now.

'I see you've been CIA trained,' he said resignedly. 'It was over Paul Stock's ex-wife with whom Patrick *was* having an affair. Paul had seen her in the car park carrying what was clearly an overnight bag, and objected strongly when Patrick came out to meet her. Patrick, I fear, would not have been able to see what the fuss was about. Paul's ex-wife was now single, even if Patrick was not, so he told Paul to keep out of it. Paul refused.'

'So who was she?'

'I have no way of knowing the truth about that, even though it was fairly common gossip at the club.'

'At the club?' Georgia pounced.

A split second reaction as Bill seemed to realize he was cornered.

'It was Janet Freeman.'

Seven

'It's a motive at least.' Georgia was mutinous. Peter was not as jubilant as she about the Janet Freeman lead. She tried to ignore the suspicion that her own jubilance was because it took the case so firmly away from 1940.

'I agree.' Peter held up his hands in surrender. 'I'm just saying it's an interesting fact, not a solution.'

'You said *cherchez la femme*. I've found you one.'

'You know why the Greeks fought so successfully, Georgia?'

'Oh, *please*.'

'They organized themselves in a phalanx, maintaining a continuous line of shields.'

'So?'

'Doesn't it strike you that Bill Dane has organized a phalanx and is deflecting you from the vital issues?'

Had he? She thought about their conversation. As she did so, it wasn't Greek soldiers she centred on, however, but a faint hangover from her nightmare. She shook herself free from it. This was daytime; her eyes were open, and fully objective.

'A test,' Peter continued. 'Did he suggest you meet the other four as well?'

'No, he didn't,' she admitted crossly. 'But he didn't try to dissuade me from seeing them.'

'He wouldn't do that. If you follow it up, however, they'll all tell you the same thing. With their armour on, Georgia, how do you tell one from another?'

She glanced at him. 'Why should we? It's a motive in 1975 we need, not from 1940. And I've brought you one.'

'And who's to say one of the five didn't have a good reason for hating Patrick Fairfax that evolved in the thirty-five years since the war? Matt Jones had, for example. But,' he said generously, 'follow up Janet Freeman by all means. And,' he added as she left to make the appointment, 'good luck to you.'

Georgia had the distinct impression she was being fobbed off, because Peter had sniffed out a scent he wished to pursue. She absolved him of the crime of wanting to go it alone, but he was certainly appealing for space. He had it. He had at least upgraded Janet on the Suspects Anonymous file to a Burglar Betty, and Georgia had promptly made an appointment to meet her. But not without difficulty.

Janet Freeman lived in Norwich, but the idea of ploughing round the M25 to the A11 was not appealing. Georgia was considering the train journey when by serendipity Luke rang up and offered to come with her.

'I've had my own survey done,' he told her grumpily. 'I need to be alone.'

'You won't be if you're with me.'

'You, my heart, are part of me. I just don't want to see delivery vans, books, invoices, jacket designs, and authors for a while. OK? In particular a book called *Catty Kent*.'

That made her laugh. He'd been in two minds whether to publish it, and had regretted his decision to go ahead. Once he'd signed the contract, the dear lady who had written it, one Mrs Letty Pinkton, turned out to have a will of steel regarding every aspect and they had fallen out over the jacket design which she insisted should be one of her sweet illustrations. Since this had resembled a Louis Wain cat during his manic period, Luke had put his foot down and exercised his contractual rights to final choice.

'Very OK,' Georgia replied. She'd like nothing more than to have his company. 'But if we go by car, you drive.'

'Done,' he agreed. 'Provided you come for the weekend and stay over.'

'Done. I thought you said a poor survey could suit your budget. So what's wrong with this one?'

'There's poor and there's catastrophic. Everything from dry rot to general dilapidation. Last wired under King James I.'

'Are you put off?' She held her breath, waiting for his reply. Would she be relieved or sorry if he were?

'No, just drawing a deep breath, getting estimates and sorting the wheat from the surveying jargon chaff.'

Since Bill's revelation, Georgia had read *Women and Air*, Janet Freeman's best-seller of 1974, with much interest. The cover showed a dark-haired, eager-eyed young woman, laughing into the camera, hands thrust in flying jacket pocket, and standing by a light aircraft. She was in her thirties then, and Peter had said that her picture adorned every magazine on the stands. She stepped out round the world following the tracks of intrepid lady Victorian travellers writing up both their adventures and hers. *Women of the Air* centred on the flights of famous aviatrixes including Amy Johnson, Amelia Ehrhardt and an intrepid lady before the First World War by the name of Miss Trehawke Davies. She hadn't been a pilot herself, but insisted on being the first woman in the world to experience a loop-the-loop and had done more travelling in Bleriots than most male pilots of that time put together. That book, she realized, must have been the reason that Janet Freeman took up membership of the aviation club.

Janet lived on the road to Earlham on the outskirts of the city, an area which was, she explained on the telephone, fast disappearing under concrete. Luke negotiated the traffic with his usual imperturbable skill and drove into the gravel driveway with aplomb.

From the dustcover photo on her book, Georgia had decided she liked the look of Janet Freeman – but that, of course, was over thirty years ago. The woman who greeted them – if that was the word – bore little resemblance to it, even given the time gap. The dark hair was recognizable, but the face wore a set expression that did not relax easily as she spoke, and the lively eyes were hard and suspicious. She was wearing trousers and casual jacket and blouse, and bore every sign of still being extremely active physically as well as mentally.

'Come in.' Her eyes shot to Luke.

'Luke Frost,' he supplied.

'The publisher?'

'I'm honoured you've heard of me.'

'Of course. You're publishing a book by a cousin of mine, Letty Pinkton.'

Georgia gave Luke full marks for self control. His expression didn't change a jot. 'Of course,' he replied. 'What an extraordinary coincidence.' Serendipity was letting her down with a vengeance, Georgia decided. Janet Freeman's hackles would be well sharpened.

'And you're publishing this book on Patrick Fairfax?' Her tone suggested this came a poor second to Letty Pinkton's.

Georgia answered for him. 'Yes, provided Marsh & Daughter come up with enough material.'

'Somewhat rash of you to sign it up before that's certain.' She returned the attack to Luke.

'I have the utmost faith in all my authors,' Luke returned blandly.

Janet Freeman let that one go, and ushered them into her living room, although her silence suggested she had heard a different story from her cousin. The room spoke not of that laughing girl but of the sharper, older woman she now was. Clinically tidy, angular and revealing little of the personality that created it.

'What are you hoping I can tell you?' The words flashed out.

'Your memories of that day.'

'What use will they be? I take it you've read my statement to the police. How can I remember more at this stage?'

Amy Myers

'I haven't read the statement itself but . . .'

'I do dislike interviewers who haven't done their homework.'

Georgia wasn't having that. 'Who sets the homework?' she countered.

'In this case, I do,' Janet Freeman returned briskly. 'Nevertheless, since there's no reason for me not to tell you, I will. My statement no doubt read that I arrived about four o'clock with three or four other people.' She frowned. 'To be correct, I think I arrived first. I saw Paul Stock drive up as I went inside. I went to the cloakroom first, and when I returned I found Paul and the other club members in the bar with the 362 pilots. I stayed there, and when the party broke up, Patrick Fairfax suggested we had another drink after he had taken the club members to see Matt Jones about investment. Patrick duly returned, we chatted for a while, then he took me to the downstairs bar to show me the memorabilia there. We stayed there until well past six thirty. Patrick realized the time was passing, said he must see Matt Jones again and that he'd be back. He didn't return so after a while I left too.'

'Left the hotel or the bar?' No mention of Paul having been her husband, Georgia noted.

'The bar. I was staying at the hotel for the weekend to be ready for flying the next day. I went up to my room.'

'According to the barman, you left a message with him for Patrick that he would find you in the gardens.'

'I don't recall that.' Very stiffly. 'And I resent the implication that I might have been around near the time that Patrick was murdered. The police had no such suspicions, I would point out.'

Georgia tried hard to appear grateful for these very small mercies. 'What brought you to the hotel? I assume you can't have been intending to invest money or you would have gone with the others to the meeting with Matt Jones.'

Little chance of catching this lady unawares. 'I imagine it was because the weather wasn't good enough for flying.

116

Besides, I'm always interested in talking to former pilots. Having just written a book about women pilots, I was considering writing one about their male counterparts.'

Georgia looked around. No photos here of her former husband, and no ring on her finger. Nothing to suggest she had a partner or husband now. What made this woman tick? Travelling? She supposed that must be it, and yet she did not seem a woman who had much curiosity in her fellow human beings, although that was a quality that travel writers must surely need.

'And did you write one?' Luke asked casually.

She looked disconcerted at this reasonable question. 'No. I became sidetracked by mountains and desert pioneers.'

'Such as Jane Digby?' Georgia asked innocently.

'*Not* like Jane Digby. Her sole purpose in life was to subordinate herself to a man. Any idiot can ride across deserts to lie under the stars with a sheikh. It takes rather more to cross the deserts for their own sake. I like to think so anyway.'

Georgia murmured something soothing and Luke quickly stepped in.

'What about a book on Kentish explorers?' he asked.

He received a terse reply. 'Men chiefly. I'm not a rabid feminist but I do have to think of marketing. I'm interested in little-known women, not men. You should appreciate that as a publisher.'

'I do,' Luke assured her.

'Now, if you have no further questions . . .' Janet said firmly.

'Just one,' Georgia said immediately. 'I see from the acknowledgements in *Women in the Air* – which I enjoyed,' she added sincerely, 'that you give Patrick Fairfax quite a big hand.'

'I was fond of him,' she replied instantly. 'His death upset me a great deal, especially since I had been with him so shortly before his death.'

117

'You acknowledge Paul Stock too. I understand you were once married to him.'

Georgia had forgotten she hadn't told Luke that, and he looked surprised. Janet was made of stern stuff, however. 'I can't see its relevance, but yes I was. It was he who first introduced me to the club. We married, we divorced and we remained on good terms.'

'Were you still married in 1975?'

'No,' came the iceberg answer. 'If you must have the exact details, we were married in 1970, and divorced at the end of 1973.' A pause. 'Have you met Paul?'

'Yes, though he didn't mention your marriage. There are various rumours, however, which of course we treat as just that, until proved otherwise. One that Patrick Fairfax accused him of fraud, and another that he was a ladies' man.'

Janet regarded her with distaste. 'If you are implying I had an affair with Patrick, please don't be so mealy-mouthed.'

'It was actually Paul I was speaking about.' Ambiguity could bring its rewards. 'Those were also the words used to me about Patrick though.'

A reluctant smile appeared on Janet Freeman's face. 'You seem to have caught me out. Well, no problem, I'd prefer it not to be in your book for the sake of Jean Fairfax, but if you feel the need to upset her, then you must do as you please. I won't deny it. As for Paul, let's say that he was and may still be enthusiastic where his sex life is concerned. And as for the rumours over the fraud, Paul always seemed to me an honest broker – financially at any rate.'

Well put, Georgia thought wryly. 'Was it a serious affair with Patrick?'

'I thought so,' was the bland answer. 'But then I would, wouldn't I? To Patrick it was probably just a Spitfire interlude. Now you see him, now you don't. That, I realized later, exactly suited me. I'd had enough of marriage not to want to be tied down in any way.'

Georgia avoided Luke's eye. 'But Paul might not have seen it that way?'

'How can I say?'

Very easily, Georgia thought. One last try.

'We were told that Patrick and Paul Stock had a row over you when Paul arrived, and I wondered if that was because you had planned to stay at the hotel with Patrick?'

'Irrelevant in the circumstances,' Janet said coolly. 'And even if poor Paul did fly off the handle in a big way, you need waste no time trying to pin Patrick's murder on him. He wouldn't have the guts.'

'What did you make of that lady?' Georgia asked Luke as they headed round the ring road to the A11 for the drive home.

'A doughty customer.'

'For all her marriage to Paul and affair with Patrick, she seems distinctly unsexy.'

'You think so?'

She glanced at his profile to see that he had that irritating smile on his face which said 'we men know more than you about such things'.

'I do,' she said firmly.

'I don't. I would say that she had a sexy youth and is now enjoying a sexy maturity.'

'If she's a passionate lady then,' Georgia began, 'perhaps the affair with Patrick was *very* serious, which means—'

'He found the guts?'

'Lunch,' declared Georgia at last, the following morning. There was only so much rapture she could extract from a computer screen.

'That's a delaying tactic, not a solution,' Peter shot back at her.

'For me it's a solution. All computers can do is produce sense from what we feed into them. They can't do our work for us, only make short cuts.'

119

'Charlie wouldn't agree. He'd disown you if he heard you speak disrespectfully of Suspects Anonymous.'

'Tell me one good thing that it's produced over this case.'

'One can't expect miracles.'

'One can hope for them. Look what this blasted screen is showing though. On second thoughts, don't. I've been eyeball to monitor long enough. It's *lunchtime*.'

The screen was dotted all over with Burglar Bills, not to mention Janet Freeman, but they were all lined up against a bar. The problem currently being thrashed out – a moderate term for the heated discussion in progress – was whether Sylvia Lee should be added only as a witness for background information or whether in view of her husband being present that day she should be upgraded.

'Are you suggesting,' she asked him sweetly, 'that Richard Vane was so concerned over what his wife had been up to thirty-five years earlier that he (a) joined the aviation club and (b) for some mysterious reason chose a public place like Woodring Manor Hotel to sort the matter out with Patrick Fairfax once and for all?'

'I don't have to prove a case for it,' Peter pointed out with dignity. 'We once agreed the rule that gut feelings are relevant.'

'Not on Suspects Anonymous, only in our thinking.'

'Suppose we compromise?' Peter suggested generously, 'and put the Vanes in, husband and wife, as one player.' He promptly created a new icon, and a Burglar Bill duly appeared on the screen with Vane emblazoned on its stripy shirt.

'Done,' she agreed. 'Lunch?'

'Not yet. Let's see how it works. Now, we're agreed that six of the pilots had left – or at least appeared to have done so – at about five o clock. Matt Jones and Patrick Fairfax remained, Richard Vane left twenty minutes or so later, and the other three club members shortly after that.'

'Yes, subject to alibis holding up.'

'Of course. Right, that's good. That gives us thirteen players, including Patrick himself. An inauspicious number. OK to run the session? I'll set the clock at three forty-five p.m.'

'Go for it,' she said with resignation. Lunch, it seemed, was not an option.

Peter, frowning into the screen, duly clicked the button and sat back as the round clock dial at the corner of the screen whirled into action, and one figure in white (Patrick Fairfax), and seven of the Bills left the bar and sprang to life. The clock worked to evidence time, not real time of course, and despite her empty stomach Georgia became hooked by what was happening. It was all going smoothly with icons gliding in and out of Matt's office and the two different bars, until the time clock reached seven o'clock, when a large red cross appeared on the screen.

'The error sign, so that doesn't fit.' Peter frowned. 'Paul Stock said the downstairs bar was empty, yet the cross must be pointing out that not only do we not have supporting evidence for that, but there must be a definite clash. I suppose it's because the barman told Patrick that Janet was looking for him out in the grounds, but Janet said she was in her room and there was no message.'

'Easily explained,' Georgia replied. 'We have only approximate times. Patrick says at, say, six forty-five that he has to have a word with Matt and he'll be back in a trice. Janet decides to use the time to go to the loo or to their room. Obviously they were going to spend the night together at the hotel, so she tells the barman to let Patrick know she'll meet him upstairs. He'll know she means their room; the barman knowing when he gave his statement that Patrick was killed in the gardens takes it that she referred to the garden doors which are right there as you come up the stairs from the basement floor. Alternatively, instead of going to the loo she uses the time to filch the gun if the barman nipped out, and she's feeling hard done by Patrick Fairfax. Computers,' she added crossly, 'are not Old Bailey judges. They are only a *tool*.'

'But a useful one.' Peter clicked Janet Freeman's Betty icon

121

again to run through her movements. 'Yes, a definite question mark over that lady. She was there with the gun, and as barmen tend to come and go she could have been alone with it. She'd only need a minute. The barman . . . Which one was it?' He hunted in the index file. 'Tony Wilson. She gets rid of him on an excuse, takes the gun . . . no, *another* red cross.'

'Ammunition,' Georgia said smugly. 'She wouldn't have any.'

He stared at her in annoyance. 'Why? Suppose she'd planned it?'

'Why should she?'

'Fairfax was giving her the boot. She thought he was more serious about their relationship than in fact he was. Bingo.'

'It's possible,' Georgia conceded. 'We're only presuming that Patrick was going to stay the night with her. Suppose he'd already dropped her and *that's* what the row between Paul and Patrick was about. News had spread. Paul was upset on her behalf and told Patrick what a scumbag he was. At six forty-five, after a final appeal to Patrick has got nowhere, Janet departs to her room, which is handy for a swift retreat. She's come fully prepared for vengeance. She'd need clean clothing, for instance, in case she got Fairfax's blood on her. She also has the ammunition – she has seized the gun when she had the opportunity in the bar – she leaves the message with the barman, goes into the gardens and waits for Patrick to come.'

'Possible,' Peter grunted.

'Then let's have *lunch*,' she pleaded.

Peter ignored this. 'Wouldn't intrepid lady travellers have guns of their own? Why go to the lengths of relying on the Webley?'

'Not traceable to her.'

'Why the dell?'

'Their special place?'

'Could be.' Peter frowned. 'Hypothesis only. It doesn't satisfy.'

'Lunch could.'

'These pilots,' Peter continued, 'are moving around in a gang on this screen. Yet they can't have done. They say old soldiers never die, they simply fade away. Did the pilots fade out *together* from the hotel?'

'Yes, according to their police statements. "Just after five" in most cases. We don't know who went first and who went last. But does it matter?'

'It matters if one of them *didn't* leave. None of them would have been asked by the police about the others' movements.'

'The police must have been satisfied that everyone save Jones, Stock and Freeman had left well before Fairfax was killed. Why on earth would any of the pilots or the club members choose the hotel to kill him in? Why not the club itself, where it would surely have been less risky? Unless, of course, it was a spur-of-the-moment murder.'

Peter sighed. 'You're getting tired, daughter. Look. You'll agree Paul Stock is a good candidate for a spur-of-the-moment murder.' He clicked on Paul Stock's icon and united it in the downstairs bar with the gun symbol; it then followed the Victim icon through the garden. When they reached the blue area indicating the dell, symbolized by a tasteful blue hyacinth – the nearest the computer could manage to a blue-bell – Peter pressed the action button. The gun was fired – and immediately a red cross came up.

'As you said,' Peter continued smugly. 'No ammunition. It was a planned murder. Someone knew the gun was there, knew it was unloaded, knew the layout of the hotel.'

'All twelve Suspects would qualify for that,' she said gloomily. 'Where do we go from here?'

'Lunch?' Peter suggested sweetly.

Leaving Margaret intent on preparing a supper for them since they had deprived her of the pleasure of serving them a midday meal (Georgia suspected she really did see it that way) she and Peter set forth for the White Lion. Haden Shaw was a typical Kent village in that its buildings were largely strung out along one street, with a few side lanes, which made it relatively easy for Peter to move around. The pub was on the same side of the road as their two adjoining cottages and it was a pleasant walk past a medley of medieval, Tudor and eighteenth-century cottages. The occasional one was set back from the road, which gave them the luxury of peering into several front gardens and being barked at by a cross-eyed terrier over-protective of his territory.

Inside the pub still had its inglenook fireplace, though the owner, Dave Winslow, had to be leaned on to light the log fire displayed within it. Even though it was high summer, it still provided a comfortable central point. It was fishcake day, Georgia was glad to see. Nancy, Dave's wife, had a mean hand with them.

'Any more from Luke about the house?' Peter asked, after he had taken his first sip of bitter.

'He said he'd put in a revised offer.'

'Foregone conclusion?'

'No. Prepare for doom and gloom and every day a new cliffhanger,' Georgia said cheerfully. 'Luke's really hooked on this house now, so he'll persevere.'

'And you? Are you hooked on it?'

Georgia studied the fishcakes being placed before her and thought about this. 'Yes,' she said firmly.

'I take it that's a yes with reservations?'

'Isn't it always and for everyone?'

'I do realize that Luke's doing this at least partly for me,' Peter said forthrightly. 'You could move to South Malling, if it weren't for me. You could anyway, but I know you won't believe that.'

'Wrong. Knowing myself, it could work the other way round. Without you in the equation, I'd be having *worse* jitters. Nothing might prise me out of Haden Shaw. "Jam tomorrow" has always seemed an excellent way of living to me.'

Peter laughed. 'Change of subject then. Do you agree Suspects Anonymous did a good job?'

'Within its limits.'

'Which are?'

'We might tend to concentrate on the evidence we've fed in and the people we've identified. What of those who slip the net? They're going to be further distanced by using that software. The more we use it, the more we'll rely on it.'

'Has anyone slipped our net so far?'

'Tom Armstrong, Lord Standing, Vincent Blake . . .'

'We can't dub people suspects just because they were there.'

'On the other hand we can't *exclude* them,' Georgia pointed out, 'so let's say they're all players in the reserve team for Suspects Anonymous. Like Alice Dane.'

Peter looked pleased at this analysis. 'Ready for transfer to First Division in her case. Ah, Dave,' Peter called out, since he was strolling over to clear the plates. 'Coffee if you please, and tea for Georgia.'

'Should know that by now,' Dave grunted. He was the laconic one of the couple. Nancy took the bubbly role. 'Weren't you off to Eynsford a few weeks back, Georgia?'

She looked up in surprise. 'Yes, why?'

'Heard there'd been a murder there. Wondered who it was.' Dave was under the impression that the Commissioner of the Metropolitan Police had a hot line to Peter as did every Chief Constable in the country, especially Kent. Dave therefore presumed that news of each body discovered in Britain and quite a few outside reached Marsh & Daughter pronto, whether the death dated from 3000 BC or thirty minutes previously.

'No idea, Dave.' Georgia looked at Peter uneasily.

'It's only because we've been talking about the case,' Peter reassured her quickly. 'It won't be Jack.'

'Of course not,' she agreed. 'Eynsford's a large village.' A silence fell which lasted until they had paid the bill and returned to Peter's office.

'I'll ring Mike,' Peter said at last, 'just to be sure.'

'Yes,' Georgia agreed. This was stupid. Not every tragedy in the world revolved round Marsh & Daughter or 362 Squadron. She tried to occupy herself with such delights as writing out cheques to the Inland Revenue – anything to make the time pass until the phone rang with Mike's reply. Eynsford wouldn't be in his area of course, it would be in Darenth Valley's, and so it would take longer. She could see that Peter was obviously feeling as on edge as she was, and only pretending to be busy on the internet – which didn't help her own fears.

By the time the phone did ring – and she guessed from Peter's expression as he answered it that it was Mike – she had managed to convince herself that the answer would be negative. It couldn't possibly be Jack. Then she realized that Peter was listening to Mike for too long a time, and by the time he put the receiver down, she guessed the truth.

'It was Jack,' he said, looking very shaken. 'His wife had been away, and found the body in his office when she returned on Sunday evening. He'd been bashed over the head with a heavy and as yet unknown object, dead for twenty-four hours or so. Their neighbour was taken in for questioning, but released this morning without charge.'

Neighbour? She clung to this thought, if only because it took this terrible murder into the realms of the real, and away from the turmoil inside her which insisted this had something to do with Patrick Fairfax.

'Some boundary dispute,' Peter continued. 'Going on for years. The neighbour came round to sort it out once and for all, and according to him, they had. Then he left. Moreover, he claims he came on Friday evening, not Saturday. There's no proof of that, however, and he had no alibi for the evening in question. Anyway, the SIO has ruled out charging him.'

The taste of the fishcakes was unpleasantly repeating itself in her mouth, and her stomach churned. Jack dead. All she could fix her thoughts on was that model Spitfire outside his door, and that ridiculous bench. Her eyes felt heavy with shock, and even tears were close. All this morning they had playing around with stupid computers and Burglar Bills, and in the real world Jack was dead.

She told herself this was illogical, that she had no difficulty in remembering what their job was all about. She also reminded herself that Suspects Anonymous served the purpose of providing objectivity away from the hideousness of whatever crime they were investigating. It was a tool, as the police had tools, to come at a case from an outside angle rather than the personal emotions that perhaps inevitably clouded the people most concerned.

She'd only met him twice, and yet the thought of that now unused office dedicated to his life's passion threatened to overwhelm her. She disciplined herself, struggling to think rationally, separating personal sadness from work. Why on earth should his death be connected to their enquiries about the Fairfax case? Jack hadn't been interested in writing another biography himself, nor had he tried to deter her from the project, as he would have done if he felt fiercely protective of the people involved. Indeed rather the contrary. Involuntarily her thoughts switched to Susan Hardcastle. She thought of Jack as he had been at Tangmere – and then inevitably she pictured what Susan had walked in on.

'Mike's keeping us informed,' Peter told her. 'And, decent of him,' he said graciously, 'the Scene of Crime is being wrapped up Thursday morning. He says you can go over and have a word with the SIO if you like. I take it you would?'

She nodded. It would be the last thing she would want to do if she had any choice. But she didn't. The tape, the chalk marks, the scene-suited figures, the memories it would bring of Jack himself, they all had to be faced. It went with the job.

Eight

'I don't believe in coincidence.' Peter had obviously guessed her basic concern. 'Was there something, *anything*, you felt Jack was holding back on when you first met him? I can't see anything he told us at Tangmere that would have led to this.'

'Yes. I still can't pin down what or how. There was his outburst about Paul Stock at Tangmere, but Paul having made a pass at his wife hardly seems a motive for his killing Jack – especially since it happened years ago.'

'But when you first met Jack?'

'He answered my questions, more or less. But, as I told you, he was ambivalent. He was talkative about the pilots themselves, and encouraged us to meet them. Then he told me that they would be of more use over information on the aviation club members since the pilots could be discounted as suspects for Fairfax's death.'

'From your notes,' he reminded her, 'he hardly mentioned the club, although he must have researched that for his biography.'

'What are you implying?' she asked edgily.

'That he was definitely trying to steer you away from 1940. All the more reason for your meeting with Sylvia Lee tomorrow, Georgia.'

Peter didn't even glory in this small victory, but nevertheless Georgia was silenced. *Had* Jack done so purposely? And if so, why?

As she drove to Eynsford half an hour later, she found

128

herself switching tack to Peter's last comment hurled after her as she left. 'Alan Purcell. Don't forget him when you see Sylvia Lee.' Or, she thought, Susan Hardcastle. Jack had given away that he'd at least met Purcell. Too fast, too fast, she warned herself. There should be speed cameras for case investigations as well as roads. First, concentrate on Jack himself. Somebody had killed him, and the priority was to discover why.

For once she wished she wasn't on her own, as she drew up near Bramley House that Thursday morning. It looked all too familiar, except for the large mobile incident van parked opposite the house. Even the roses bloomed on regardless. There was no Susan popping up from behind the hedge now, however. Instead the door was open and a man, not scene-suited, which meant the main investigation must be over, was walking up to the gate. Thirties, weasel-faced, the sort who, like the cross-eyed terrier in Haden Shaw, would guard his territory.

'Georgia Marsh? DI Pullman, Darenth Area. I gather you knew Hardcastle. You wrote that book about Wickenham, didn't you?'

The eyes seemed to be drilling into her, and his tone of voice indicated that books were not only sidelines but full of fairy stories and a world away from his.

'We did. My father was a Kent DCI, Stour Area.' She needed to lay down credentials here. 'Jack Hardcastle was helping us on a cold case we're looking into.'

'So Mike Gilroy said. Patrick Fairfax, 1975. I deal with facts like Gilroy. Have you any evidence that the Fairfax case has anything to do with his death, or is it just a hunch?' He kept a straight face, but the implication was there: she might be too young for a Miss Marple, but was obviously tarred with the same brush. So what, she thought. Miss Marple did a good job.

She answered him suitably earnestly. 'I don't blame you for thinking we might be barking mad at this stage.' Slight

129

emphasis on the last three words. 'To tell you the truth, I hope we're wrong about any connection. We liked Jack Hardcastle and, really, I'm only too anxious to be able to rule out that slight possibility.'

A pause while she was weighed up. 'You'd better go in. Mrs Hardcastle says it's OK.'

'She's here?' Georgia hadn't expected this.

'Only for a few hours to double check there's nothing missing. The place was a mess.'

Could robbery have been a motive, she wondered. Robbery of what, though? The insidious thought crept in that Jack's files might have been the goal.

'Do I need to be scene-suited?'

'No. Mrs Hardcastle's got a PC with her. We've bagged everything we need, but don't walk off with anything without her say-so.'

She assured him she would be good, while wondering how far her understanding of the word 'good' might stretch. As she entered, she could hear voices coming from Jack's office. Susan Hardcastle must be a brave woman to face that. When Georgia joined them, she could see that it was indeed a mess: chalk marks still evident on the carpet, blood spatters now being cleaned by the police constable, who was a formidable-looking girl in her early twenties.

Susan was sitting in a chair behind the door, only contributing the odd word. She looked up at Georgia and managed a nod of welcome.

'It's good of you to let me come,' Georgia said quietly.

'The more the better,' Susan replied wearily. 'It takes away the need to think. This is PC Jane Diver. She's been a brick.'

The brick greeted Georgia cautiously, to her amusement but not surprise.

'Just tell me if I get in your way,' Georgia said.

The answering look said that there was no doubt about that, but Jane warmed a little when Georgia offered to make

130

coffee for all of them if Susan so wished. It proved an ice-breaker and when she returned with a tray the atmosphere was considerably warmer.

'You'll think I'm weird sitting here, taking part in all this,' Susan said gratefully as she drank the coffee. 'But it puts off the . . .' She hesitated.

'Telling people,' Georgia supplied. She could remember only too well the agonizing she and Peter had been through over whether and what to tell friends and relatives about firstly Rick's disappearance and then Elena's departure a year later.

'You've no idea. The phone at my son's house where I've been staying is ringing non-stop. The mobiles are jammed with messages. And the funeral – well, there's no funeral in sight, but that has to be thought about. He has – had – relatives in Australia. Do I phone . . .?'

'Take time,' Georgia advised her. 'You can't do it all at once. Cope with what you can.'

'I want them to find who did this.' Susan's face was set hard. 'That's why I thought I'd come home. And that's why I don't mind seeing you, just in case you had any ideas.'

Georgia gratefully took the opportunity. 'Is it possible it could have had anything to do with his work?'

She hesitated. 'Jack *was* his work. Our friends came from that world, fellow historians, that sort of thing. Why would any of his relatives want to kill him? Or mine?' She looked hopelessly at Georgia with this rhetorical question.

'The police mentioned a neighbour.'

'Simon Pollock's a pain in the – well, you can guess what Jack used to say.' The memory of the joke obviously nearly finished Susan, but she made another effort. 'When I spoke to Jack on the phone on Friday he said that Simon was coming round to sort things out.'

'Did he mean that evening or Saturday?'

'He didn't say. And I didn't speak to Jack on the Saturday. We were out all day and didn't get back till ten o'clock. I

thought I'd ring early in the morning instead. There wasn't
a reply, of course.'

Jane Diver glanced at Georgia as Susan choked, and
Georgia interpreted the message. 'Do you want me to help
you put these files back, Susan?' Action, she reasoned,
would help Susan, and there was plenty needed. Many of
the files lay on the floor and had burst open, spreading their
contents over a wide area. Photographs lay scattered everywhere where one box had emptied itself. It would be impossible to tell what the murderer or the police had removed.
Where to start was the question.

'It looks to me,' Georgia observed to Jane, 'that this isn't
the result of trashing the place. It would have been worse
if that were the motive.'

'We took a lot of stuff with us,' was the non-committal
reply.

Georgia pressed on. 'Whoever did this,' she said to Susan,
'could have been hunting for something in particular, such
as the 362 files.'

'Good luck to him,' Susan said bitterly, then winced at
her own words. 'Jack could never find anything he wanted
himself, so no one else would stand a chance.' She glanced
at the shelves. 'They were up there. They've gone.'

Georgia could see that, and resigned herself to sorting
through the pile on the floor. Susan began to help, picking
up stray photos and documents. Georgia lifted one heap at
a time, dumping it on the desk to examine. She began with
the complete files, which didn't take long. There was none
marked with anything she registered as relevant to 362, and
a swift peep inside revealed nothing. If Jack's death had
nothing to do with 362 the files should still be here, unless
the police had taken them after Mike's call. But she found
nothing, save a few photographs that looked familiar.

Her heart sank. If the files had disappeared into evidence,
not even Mike would be able to get at them without pulling
out every stop in the book. She squatted down to pick up

some of the loose photographs, and it was only then she realized what was so obviously missing from the room. 'Was his computer taken?' she asked Susan.

'We took it,' PC Diver announced flatly. Georgia loved the universal 'we'. If Lord Lucan were found at long last, she was sure that 'we' would have made the breakthrough. 'It had been used.'

'Did anyone other than Jack regularly use the computer?' she asked Susan, who was regaining some colour in her drawn face.

'My son did. I did occasionally, and there's a computer guru who comes in from time to time.'

Not helpful. Georgia tried Jane again without much hope. 'Do you know what was on the screen when it was found, apart from a screen saver?'

PC Diver looked as though her integrity had been attacked. 'Of course. The screen manager.' She hesitated, then obviously couldn't resist displaying her knowledge. 'The recycle bin was empty.'

'But all the files were still there?'

Well, it had been a stupid question, she realized, as Jane smirked and gave the obvious answer. 'How would we know if it was *all*?'

'Stupid of me,' Georgia said brightly to Miss Brain of the Year.

'I could probably tell you,' Susan said hesitantly, as Georgia spun round in surprise. 'I took the laptop with me. We both used that, you see. I used it for household stuff and Jack used it both for back-up and note-taking,' she explained. 'There's some sort of data transfer cable some-where.'

Could there possibly be a glimmer of hope, Georgia wondered. If Jack used it for back-up, he would have exported files from the desk computer to the laptop as well as importing them. 'Do you have it here?'

'I brought it back. To send emails . . . Shall I fetch it?'

Amy Myers

'Oh yes, please,' Georgia said fervently. Then she remembered the all-seeing eye, Jane, as Susan went to fetch it. 'There wouldn't be any prints of interest if the laptop wasn't here.'

'But—'

Georgia cut her off. She could see the way out of this. 'I'll open it here, and Susan or I could send anything I needed to my home computer by email attachment. Then you could take the computer if you need to. You might, for instance, want to check the contents against any that don't appear on the main computer now. The murderer might possibly, only possibly, have deleted them there.' She hoped this was enough to suggest to Jane that she might receive quite a few brownie points if this proved to be the case.

There was silence, then: 'We'll open it together.'

A deal had been struck. Never had Georgia felt so pleased to see Microsoft Word. With her heart in her mouth, she clicked on Jack's user name, with Jane breathing heavily over her shoulder and Susan sitting some way away. Open Sesame, she breathed to herself, and lo, the magic cave opened. There were the yellow folders including several for 362 Squadron, differentiated by years.

'Do you mind if I look?' she asked Susan.

'No.' Susan obviously did, but was doing her best to be brave.

She opened the folder for 1940, and then the document for the list of squadron personnel. That looked promising. Next she tried Patrick Fairfax, and was disappointed. This was clinical technical stuff – what each pilot did each day, addresses, dates interviewed, interview notes. There was nothing here that would help Marsh & Daughter with his death in 1975, because when Jack was interviewing them that had not been the main focus of the interview. Mindful of Peter's instruction, she tried Alan Purcell and was rewarded by an instant sight of his contact details, which for double safety she wrote down under Jane

Diver's suspicious eye. Then she had to ask for Susan's co-operation over emailing the material. It was willingly given – on her part anyway.

'Anything you discover . . .' Jane began warningly.

'There'll be nothing that you won't have access to if you need it.'

Susan was looking worried. 'Do you really think Jack's death had anything to do with 362 Squadron?' she asked.

'Probably not,' Georgia answered. 'Jack had finished all his work on that squadron. He told me he didn't want anything to do with Martin's new edition of Fairfax's book.'

'No. He was very firm about that. He told Martin Heywood that he had a clear field and never mentioned anything more about it.'

'Susan, what took Jack to Tangmere that day? He told me it was work, so was it another book?' A straw to clutch at. If 362 had nothing to do with Jack's death, then this responsibility might lift a little.

'He had a commission for writing another book on the Battle of Britain itself. Eddie Stubbs was helping him with it.'

So 362 *was* involved in a way. 'Would Alan Purcell come into that?' Georgia asked, trying to make it sound a casual question. She didn't want to upset Susan or set Jane's nose twitching. 'He lives in France now.'

'I don't know the name, but Jack did go to France recently.'

'You may be barking up the wrong tree again.' Peter was irritable. He had pounced on Georgia's immediate deduction about Alan Purcell and read Jack's computer file on him, now safely saved in both their own computers. 'There are only the details of his wartime career in this file, and no interview dates. Lots of ex-pats live in France. It could have been someone else Jack went to see. You're jumping to conclusions – as usual.'

That was unfair – which, she grudgingly conceded, was unusual for Peter, and so did her best to work out whether or not he had a point. 'I still think it's worth following up.'

'Alan Purcell wasn't at the 1975 reunion,' Peter howled.

'Nor was Sylvia Lee, and it was you who insisted I saw her for background material *and* to ask her about Purcell.'

Peter glared at her. 'I've changed my mind.'

'Let's try his number.' She checked the contact details. 'Ste Marie de Faux . . .' She broke off, deflated. 'My French isn't particularly good, but doesn't *faux* mean false?'

'It does,' Peter rejoined grimly. 'Which suggests this is a deliberately false address. I'll try the phone.'

By the time he had put the receiver down, the question was answered. 'That,' he informed her, 'is the residence of a truffle farmer in the Auvergne. He has no connection whatsoever with any former RAF pilot.'

'Why *do* that?' she exploded. Their every move seemed to be checkmated.

'Don't despair,' he said kindly. 'This helps your case, because it suggests Alan Purcell is a person of some interest, and it helps *our* case because it indicates that Jack was very wary of someone – so wary that he couldn't even put information on a computer. Which raises the question of—'

'Where he put it.' Georgia felt better.

'It was either elsewhere in the room, or more probably . . .' He looked at her. 'It wouldn't be Susan. Trusted friend?'

She answered simultaneously with his next offering: 'The computer guru?'

'And one more thing,' Peter added. 'Our truffle farmer was not pleased to be called. This was the second time he'd been asked about Monsieur Purcell.'

'Jack?'

'More likely his murderer.'

* * *

Would this be another Grande Dame of the theatre, Georgia wondered as she spoke into the entry phone of the South Kensington house on Friday afternoon. At last she'd be meeting Sylvia Lee. She was glad now that Peter had insisted this visit was necessary. If by any chance Jack's death had been connected to Fairfax's, she owed it to him to explore every avenue. It was a high, terraced, white-painted building, which looked a world away from the Fairfax home, and she pushed the entrance door open with a pleasant sense of anticipation. A woman in her sixties opened the first-floor door with a friendly grin.

'Come in, my mother's waiting. I'm Helen Vane.'

This tall slender woman had obviously inherited her mother's grace, and was no Mary Fairfax. Nor did Sylvia Lee prove to be anything like Jean Fairfax. The fragility of the woman who rose to meet her in the living room did not stem just from her age. It came from a vulnerability that displayed itself in her roles and which had probably contributed to her acting abilities. Georgia had seen her in several small roles recently on TV and at least two of her films from the 1940s and '50s. Her favourite was *Blue Moon* which had joined the ranks of the romantic musical classics such as *Maytime in Mayfair* and had the charm and whimsicality of *Salad Days*. With her figure and fair hair Sylvia had something of the screen star Ann Todd's faun-like appeal, but this, Georgia decided, was a woman who could laugh at life too. Did vulnerability go with laughter? Perhaps in this woman it did, Georgia thought. It was easy to respond to the warmth put over by Sylvia Lee.

'I'm not sure I can help you,' the actress began doubt-fully. 'I knew Patrick Fairfax so very long ago, and only occasionally bumped into him after the war. It was my husband who saw him regularly for a time at the aviation club.' Her eyes grew sad. There were plenty of photographs of Richard Vane in this room, and an oil portrait of Sylvia

137

painted in her heyday. Georgia picked one of the photos to comment on.

'Is this you and your husband with Helen, Lady Vane?' she asked. Helen, unlike Mary, showed no signs of wishing to be present and had disappeared after showing her into the room.

'No, that's my son Harvey. This is Helen with her twin Hilary.' She pointed to a snapshot of herself with two babies. 'I was married twice. A brief wartime marriage to their father and then I married Richard in 1945. Harvey was born the following year. But I won't bore you with that; you're here to ask me about Patrick.'

'I realize it's a long way back.'

'My memory is good, even if it can't help you a great deal. At the beginning of the war in 1939 I was only nineteen and very much intent on making my way on the stage. I'd already had one or two minor roles in British films and plays. Unfortunately I thought my talent lay in the Lady Macbeths of the drama world and it took a year or two to realize I was better suited to comedy, and musical comedy in particular. At the time of the Battle of Britain, I'd been appearing in a local theatre in Tonbridge and went to stay with my uncle and aunt who ran the Plough pub in South Malling. Their daughter Jenny was working at the Rose and Crown in Town Malling, where the pilots used to gather. As a result we were often invited out, and one night went to a station dance at the Manor House.'

'Woodring Manor?'

'No. The other one. I knew it just as the Manor House. That's where I met Patrick, although met is hardly the word. I suppose it is more truthful to say that he pursued me, and my head was not unnaturally turned. Indeed why not? He was a glamorous pilot, symbolic of those whose exploits were in the press daily. He continued to turn my head for a couple of weeks until I went back to London.'

Georgia felt she could hardly leap in with: 'Why did you

split up?' and was preparing a roundabout route when Sylvia
pre-empted her.

'You'll want to know what happened.' Sylvia frowned.
'It's hard to explain. Those weren't ordinary times – though
I expect you're tired of hearing that. But it was true enough.
One lived so much faster that relationships kaleidoscoped.
They came, they were enjoyed, they finished. One could
never be sure if the man one kissed one evening would be
shot down by the next. It was as hard as that. Anyway, he
was so . . . gentle, so loving.' She paused, then said
hurriedly, 'Patrick was an interesting person, but we both
knew it wouldn't last. We were just fascinated by each
other. Perhaps it would have gone on longer, but I was
offered a part on the London stage that I couldn't refuse.
I went back, met Norman Lake, my first husband, and we
married that Christmas, a rushed wartime marriage.'

'Was he an actor or in the services?'

'Both. He was on stage when I met him in the same
show, and then he was called up. He was killed in 1944.'

Bang went Georgia's airy-fairy conjecture that the twins
could have been Patrick Fairfax's children. Not entirely
ruled out, but unlikely.

'So you see,' the famous Lee smile shone out, 'Patrick
receded somewhat to the back of my mind. I'd forgotten
all about him until my husband mentioned his name in
connection with the aviation club he'd joined. I'm afraid I
was busy on the stage and didn't share his hobbies.'

'What was his work?'

'He was in the City. Look.' Sylvia walked gracefully to
the piano top, where only one photo stood. 'This is Richard
on his eightieth birthday, He never made ninety, I'm afraid.
He was so looking forward to it.'

Georgia saw her hand tremble as she put the photograph
back. Richard Vane too had a kind face, she thought. An
intelligent one and shot through with humanity as well.

'This is Richard in his beloved Cessna at the club.'

139

Georgia came to stand at her side as Sylvia held out another photo. Richard was much younger in this, clad in overalls, and it was easy to see why Sylvia Lee had fallen for him.

'Is that Patrick Fairfax with him?'

'No. Paul Stock. It's written on the back.'

'You knew him?'

'I met him at Patrick's funeral and I suppose on a few other occasions.'

'Do – did – you know Jack Hardcastle too?'

'Yes.' The briefness of her reply suggested she didn't like him and Georgia had to discipline herself not to come to Jack's defence.

'I'm afraid he's been found dead – murdered,' she added.

Sylvia looked up sharply. 'Murdered? Why?' She looked surprisingly shaken. 'That's horrible.'

'Did he come to see you when he wrote his biography of Patrick?'

'Yes. I asked him to keep my name out of the book and he did. That was good of him.'

'But you haven't seen him since.'

'I had no reason to run into him.'

Georgia was puzzled at her obvious unwillingness to discuss him. It seemed an unusual reaction to someone who was unthreatening. She tried another tack, feeling she was heading down a cul-de-sac. 'I met several of Patrick's co-pilots, five of the seven officers who were there at Woodring Manor with your husband on the day Patrick was murdered. Do you remember an Alan Purcell, though? I'm trying to trace him. He lives in France but has cut himself off from the rest of the squadron and doesn't attend the reunions.'

'I think I do,' Sylvia replied after a moment. 'A kind man. Moral. I met him during the war.'

'You haven't been in touch with him recently?'

'No.'

'I think Jack Hardcastle met him once,' Georgia ventured.

'Then you must ask—' Sylvia looked apologetic. 'I'm

so sorry. I forgot. Old age, I'm afraid. You said he'd been killed. Perhaps the other pilots of 362 might know where Alan is. Have you met them?'

'My father and I met five of the officers at Woodring Manor, and later at Tangmere, together with one of the sergeant pilots, Eddie Stubbs.'

Sylvia's eyes were fixed on her, but she did not comment so Georgia continued uncertainly, 'He has always remembered seeing Patrick dancing with you, so beautiful you seemed to him a symbol of hope. It's stayed in his mind all this time.'

'Perhaps,' Sylvia said briefly. 'But a subjective valuation on his part, I fear. I didn't feel a symbol of anything except my own wishes.' A pause. 'He was in the same squadron as Patrick? And at the same time?'

'Yes.'

'Stubbs,' she said reflectively. 'I remember one sergeant pilot, but I don't know if it was he.'

'There were four of them in the squadron during the first part of the battle. Two of them were LMF.'

'Cowards, Patrick called them.'

The flat statement surprised Georgia. 'Do you believe that?'

'Not now.'

She was beginning to look tired, almost grey, Georgia saw with concern, and was about to say that she'd leave when Sylvia sat down and was obviously ready to continue. 'It's Patrick's death you really wanted to talk about, wasn't it? My husband was there that day. What did you want to know?'

'We gather from his police statement that he left early, because he was unwell.'

'I believe that's so, but it's many years ago,' she said apologetically. 'I recall John Standing ringing to tell Richard the news, and we talked about it at length, but the details of what we said obviously escape me.' She made a visible effort. 'Richard was very upset. He thought highly of Patrick, although not, I fear, of his business skills.'

'Did he ever talk to you about Paul Stock, either about his marriage or the fact that he might have been fiddling the books?'

She looked puzzled. 'I don't recall either. My husband had a shrewd financial eye, as you can imagine. I don't think any fiddles would have escaped his eye – or,' she chuckled, 'scandal about his marital life.'

'He was willing to invest in the hotel as well as the club?'

'Only to persuade Patrick to pull out of it, in order to give Matt Jones a free hand. If he could achieve that, Richard felt he could then safeguard his investment in the aviation club by getting Patrick to concentrate on the one project. The other two, John Standing and Vincent Blake, felt the same. Alas it was not to be, and Richard lost quite heavily over the club.'

'So none of the three would have had reason to kill Patrick, in fact rather the contrary?'

'Indeed. The club was in so much debt that only Patrick with his charm and contacts could have pulled it round, provided he accepted the necessary financial discipline. The hotel was not in the same position. There he was a liability.'

'I understand that Patrick was not the most faithful of husbands,' Georgia began tentatively.

'I imagine not. Richard kept a strict silence before me on such matters, much as I know he enjoyed them with his friends. "Honour among gentlemen" I believe it's called.' Sylvia laughed. 'Being on the stage with its constant beady eye on such matters, that highly amused me. He did mention that Patrick had had an affair with somebody, which was causing trouble. He wouldn't say who – and,' Sylvia smiled, 'I can see you already know about it. Just as you found out about my having been his girlfriend for at least two weeks.'

'I absolve you of coming back thirty-five years later to take your revenge,' Georgia laughed.

'Elephants and women have long memories, Georgia. But you're right to exclude me. I only went to the aviation club once or twice when Richard asked me to attend open days. I opened an aeroplane, if that's the term. I wasn't keen on posing on the wings as the semi-naked young ladies do on car bonnets, but I am extremely good at opening shows, cutting ribbons and signing my name. That's how Richard and I first met in fact. He was a great autograph collector. He asked me for mine after a show, so I always sign everything handed to me now, in memory of that day. Save for blank cheques,' she added gravely.

Georgia laughed. 'On that I'll leave you.' She rose to her feet and Helen appeared as if by magic to show her out. 'Do you live upstairs?' she asked. 'Do you have a Wallace and Grommit contraption to shoot you downstairs instantaneously?'

Helen laughed. 'No such fun. I've been in the kitchen.'

'Mary Fairfax, Patrick's daughter, told me rather wryly about her brother leaving the work of caring for her mother to her, so I thought you and your sister might both be installed here,' Georgia explained.

'Not quite the same set-up. My mother hasn't done quite so well. I live in Buckingham, my twin emigrated to Australia and my brother Harvey and his wife Anne only live here part of the time. Fortunately my mother has a series of devoted slaves who daily press unneeded attentions on her.'

'I can see why they're devoted,' Georgia said sincerely.

'Yes. We all are,' Helen said simply.

Georgia left the house for the tube station, glad she had at last spoken to Sylvia Lee, even if the meeting had pinpointed her as witness only, which was all Peter had claimed to want. It was odd, however, that if she had so little to say about Patrick, she should have been so instantly willing to see her. Probably for no reason – she must be used to making herself available to the world and his wife. Nevertheless, she should

not forget that, genuine though that charm was, Sylvia Lee
was an actress. Had there been more to discover beneath that
charm? For instance, wasn't it odd that her first comment
when told of Jack's death was: Why?

She glanced at the platform indicator. Upminster train,
one minute. That would take her to Embankment to change
for Charing Cross main line station. The rush-hour crowds
were gathering now, and used though she was to it, she had
a sudden feeling of claustrophobic panic as people gathered around her, all peering forward to see if the train was
approaching. One push from behind and – the perfect
murder. It had happened in fiction, as it had happened no
doubt in real life. Train approaching, people pressing harder
now. She couldn't move. Yes she could – and *must*. She
turned, just as the train approached, fighting her way to the
rear of the crowd, oblivious to angry murmurs of disgust.
She was breathing heavily, sweat running down her face,
legs trembling as she ran to squeeze into the next carriage.
No way was she getting in the first one. As she leapt through
the door, she glanced over at the crowd pushing into the
adjoining carriage, anonymous-looking raincoats, hooded
anoraks, young, old, teenagers, men and women. One of
them – had she imagined it? – had had a hand placed ready
at her back.

Nine

They used to be called the dog days. The weeks in July and early August during which the Dog Star rose, dogs went mad, and the days were so hot that the mind was becalmed like a sailing ship on a flat sea. That didn't seem to happen too much nowadays, but today was the exception. Which way to go and did it matter? Georgia restlessly tried to force herself into mowing her tiny patch of lawn. Too much effort. She'd do it later. Weed? It was well into July, they could grow a bit longer. Dead-head the roses? Now there was a job for a would-be Miss Marple – perhaps later. It wasn't that she herself felt flat, but the case most certainly did. The spur that meeting Sylvia Lee had brought with it had evaporated into the wake of Jack's murder. Even her chilling experience at the tube station had receded in her mind. Ten to one it was only her reaction to a somewhat emotional encounter.

Today everything seemed to be waiting. Peter was still waiting for news on the phone number of Alan Purcell, and Luke was still waiting to hear whether his revised offer on the house would be accepted. It was the holiday season, so the agent had said apologetically. Well, good luck to those who *could* go on holiday. She and Luke hoped to squeeze in a few days after the fate of the house was known, so that too was in limbo. Meanwhile Marsh & Daughter were waiting for something to take them forward. Every time she stared at her notes, each avenue seemed blocked. And yet she sensed the way through lay there somewhere.

145

Overgrown it might be, but the yellow brick road that would lead them to their own particular Land of Oz must exist somewhere. All they had to decide was where it lay.

She had a nasty feeling that Peter shared her frustration. It was a tell-tale sign that for some days now Suspects Anonymous hadn't been on the screen, and Peter was involved in reading something that had nothing to do with the case. When she had asked what it was, he had merely replied, '*The Mammoth Book of King Arthur*, darling. Edited by Mike Ashley, published by Robinson. Anything else you'd like to know? The ISBN perhaps?'

She had been silenced except to mutter that this had little relevance to Hell's Corner in 1940, 1975 or even today. He had agreed, and the discussion ended.

Yesterday had proved the last straw in her becalming. She and Peter had gone to Sevenoaks to meet Jack Hardcastle's guru. He was no Charlie Bone. Michael Hastings looked as though he would be more at home in the Bodleian Library than enmeshed in the web of computers that surrounded him in his ground-floor office in a rambling Victorian house. In his fifties, with a high forehead and forbidding look, he could well have been a retired academic – but then academics never retired. They were like old soldiers, and just faded away. They didn't turn to computers, save as a tool for advancing their pet theories.

Michael had proved friendly enough, and they had spent some time talking about Jack and his death, before explaining their own role.

'Jack told me,' he had said at last, when they had finished. 'Are you getting anywhere?'

'Yes and no,' Peter blithely stonewalled.

Michael had seemed to be brooding on this equivocal reply as though Pythagoras had just put forward a new theorem. 'Do you believe there's a link between Jack's death and what you're investigating?' he said at last.

No brooding for Peter. 'There's nothing to support it

except the fact that we'd seen him recently and that although he claimed he wanted nothing to do with the new biography of Patrick Fairfax, we now know he was involved in a new project with one of the 362 Squadron pilots. It was one in which his earlier material about the squadron would be relevant.'

Georgia had watched Michael Hastings carefully as he thought this over too. A chess player perhaps, or was he just cautious?

At last he spoke. 'You said on the phone that you thought Jack might have left back-up files with me. Had they been wiped from his computer?'

'We don't know. The main computer is in police hands,' Peter had answered, and had then explained their problem over Purcell's address. 'Jack must have kept the real address and phone number somewhere. I hope with you.'

'Why me? He could have jotted it in a notebook, memorized it even.'

'That's true, but he was obviously a computer-conscious worker. I should warn you though that if anyone else asks you for this information it might just be Jack's murderer.'

Michael Hastings wasn't easily shaken. Again he took his time in answering. 'Look,' he said. 'Jack was worried about something. I don't know what, but he was edgy the last time I saw him. That does suggest it might be work-related. So if it helps . . .' He pulled open a drawer, which Georgia could see was full of floppy disks. 'Jack still used floppies, as do a lot of my clients. I keep back-up files for them all, and here are Jack's.' He showed them a batch of about thirty floppies. 'Where do you want to start?'

Georgia had looked at them. Even then she had had a terrible feeling that this was going nowhere. Still, they had had to do it. Hastings had slotted the disks into his machine, and they watched in silence while he studied the contents list of each one. When it came to the now familiar files on 362 Squadron, they opened up each pilot's document,

147

each of which looked depressingly familiar. Even Alan Purcell's. There it was: Ste Marie de Faux. The same old false avenue.

'Do you mind if we open them all up to see the actual texts?' she asked Michael in desperation. 'It's possible Jack might have slipped something into these back-up disks that he didn't want on his home computers.'

'Go ahead. I'll leave you to it.' Michael allotted them a computer on another desk, but two hours later they had come up with nothing. 'These are the only files he's left with me, I'm afraid.' Michael seemed genuinely regretful.

'Thanks anyway,' Peter said, and Georgia added her own, even though she was fuming at the waste of time and lack of progress.

'I liked Jack Hardcastle,' Michael had said unexpectedly as they left. 'Keep in touch, will you? If there's any chance his death was connected to this case you're looking into, let me know. I'll ring if anything occurs to me.' He fidgeted as he politely watched Peter manoeuvring himself into the car, and Georgia noticed that he was still watching as they drove off.

And that had been that. The chances of anything at all occurring now seemed to be zilch. Georgia could hear the internal phone ringing on her office desk and, glad even of that distraction, she abandoned the garden and went inside to answer it. After all, it might be *good* news.

It wasn't.

'Jacob can't find any trace of an Alan Purcell.' Peter's voice betrayed that he was feeling as glum as she was. So that was that. The online French telephone index needed an address for a search, and so they had rung Peter's old friend to check the French Minitel computer terminal system, which wasn't so picky about its prior requirements for searches.

'So what's next?' she asked Peter.

'I'm going back to King Arthur.'

She put the phone down, and wandered back into the garden. Almost immediately the landline rang. Probably a phone call from Luke to say the house deal had fallen through. She picked up the receiver.

'Don't tell me. It's all off,' she said.

A surprised silence greeted her. Then: 'DI Pullman here, Kent Police Darenth Area. Are you around if I come over?'

She laughed at herself and apologized. 'Of course. Is it about Jack or Patrick Fairfax?'

A pause. 'Hardcastle *and* Fairfax.'

'Well, at least something's *happening*,' she said brightly to Peter, having deflected him from King Arthur with some difficulty.

'I doubt it,' he grumbled. 'He isn't coming to help us, only I suspect to clear Patrick Fairfax from the frame. It'll be sticky going.'

'Then I'll get some strawberry tarts for tea from the butchers.' Pat Mulworthy, the Haden Shaw butcher's wife, did a good sideline in savoury pasties, but had recently added a summer specialty of cream and fruit tarts to her repertoire. 'No one can be sticky going while struggling with one of them. It puts us in control.'

'Very funny.' Peter wasn't amused. 'Just be sure Pullman isn't coming to put you in the frame.'

Pullman was definitely the 'spies everywhere' sort of policeman, Georgia thought as he arrived. Watchful, suspicious, and dour. He was dubious about sitting in the garden, but since Peter's office was hot this afternoon, he was persuaded.

'You don't have neighbours who'd want to sell the story to the press, do you?' he asked suspiciously as he dubiously took a garden chair.

'Only me,' Georgia said blithely. 'There's a lane the other side. The village chat machine might be lined up, ears pressed to the wall, but I doubt it. Anyway Haden Shaw's idea of gossip is whether the village shop will close down. And at the end of this garden there are only sheep.'

'Long may that continue,' Peter said. 'Have a strawberry tart.' He proffered the plate to Pullman.

'Not for me, thanks,' Pullman said. Obviously he intended to remain in control. 'I'll wait. Business first.' Signs of humanity at least, she thought hopefully.

'We're following up this Fairfax line of yours,' he began. 'I've read the files from Downs Area, and Mr Manners and I have talked.'

'What persuaded you?' Peter munched happily. 'All other lines closed?'

He received a cross between a glare and a reproving look. 'PC Diver told us about those files you copied, Miss Marsh, so we compared the laptop with the computer files. The files about Patrick Fairfax had vanished from the main computer, but it could have been Jack who deleted them, of course.'

'Why should he, and if he did then why not the laptop too?' Peter asked.

'Perhaps he hadn't got round to it,' Georgia suggested, playing devil's advocate.

'Fair enough,' Pullman conceded. 'It's worth looking into though. The timing could just be coincidence, but if not there's a link with Fairfax's death. Which leads to the possibility at least that Jack Hardcastle had evidence pointing towards who killed Fairfax.'

'True.' Peter poured more tea.

'Which means that whoever killed him was probably present at that hotel in 1975, and probably guilty of Hardcastle's murder.'

'A lot of probablys there,' Peter observed.

'You think I'm building up from thesis to facts rather than the other way round, do you?' Another glare.

'There's always a risk of that with cold cases in my experience.'

'Not with me. You can be sure of that,' Pullman said drily. 'I've read those files on the laptop.' A grudging nod towards Georgia. 'I can't see they're relevant to Fairfax's death, save one perhaps.'

'We agree,' Georgia said frankly. 'Loads of information, but not leading anywhere – yet, at least. Which did you think relevant?'

'Easy. Those pilots are all in their dotage now; I don't see any of them dotting a healthy younger man like Hardcastle on the head. But the file on the Wormshill Aviation Club had also vanished from the main computer. Paul Stock appears on that, and there's evidence there were words between him and Fairfax on the day of his death, so we had him in for questioning. His statement for 1975 admits he was with Matthew Jones and still in the hotel at the time of Fairfax's death. We checked the forensic evidence, though, and there was no residue on Stock's hands, and the footprints didn't match, so despite the fact that there was trouble of some sort between him and Fairfax, there was nothing to hold him on.'

Peter glanced at Georgia, and she nodded. 'There were two stories about that row,' Peter said. 'One that they'd fallen out over the finances of the club, because he'd been fiddling the books, and two, that they had a row over Paul Stock's former wife, Janet Freeman. We believe the second.'

'Who did you hear that from? Nothing in the statements about it that I recall.'

'Various sources,' Peter replied. 'It wasn't in the statements because even if they knew about it, gentlemen didn't prattle about fights over mere women.'

Pullman frowned. 'Janet Freeman? She made a statement too. I remember the name. Nothing about this. What was the fight about?'

'Probably because she was having an affair with Fairfax and intending to spend the weekend at the hotel with him.'

Pullman looked interested. 'Lovers' tiff? That could put her in the frame, as well as Stock.'

'For killing Jack?' Georgia reminded them.

'Depends. If Hardcastle knew that together or separately they were mixed up with killing Fairfax, why not? Fairfax was married, so it could be she thought him more serious than he was. Happened before.'

'She told me serious is what she didn't want at that time,' Georgia put in.

'She would, wouldn't she?' Pullman said stiffly. 'I'll check where she was when Hardcastle was killed.'

'Any idea yet what the blunt instrument was?' Peter asked.

'Mrs Hardcastle has realized there's a bronze sculpture of a Hurricane missing. If this Janet Freeman is a strong woman, she's not out of the wood because of her sex.' He said that with some satisfaction, Georgia sensed.

'Nor perhaps should the pilots be because of their age. Besides, they all have family and carers,' Peter pointed out. 'Someone could be acting on their behalf.'

Pullman, to Georgia's surprise, burst out laughing, an odd sound from such a contained man. 'You think they've all got six-foot-five minders to do their dirty work for them? I suppose we should follow that up though. I spoke to Martin Heywood, your rival biographer . . .' Georgia let that pass. 'He said there was one you couldn't trace,' Pullman continued.

'Alan Purcell, who's apparently lived in France since the 1940s and never comes to Britain.'

'If he wasn't here in 1975, I can't see he could be involved.'

Georgia hesitated, then, mindful of Marsh & Daughter's rules, said, 'We think Jack might have gone to see him recently; the address in the Hardcastle files is a false one though.'

'I'll see what I can do.' Pullman's eye fell wistfully on the strawberry tart.

'Do have it,' Georgia urged.

'I will.'

Pullman engaging with crumbly strawberry tarts would be an interesting test of his character, Georgia thought. She watched as he attacked the tart straight on, regardless of crumbs, going straight for the central strawberry. Was that an encouraging sign, or an indication of a blinkered mind? It could, she supposed, be either. It would depend on whether the strawberry was the real McCoy or a plastic one for decoration.

'Are we still downhearted?' Peter asked, after Pullman had left (with what seemed genuine gratitude – for the strawberry tart at least).

'Yes.'

'Why?'

'I feel that he's on the wrong track pursuing Paul and/or the other aviation club people.' That, she thought, might be Pullman's plastic strawberry.

'That's a new track for you. That's where you originally thought the answer lay. Is it the right track though?'

'I don't *know*,' she answered in desperation. 'What Pullman says does make sense. If Jack's death is linked to those reunions, it follows that his killer was likely to be one of the aviation club contingent, and we should be following up Vincent Blake and Richard Vane, and yet it doesn't feel *right*.'

Peter thought for a moment. 'Perhaps they'll get Purcell's address for us.'

'And perhaps they won't. Has it occurred to you that he might not be living under that name?'

'I was hoping you wouldn't think of that. It would turn a mere nightmare into reality. Anyway, Purcell might possibly have a line on Jack's death, but not Fairfax's.'

'Wrong,' she said instantly. 'If the former, then the latter must be relevant. What else would Jack have seen him about?'

'General Battle of Britain stuff for the new book.'

153

'Then why was Jack so cagey about it? Why the false address, and why, if we're right, has Purcell taken a false name?'

'Because he's a nutter about secrecy.'

'Make my day complete,' she said gloomily. 'You might be right.'

Her day was made as soon as Georgia returned to her own home. There was a message waiting for her to ring Martin Heywood. What could this be about, she wondered. Exchanging sob stories about police interviews? Intrigued, she rang straight back. It was a mobile number and he answered almost immediately. She was right, as it turned out.

'I've had the police on my back,' he said abruptly. 'The last thing I need at the moment.'

'So have we, but they're still fishing around. I don't see why it should affect you, however, apart from the time point of view. You're not dealing with Fairfax's death to any great degree, let alone Jack's. Anyway, they seem to be going down the aviation club road,' she said comfortingly.

'You have no idea.' His voice sounded bitter. 'I was going to ring you anyway to let you know we're beginning to plan the campaign.'

'What campaign?'

'The press.' He sounded slightly surprised that she hadn't realized. 'We want to launch the publicity on Battle of Britain Day, September fifteenth. I'll send you tickets. *For Earth Too Hard* is to be released next year.'

'That's your film?' It had to be. It sounded lofty and learned.

'Yes, a quotation from Browning. Aspirational. Really aspirational. We need press build-up, interviews and so forth.'

'Why are you worried about a police investigation? After all, there's no such thing as bad publicity, so they say.'

'It depends how bad. We want the public to concentrate on Patrick's life, not on who might have killed him. It affects the final shots anyway.'

'You mean if we or the police discover who did kill him your film might be invalidated?'

'Not necessarily. We might end with just a gun, exploding into darkness. The death is symbolic. Do you see what I mean?'

'I think so,' she lied.

'We might choose to have just that, followed by silence and a screen relating what happened. That can be done at the last moment, and the new edition of the book wouldn't be affected.'

'Then what's the problem?'

'I'll tell you. You should know, anyway. It sounds crazy, but I think I'm being watched,' Martin blurted out. 'I've had some threatening letters, warning me to keep off. I have had plenty of them in the past, and usually bin them, but this time it's different. I get the impression that this is serious, and I've a wife and kid to think about. I wondered if you were getting the same treatment. Do you think there's some maniac out there who doesn't want Fairfax resurrected – and that's why Jack was attacked?'

The receiver felt clammy in her hand, as the memory of that tube station came back. 'I haven't had warning letters, but I've had the feeling of being followed too,' she admitted. 'Peter hasn't, to my knowledge, but I'm the more visible presence.' Although he, she thought with a shiver, was the more vulnerable.

A silence. 'That's bad, then. For all of us. When were you aware of it?'

'The day I went to see Sylvia Lee,' Georgia said. The first time she was sure about it, at least.

'Why did you want to see her?'

'Background. And her husband was there at the time of the murder.'

'Aviation club again. That's what Pullman's interested in, you say. By the way, you told me you were interested in the sergeant pilots, as well as the officers.'

'Yes.' For a moment she couldn't recall doing so, and then it came back. Tangmere. She was surprised he'd remembered. 'We need the full picture, and Eddie Stubbs is still around, of course.'

'Sylvia talks about them sometimes,' he commented.

'She spoke briefly about them to me too. Did you interview her for your film?'

'Of course. She agreed to be represented in it, so to speak. Dancing with Patrick.'

'I know where you got that idea,' Georgia laughed. 'Eddie.'

'Right. I might be able to help over the sergeant pilots,' he continued. 'I talked to Vic Parr before he died, as well as Eddie and the other surviving officers.'

'Including Alan Purcell?'

'The great recluse? No. Not from my point of view essential. I had Hugo Barnaby for the evasion story. He was in the same group.'

She'd forgotten about Patrick's later career, and his being shot down in France. 'Are you covering that in the film?'

'Of course. It's a great story.'

Was this something they had been overlooking? Could there have been anything in that relevant to 1975? Not likely. The reunion was focused on the Battle of Britain, not the remainder of the war.

'We have to concentrate on the pilots,' she said, 'which means the Battle of Britain.'

'Just as well. Barnaby died last year. I could send you his account of the evasion if you want it. He was on the same party as Patrick. If I get a line on Purcell, I'll let you know.'

'Martin implied that Purcell could tell us about Fairfax's evasion when he was shot down in 1941.'

'Did he?' Peter reached for Jack's biography and flicked to the relevant chapter. 'Shot down in a village outside Lille, evaded via the Garibaldi line to the Pyrenees, captured by Vichy police, interrogated, escaped, and made it – with Hugo Burnaby – over the Pyrenees to Gibraltar early in 1942.'

'No mention of Purcell?'

'Odd. I'll look into it. If we ever do trace Purcell, it might be useful. Meanwhile, we'll have to hammer on at the other pilots.'

'Not Bill Dane again,' Georgia decreed.

'I agree. He could stonewall for England. Who do you reckon then?'

'Not Matt Jones.'

'Poor old chap. Again, I agree. Take your pick of the canny reliable Scot, McNee, jolly old Harry Williams, or doom-laden Jan Molkar.'

'I'll pick jolly Harry Williams,' she said promptly. He lived in Lewes, and Sussex on a summer day was preferable to the London area.

'Don't see how I can help, dear lady. Delighted of course. Not often a pretty woman comes begging to see me at my time of life.'

'Difficult to believe that,' Georgia rejoined automatically to Harry. With a mane of grey hair, and strong if florid features, Harry Williams was still a fine-looking man, and although he was not able to walk too far he radiated energy, rather than shadows of a life past.

'Still looking into Patrick's death, are you?'

'You liked Patrick?'

He looked at her in astonishment. 'Splendid fellow. Still miss him. That laugh of his. I can still hear it. His voice over the intercom: "Tally-ho! I spy bandits."'

'You all seem very different in temperament, although you're so close-knit now.'

157

'We've been through a lot. Like being at school. You don't pick your chums, they just arrive. Like poor old Ken Lyle. You stick, because you don't question them.'

'Ken Lyle? He was in 362, wasn't he?' She remembered the name from the photograph.

'Killed in the battle. Remember him as if it were yesterday. What we went through.'

Was that the only reason that the magic circle was so hard to break into? It was the iron band born of common experience. Perhaps, yet she'd been to the occasional squadron reunion with Peter's father when he was alive, and had no such impression. But she wasn't looking into a murder then. Could murder be holding this group together? It was hard to believe a group of men of nearly ninety would be protecting a murderer in their midst, but it wasn't impossible. Save, she thought, that the reason for the murder would surely have to be in their common interest and there was no hint of that.

'How do you remember the day of Patrick's death? It must have been terrible.'

He thought about this. 'Clouded.' He leaned back, eyes closed. 'Trying hard, m'dear. Trying hard. Can't remember the lunch – had so many since. I remember old Patrick being upset because those club members of his came.'

'I heard about that. I met Janet Freeman.'

'Oh-ho!' His eyes gleamed. 'He wasn't upset about her. Far from it. Had a dirty weekend set up, in my view.'

'You knew about his affair with her?'

'Seen it all before. Talking of my own parade ground here. I recognized the signs. Crazy about her, he was.'

'And she him?'

'No doubt about it. The lady didn't beat about the bush.'

'But it wasn't a serious affair between her and Patrick?'

'Not so sure about that. I got the impression Patrick was serious this time. His kids were grown up and off his hands, and Jean – well, she must have taken some living with. Intense sort. Patrick liked a good time.'

'Janet Freeman didn't strike me as a good-time girl.'

'She was in those days, believe me. A very flirty lady. Had a bit of a fling with her myself, as a matter of fact. She dropped me like a hot potato when Patrick turned his blue eyes on her.'

'Mrs Fairfax thought Patrick's row with Paul Stock that afternoon was in fact with Bill Dane and over his wife.'

He blushed. 'Afraid that might have been me. Tried to cover up for Patrick even though he was dead. Didn't want to upset Jean. She was used to Patrick's fly by nights, but a serious affair was a different kettle of fish. So when she tackled me about what had happened that day I said the first thing that came into my head. Patrick was seen around with Alice quite a bit, so I told Jean it was over her. Rotten of me. Confessed to Alice. She and Bill hauled me over the coals and that was the end of it. All forgiven. Alice was a good sort. If she wasn't married to Bill I'd have made a play for her myself. Don't worry, m'dear. I'm past all that now.'

Georgia laughed aloud. 'Good.'

'About time, you think?' His own laugh bellowed out. 'With the old woman I've got I wouldn't dare make a pass. She's out with her active pensioners group climbing Box Hill this afternoon. You should see them, sticks to the fore, charging around. She's active enough with her mouth too, I can tell you. Keeps me in my place. Tell you what, m'dear, you give me a hand and we'll take a turn round the Grange Gardens. Only just round the corner and with a bit of help I can make it.'

Obediently she helped him out of his chair and into his coat, put the sticks in his hand, tucked her elbow under his arm, and set off with him at a slow pace across the road. This lower part of Lewes was quiet and residential, the older part of the town. It was here that Henry VIII had provided a house for Anne of Cleves, and the monks had once pursued their meditations in the now ruined priory. In the higher part of the town, the castle and battlefields spoke of a former, bloodier past, but here it was still possible to imagine monks walking, despite the close bypass and railway.

The gardens were indeed lovely, with bricked paths and water features, but the steps took time to negotiate and Georgia tactfully steered Harry towards the flat grassy part of the gardens. 'Recreation ground.' He turned and pointed behind them. 'Monks played football there.' Wheezy laugh. 'My football days are over. This is as far as I can get. Now then.' He paused to rest. 'About poor old Patrick. He wasn't one for money details, but he saw the broad picture. I remember him winking at me as I left the hotel that day. "I'll leave it ten minutes or so till precious Paul gets going with Matt and Alice, then I'll blow in with my answer to their prayers. Cash input from Vane, Blake and Standing." He just couldn't see that he was the source of the trouble and that cash wouldn't help.'

'But you don't think Matt had anything to do with Patrick's death?' she asked bluntly.

He looked horrified. 'Good grief, no. Matt was all talk. That's why he let Patrick get away with it for so long. The idea of his picking up a gun and shooting anyone is ludicrous and even the police thought so. Must have done. They tested his hands, you know, for powder burns. Nothing. All clean. And before you say gloves, where would you find a pair of them on a May evening?'

'It was a planned murder,' Georgia pointed out.

'Then,' Harry said with simplicity, 'it can't have been Matt. He lost his rag at the meeting, not earlier. Half an hour or so isn't long enough to plan that sort of thing.'

'But suppose he had planned it, guessing that the meeting would achieve nothing, and just went through the motions of discussion.'

'You're on the wrong track, m'dear. Not Matt, not any of us could have done it. The police saw that.'

'Are the sergeant pilots ruled out too?' she asked without thinking, and felt her arm jerk.

'What?' Harry looked horrified. 'It was an officers-only do.'

'They might have been somewhere else in the hotel,' she continued uncertainly, thrown by his reaction. 'They would surely have known about the reunion, since you all went to the aviation club together.'

'No reason to want to come, m'dear,' he replied easily. He stopped at an old mulberry tree, now roped off to the public with a safety notice attached. 'Look at that,' he continued. 'Would you believe it? Centuries old. Now it's a danger to the public, roped off. Next thing we know it'll be chopped down like the tulip tree that used to be here.'

Georgia was shaken. Was this some kind of warning to her, or was she imagining it? 'I felt like that in the dell where Patrick died,' she persevered.

He looked his full age. No laughter in his eyes now. 'Perhaps, my dear. Perhaps. Out of bounds, you know.'

With a man so elderly it was hard to guess at his thoughts, but the warmth had gone from the meeting. The magic ring had closed tight shut once more.

Ten

'Would you prefer to go out?' Georgia asked. Eddie Stubbs lived in a sheltered-housing complex in Dover, and after her experience with Harry he had been their obvious next choice. There was no point in tackling any of the four other pilots in the magic ring.

'No offence, but I thought that was the idea.' Eddie immediately perked up.

'We could take a run up to the castle if you fancy,' Peter chimed in, 'and take a look at old King Arthur's Hall.'

Georgia's heart sank. Would King Arthur *never* go away? Fortunately Eddie had other plans.

'How about the old Coastguards? That's if you don't mind a bit of a drive.'

Dorset, she wondered wildly. She suspected Eddie was quite capable of it.

Luckily it proved somewhat nearer – at St Margaret's Bay. It was just as well that Peter had chosen not only to accompany her but to drive his own car, which meant that she could now climb in the back to leave room for Eddie in front. It was also just as well that Peter was more than usually equable since Eddie's navigating didn't suggest he had missed a career in the RAF in this respect.

'That's it!' he shouted after the car had whizzed past the narrow turning for St Margaret's at Cliffe, but Peter surmounted the problem and drove through the small village.

Georgia hadn't been here since she was a child and had visited the beach at the foot of the cliffs with Peter and

Elena. Eddie directed Peter to turn off before that, however, towards the open cliffs, where the dramatic former coast-guards' tower was operating as a small café and restaurant, overlooking the sea and the coastal path to Deal. It was packed to the gunnels on such a fine day, but at the sight of Peter's wheelchair accompanied by Eddie's small frail figure, room was hastily made for them outside, where they had one of the best light lunches she had had in ages. With the magnificent view of the bay and cliffs and butterflies to be seen everywhere in the gorse heathland, it was easy to feel that 1940 was only yesterday.

'Nothing like the old ozone,' Eddie said contentedly. 'Not a patch on flying up there in the clouds, but at my age I'll settle for the old sea. Look at it, eh? Hard to imagine it all roped off, radar stations, mines, guns. I can tell you, I wouldn't have wanted to be down here. Up there's better. You can see what's coming.'

'Even considering what you went through?' she asked.

'Each to his own,' he rejoined. 'Glad you suggested coming here.' There was a glint in his eye. 'It's like going back to Malling. Easier to remember it all. I went with Jack to that golf clubhouse – know it?'

'Yes.'

'Looking out from those windows brought back what it was like taking off in the Spits. You don't forget things like that. Mind you, most of the time we were looking down at the craters in the runways, not up in the sky. Once you were up, half of you was wondering what you'd done to make God so good to you, giving you the Spit to fly up in His clouds; the other half was wondering when the black specks would appear, and those Stukas scream down for another go. Ever heard a Stuka, have you?'

'On a museum recording.'

'Well, imagine six of the bastards heading for the airfield. I was down there one day when we caught the lot. Stays with you like the air-raid siren, etching into your mind.

Another time it was eighteen blooming great Dorniers. Now, what was it you wanted to know?'

'About your fellow sergeant pilots, Eddie.'

'What about them? Told you most of it.'

'That's the problem. We don't know. We just don't want to miss anything. So you talk away.'

'There's an offer my old lady never gave me.' Eddie grinned. 'First thing, you make it sound as if we were two groups. We weren't. Slept and ate separately, but that's no more than most people who work together anywhere, any time. It's what you do together that binds you. Take Tanner. His two mates were Ken Lyle – officer – and Joe Smith, sergeant pilot. We were all one. Vic was the son of a bespoke tailor, and there's a word you don't come across now. We thought he was posh, one up on us. My dad was in the Thanet mines, Tanner's was a porter – another word you don't hear much now – and Joe Smith . . . can't recall. Yes, I can. Gardener somewhere. We were all in for hostilities only. We all got to do some training before the war, so were first in the queue for pilots. My pal was Vic. Joe was a loner, and Tanner – well, never knew really. A quiet sort, who hung around with Joe a lot. I liked Tanner, though I hardly saw him in the mess. He was in love, met some girl in Malling and that was that. Rarely saw him and never saw her. Off out whenever he could get a pass. Fat lot of good it did him. We'd met up in June when we joined the squadron. Some of the chaps had been in France, not on holiday either. Nasty do that. Patrick had been flying convoy patrols, so had Matt Jones.'

'And Alan Purcell?' Georgia asked.

Eddie squinted at her in the sun. 'Same as Patrick, if memory serves me right.'

'Have you ever heard from him again?'

'Not a dicky bird.'

'Did you get on with him?'

'He was in B Flight. Tanner and Smith were his buddies amongst us NCOs. He was interested in the LMFs. The news went round dispersal one day that Smith and Tanner had been up before the CO late the afternoon before. Smith was proven LMF, Tanner was to return next morning for the verdict. He didn't wait. He deserted that evening.'

'Did he tell you?'

'Nah. Wouldn't have had the guts. Adj came for their effects the morning after, and by the evening we had two new chaps. Purcell thought we were too hard on the LMFs. He didn't have much time for Smith, but Tanner was in a different class. An oddball like Purcell.'

'What was odd about him?'

Eddie considered. 'Not a mess chap. Anyway, he told me he tried to intercede with the CO on the Sunday.'

Georgia winced at that name again.

'No use though,' Eddie continued, 'except that might have been why CO King Arthur postponed the verdict. His family reckoned he drowned himself. Bodies were being washed up all the time and not all of them could be ID'd.'

'It must have been a shock for you and Vic.'

'Nah. Not really. We were losing mates every day. Never had time to mope about it – not till later, anyway. Some of the lads never went to funerals; that way they could think blokes had just gone for the famous Burton, rather than died in flames or in a thousand bits. If they stopped to think what they were doing, they'd all be LMF.'

'When did all this happen?'

'Let's think now. We flew in to Malling on July twentieth – know the date, doing my homework for Jack, see.' Eddie stopped for a moment. 'Poor old chap. Never did harm to no one did Jack.' He looked at them. 'You thinking that 362 business had anything to do with it?'

'It's a possibility that Fairfax's death could be involved,' Peter said matter-of-factly.

'Then ask on, mate. Anything I can tell you, I will.'

'Did you realize there was a big battle coming when you arrived?'

'That and invasion, yes. Invasion was the word of the day, believe me. Oh-ho, we're for it. We flew in on the twentieth, like I said, to replace a squadron of Defiants. Or what was left of it. The poor devils in 141 copped it in those death traps. No way out for the gunner, you see. Eleven of them left Malling one day for an advance landing field. Only four landed back there. Fodder for Jerry guns. They'd all have gone if some Hurri squadron hadn't come in to save them. Well, they were posted away and in we come with our Spits. There was action right from the word go. In the Channel, not over Kent, because the Jerries were softening up the target by attacking shipping. From then it escalated . . . Well, you know the story. Eagle Day, was it? Göring telling his chaps to attack the airfields to put them out of action. He didn't specify Malling, but he might as well have. The chaps no sooner got the runways back in order than back the bombers come again. We began to get a bad name in the luck states. 'Course, I have to be fair, Biggin on the Bump was worse hit. Then Hitler gave the go-ahead to attack London and it was all systems go to stop the bombers getting through. Like the blooming trenches, it was. No sooner get a fag in your mouth, a drink in your hand and your arm round a woman than Hitler asks for 362 in person. Vic and I were there for the duration. Tanner and Smith were long gone by then.'

'When exactly?' Peter prompted when Eddie paused.

'Not long after the station dance. I kept a sort of diary – well, we all did, and no, mine's not the sort you can quote from, full of poetic thoughts about life. Just odd jottings of dates and things. Got the dance written in big letters, at the Manor House on August thirty-first. We all spilled out into the gardens, a couple of us went for a dip in the lake – that sort of thing. Ken Lyle had been shot down that day, so we had to do something. Patrick had a spat with Tanner at dispersal after – tearing him off a strip, I reckon – and it was the day after that the LMF thing blew up. Blew up's not right, though. All very hush-hush it was, which meant more and more rumours.'

'How did they start?'

'The MO might report chaps are calling in sick without reason. One too many engine failures. The CO might pick up something, or the IO. Who knows?' Eddie was puffing away, looking out to sea.

'Did other pilots make complaints?'

'Rarely. Only if something happened in the air maybe. In dispersal you wouldn't always notice who wasn't there and should be, or who didn't get to their Spit quickly enough and someone else grabbed his place. Weren't supposed to, of course, but it happened, especially when the airfield was under attack. Most of us were all too keen to get the hell off the ground and into the air then.'

Georgia misunderstood. 'Because of the invasion threat?'

'We didn't stop to ask ourselves why we were doing it. We just went. It was them or us. You don't stop to wonder in the middle of a dogfight whether this is a worthy cause.'

Peter chuckled. 'Point taken. Were you surprised about Smith and Tanner and the LMF?'

'No. Too many rumours around. They were in Fairfax's section as a rule, in B Flight under McNee. Sometimes they flew with A Flight, though, to fill in gaps. No time to think at the time, but afterwards you put two and two together, when the chaps talk in dispersal. The times he wasn't there when he should have been. Now Vic was a different case. He was right there at your side. Salt of the earth.' Eddie sighed. 'It's a long time ago,' he continued. 'I don't reckon either of you were born then.'

'Did Jack spend a lot of time talking about 362?' Georgia asked.

'He would, wouldn't he? That's what I know about best.'

'Did he ask you about the other sergeant pilots?'

'Why not? We were part of it. He talked to Tanner's brother, he said.'

'When did he do that?' Georgia asked curiously. 'When he wrote the squadron history, or recently?'

'When we started this new thing,' Eddie said impatiently. 'Look, what's this about? The chap's dead. Drowned. You think his blinking ghost came back to kill Fairfax?'

'I don't know,' Peter said. 'Do you believe in ghosts?'

'Nah. And even if I did they don't shoot with Webleys.'

'Rainy days are sent to make us appreciate the sunny ones,' Peter said sanctimoniously.

'It works,' Georgia grunted. She was sick and tired of computer screens.

'There is a certain pleasure,' Peter remarked irritatingly, 'in bringing one's records up to date. Boring though it might seem, it has its own fascination. I for instance considered it worthwhile to reread all Jack's notes again, since he was asking Eddie about those sergeant pilots.'

'*All* the pilots,' Georgia reminded him. 'And *all* the pilots would be relevant to this book that he proposed to write.'

She was ignored. 'Both Vic Parr and Eddie went on flying right through the war, which is remarkable, but they weren't present on May tenth 1975, and even if we follow the theory that they were hiding in the Woodring Manor broom cupboard on that Saturday, we haven't a ghost of a motive for them, so let's rule them out. Alan Purcell is in a different category, even though he wasn't there in 1975 because—'

'Jack went to see him because of the new book,' Georgia finished for him.

'Which is apparently so secret he has to hide his contact details so efficiently that they can't be found.'

'Touché,' Georgia admitted. 'Moreover, if his guru Michael Hastings was right and Jack was edgy, then there was concern on both sides, not just on Alan's.'

She had even gone so far as to think that France was a double bluff and that Alan Purcell was alive and well but living in England. The number of Purcells even in the local telephone directory was daunting, however, and after trying several she had given up the attempt. First prove he did have something to contribute on the subject of Fairfax's death, and then put in the spadework.

'I've been piecing together Purcell's wartime career,' Peter said, 'including reading about evasion in occupied France. That's quite a story. Selflessness on the one hand and betrayals on the other. Alan Purcell himself was shot down just after D-Day, and though you might think it would be easy for him to slip through the lines to the Allied forces, it wasn't. Evasions by then had changed. Before that servicemen had to find an evasion line that would take them through either to Switzerland or the Pyrenees. By the time Alan Purcell was shot down behind Boulogne, at a village called Wierre Effroy, there was another plan to gather all the evaders together in camps at certain spots so that when the Allies reached them they would be ready to help the war effort. Alan was in Camp Sherwood, near Châteaudun. In fact the camp was there for longer than MI9 anticipated.'

'Interesting, but what does this have to do with Patrick Fairfax?' Georgia demanded. 'I can see that if Purcell had good help from the French it could have bonded him to the country, but Fairfax was safely in London at that point helping to plan D-Day.'

'True, but you know what? These computers are damned clever machines. In an idle moment, waiting for my coffee,' Peter roared out in the hope that Margaret would take the hint, 'I followed up that apparent implication by Heywood about Purcell knowing a lot about Fairfax's evasion, and did a search for Purcell in Jack's Fairfax files. And guess what?'

'Fairfax was a classical music fan and was particularly fond of Henry Purcell.'

'Wrong. Purcell came up in a file I hadn't looked at before. The sources, not his career notes. We were too busy thinking in terms of 1940.'

'Really?' Now this was interesting. 'Tell me, and I'll get your coffee myself.'

'The name Purcell does crop up in the story of Patrick Fairfax's evasion.'

Curiouser and curiouser. She meant it.

'Don't get too excited,' he warned her. 'I failed to cross-reference that with Alan Purcell's own file, so I've had to do some more digging. The Fairfax evasion was covered in Jack's biography, and he calls Purcell Alan in that, but when I read the story in another source, it referred to Maurice Purcell. Could be a mistake, but interesting.'

'Why? Could I remind you that neither Alan nor Maurice Purcell – if he exists – was present in 1975?'

'I don't need reminders.'

She was forced to eat humble pie. 'The story as I recall was that he went down the Garibaldi line, presumably so called after the gent who evaded the Germans by flying his balloon out of the Siege of Paris.'

'Correct. In the summer of 1941 Fairfax crash-landed on the Belgian border near Lille. He was slightly injured, was lucky in the folk who found him, was sheltered and his wounds tended. As soon as he was fit to travel he was sent to join a group travelling south to the Pyrenees. The first stage, to a safe house near Etaples, was with a Belgian woman called Marie. Her husband was a bilingual Englishman, who was the chief organizer and code-named Garibaldi. They had contacts all the way down to the Franco-Spanish border, and the main courier was a girl called Roseanne. It worked on a system of safe houses, and on the usual plan of each safe house not knowing the names of the next in line. Roseanne took them to a safe house in the Pyrenees, near St Jean de Luz, from which they were handed over to a Basque guide.'

'One of the servicemen in Patrick's group was Purcell, either the unknown Maurice or Alan himself. I presume the former since Alan was shot down again later, and was

never in a POW camp. They were captured just after they
set off for the Pyrenees, and taken to the local police
station – even in Vichy days working with the Germans –
to wait for interrogation by their very special inquisitor-
ial squads who were usually eager to out-Gestapo the
Gestapo. Then they were despatched they knew not where,
but Patrick and one of the other pilots, Hugo Barnaby,
managed to break out of the train van. The guide was
shot, so were the owners of many of the safe houses, so
were the organizers of the line. The pilots eventually ended
up in a POW camp.

'Patrick and Barnaby lay low after their escape, went
through a rough time and Patrick persuaded Barnaby not
to surrender but that they should have a go at crossing the
Pyrenees themselves. Madness, of course, but somehow
they managed it. They had a rough time with the Spanish
on the other side, but once through that they reached
Gibraltar, where the new MI9 agent was by then installed
to organize travel onwards. They got back to England by
the early summer of 1942.'

'Does that tell us anything about Patrick Fairfax in 1975?'
'I don't know, but it makes me keener to talk to Purcell.'

She heard the familiar car draw up, and couldn't for the
moment believe it. Surely that was Luke's car, and this was
a Wednesday morning? No way would he be here.
Nevertheless she ran to the window and peered into the
street. It was his car, and, moreover, it was Luke as well.

She flew outside just as he climbed out. One slam of the
door and she was in his arms, being whisked off her feet,
spun round and placed back again for a long kiss.

'I've got it,' he said.

No need to ask what.

'That's wonderful.' Doubts fell away; it *was* wonderful.
It was a step forward into a new life.

'Happy?' she asked.

'You ask me that? Woman, I tell you, I'd move in tomorrow if I could.'

'Can't you?'

'The deathwatch beetles are lining up with their spears and body armour to prevent me. A month or two yet I'm afraid, but you can start packing.' He must have seen her face. 'You are moving in with me, aren't you?'

'Luke, I . . .' She mustn't spoil this moment. 'I hadn't realized that's what you wanted,' she finished weakly.

'Georgia,' he said warningly. 'Decide *now*. Realize *now*. Sorry if I hadn't made that clear. I thought it was a done deal. You will, won't you?'

Decide now? How could she? It was too much, too soon. No, this wasn't fair of Luke, even if he had made a genuine mistake. Even if she had. She couldn't be expected to give him an instant yeah or nay. She turned to see Peter's wheel-chair in the doorway.

'Don't let her back out, Luke,' he called cheerfully. Damn him, she thought savagely.

'I'll walk round the block,' she announced. Not that there was a block, but she could walk. Anywhere to escape those four eyes scouring her face.

Luke said nothing, but she had to go, despite his expression. She walked down the lane by the side of Peter's house which led to Pluckett Farm. How could she move in so quickly? Did she want to move? Had she imagined the status quo would go on for ever? Was she crazy or just selfish? She had to be sure. She gazed into the stream trickling away under the bridge. Here as a child she used to play Pooh sticks with her mother. She had played Pooh sticks here *only last week* with Luke. She'd always wanted to float along with the sticks, not get stuck under the bridge. And that's where she appeared to be now. But round the corner the Pooh stick might run into a Zac. So what, she reasoned, if Luke were there too? No, she should manage on her own. But why? It was only one tiny step to Medlars,

172

Cot Street and Luke. She wasn't burning any bridges; she would be *making* one.

She found herself running, and this time running back. Luke had begun walking down the lane towards her, so it wasn't too far to go. No time to change her mind now, and in any case she didn't want to. This time he just held her.

'Sure?' he asked.

'Quite sure.'

He drew a deep breath. 'Thank heavens for that. I thought I wouldn't be needing that double bed again.'

'You'll be needing it. We could try it out tonight.'

'We're not moving in tonight.'

'South Malling. Trial period.'

'Trial periods are over, remember?'

'I do, I do.'

'OK, that's settled. Now we can go celebrate at the pub. Anyway I've some business to talk about.'

'Deeds to sign?'

'That you should be so lucky. Wedding banns?'

'That *you* should be so lucky,' she retorted cheerfully. 'One day. House first.'

With lunch over, and as they reached Peter's office, she thought to remind Luke about the business he'd mentioned.

'Oh yes, I've found Thomas Langley for you,' he told them.

'Who?' Even Peter looked blank.

'The aged barman from Woodring Manor who was there in 1975. Lives in Maidstone now.'

'That's very good of you, Luke,' Peter said, gratified.

'Not at all. He's the brother of the owner of Medlars.'

'This is a remarkable amount of good news for one day,' Peter gloated. 'Anything else? You don't happen to know what name Alan Purcell's living under in France, do you?'

Luke looked blank. 'Purcell?' He laughed, picking up Peter's favourite current book. 'Try Arthur.'

'Very funny,' Georgia said sourly.

173

'No, really. If Purcell changed his name it might have been something related to the composer. His work for instance. You never know. *Dido*, *Aeneas*, *King Arthur* . . . I'd say Arthur was the most likely.'

'You know, Georgia, he's got a point,' Peter said, excited. 'Let's try that at least.'

He was already reaching for the phone when it rang. He glanced at Georgia and as he answered it he held the receiver briefly towards her so that she could hear the familiar tones of DI Pullman.

She couldn't work out what he was saying from Peter's end of the conversation. 'More good news?' she asked when he rang off.

'Depends. He thought we'd like to know that they've charged Paul Stock with Jack Hardcastle's murder. He's admitted being at the house that evening.'

Eleven

'That must mean,' Georgia said, 'that Jack's death *is* connected to Patrick Fairfax's.' They had been talking about the arrest for what seemed like hours and still they came back to this starting point. Not long after Pullman's call, Paul's wife had telephoned.

According to Paul, Jack had rung him quite peaceably to ask if they could have a chat about the aviation club. Paul had assumed he meant over the phone or for a drink, but Jack had asked if he could come over right away. He'd something he wanted to talk about. When he got there, Jack was his usual hale and hearty self. They had a glass of beer, and Paul was intrigued, but all Jack wanted was to talk about Patrick Fairfax and 362 Squadron. Did Patrick ever talk about the war to him? Paul had answered truthfully no. The drink came to an end, and so did the meeting.

Odd, Georgia had observed.

'Just what Pullman probably thought. He showed no signs that he believed the slightest word Paul said.'

'Why did his wife ring us?'

'Ah. Pullman is, Paul fears, making up a case that it was he who killed Fairfax in 1975 and that Jack was threatening to expose that, having just discovered the Janet Freeman angle.'

Georgia couldn't see this. 'Even if they could make a circumstantial case for his killing Jack, they couldn't find proof for his killing Patrick. If it was as easy as that, the police would have found it at the time. As it was, it

175

Amy Myers

appears he wasn't even suspected. So where do we stand on this?'

'Jack's death is a moral responsibility for us if it was we who stirred him up over 1975. Our focus is still Fairfax, and Paul is still therefore in our sights. Even so, I can't see him murdering anyone, can you?'

How could one possibly tell, she wondered. She remembered Jack's 'That bastard!' Would he really have an amicable discussion only a week or two later with said bastard?

'Yes,' she said finally. 'I could. But only impulsively. Jack's death would fit with that, but not Fairfax's. I could see Paul having a fight with Fairfax on the spot, but not then attending the reunion and having a business meeting, and all the while planning to spirit up some ammunition, seize that gun and stalk Patrick until he got him on his own. It doesn't add up.'

'Pullman thinks it does. We've no idea what forensic evidence he might be sitting on. The only point in Paul's favour is—'

'The weak story he gave his wife to tell us,' Georgia finished for him. The advantage of a long partnership is that minds think alike. And in long marriages too, she thought. A vision of herself and Luke as grey-haired pensioners popped into her mind, not entirely to her horror. A good sign?

'Beer in an English pub garden on a summer's day, with the sun above, the river in front and the knowledge that all the world and his wife could pass you by, kings, road sweepers, prime ministers. One of the great signs of anonymity,' Peter observed as he sipped his drink.

'Drinking beer?' Georgia enquired.

'Quite. It bestows a cloak of invisibility. What the butler saw. Some day I'll write a history of Britain written entirely from the butler's diaries, only in this case the barmen,'

176

Peter said. 'Has it ever occurred to you that the *real* history of any country remains untold because those who can write don't write the truth, only their political slant, and those who could tell the truth either couldn't or hadn't the time to write?'

Georgia laughed. 'Then how will you write this great history, Lord Macaulay?'

'Macaulay had a sweeping overview in his *History of England*, but I would have a worm's eye view from beneath. And to answer your question, I've no idea, but you consider what the chambermaids and butlers could tell us about the events of history. Napoleon, we are told, had piles that affected the course of Waterloo. Suppose Henry II had had a row with his wife before he so irritably told four of his best knights to rid him of that turbulent priest Thomas à Becket. Or that the Earl of Leicester had a stomach disorder the day he went a-wooing Good Queen Bess. Or that Queen Victoria's stays were laced too tightly on the day she was not amused. Yes, gardeners, ladies' maids, butlers . . .'

'Barmen,' supplied Georgia. 'Seeing that's why we're waiting here today. To be exact, a retired barman. This might be Mr Langley coming now.'

Strolling towards them in a determined fashion was an affable-looking man in his sixties with an equally affable-looking spaniel on a lead at his side.

She and Peter had followed up Luke's information, and this had proved the first opportunity Thomas Langley had free, a week later. Such was retirement, Peter said somewhat sourly, to which she had replied that he would be even more unbearable if he retired.

'Mr Marsh, Miss Marsh. Glad to meet you. You're moving into Stan's place, aren't you?'

Stan, Georgia realized, must be the current owner of Medlars, a house which, like the fruit it was named after, was best appreciated rotten. That had been Luke's joke, not hers, and she could see his point.

'I am,' she answered. And how strange those words sounded. As solemn as a contract.

'How is the old place nowadays?' he asked after drinks and menu were before them.

'Medlars?'

'Woodring Hotel. The Old Woodpile I called it.'

'Didn't you enjoy working there?'

'Not bad. A job. Wouldn't like to be there now. Started there in 1969 when I was still wet behind my ears. You have to be dry to be a barman, in all senses. Still, I learned quickly. Now that young gentleman of yours, Luke Frost . . .'

She'd pass that on to Luke later, Georgia thought.

'. . . said that you were writing a book for him about the death of that pilot chappie.'

'That's right. We need all the material we can get.'

'Do my best,' he remarked promisingly. Thomas sat back, licking the foam of the bitter on his lips. 'Tastes all the better when you don't have to draw it yourself.'

Like cooking, Georgia thought, then firmly stamped on thoughts of her looming life at Medlars.

'They came every year, did that group of pilots. I'd come to recognize them after a year or two. We had a lot of these reunions, but that was the one I remember most clearly. I suppose it was because of him, the chap that got murdered. They'd all have been in their fifties by the time I knew them, but you would never have known it. Always roaring the odds, they were, but nice about it, if you know what I mean. Fairfax was the leader of the pack all right. Seemed a nice chap though, and right from the beginning my boss told me he was a war hero. Matt Jones being the owner and one of the group himself, we treated this group special. Not free drinks – well, not unless Fairfax said so, and then there was a right royal fuss. We had orders after a while from Matty to chalk them up to Fairfax.

'Anyway that day we had both bars going, being a Saturday. I had two sidekicks then, both casuals or students, can't remember which, Jimmy Potter and Tony Wilson. Both of them were bright lads, well spoken, Tony a bit older than Jimmy, early thirties maybe, and more serious like, not given to larking around. They weren't the rough sort; Matt wouldn't have that in his hotel. Well, it was pretty busy and we all stayed on most of the day barring the odd ten-minute break. I was on the upper bar, and Mr Fairfax was rampaging around in fine form most of the time. After most of his mates left, he joined this lady, a guest at the hotel. He was in a black mood by then. Go careful with him, I said to Tony. So we arranged to keep an eye on him, Tony in the downstairs bar, two of us upstairs, with the odd break now and then.'

'Were they arguing?'

'Not really. More talking hard, if you know what I mean. Then they went downstairs and I didn't see Fairfax again. Not in the bar, anyway. I saw him rushing by the door about seven and assumed he was off downstairs. Some chap came in asking for him later and I sent him downstairs. He wasn't there, of course, because Tony had passed on the message that his lady friend was in the garden. Tony was switching with Jimmy at the time, so when this chap went downstairs, one bar was empty. No Patrick. No lady.'

'Any chance of tracing Jimmy or Tony?'

'Casual workers. No way after all this time. They both made statements, I'm pretty sure.'

'Anything else you can tell us?' Peter asked. 'Did you see this lady or any of the guests from the reunion still around, apart from Matt Jones?'

'Ruby might have. She was on the desk that night. Used to be a barmaid there. Some maid. She was in her fifties when I joined. Been at Woodring for ever.'

Georgia pricked up her ears. 'Would she have been there during the war?'

'She couldn't have been, Georgia,' Peter said. 'It would have been run by the military.'

'Wouldn't she indeed?' Thomas commented. 'She was there; that's how it started. Matt bought the hotel after the war, and her being a local girl Matt was thrilled to bits to see her, and brought her back. Favourite with the customers, she was.'

'When you say she could tell us, does that mean she's still alive?' Georgia asked.

'In a retirement home, but lively as a cricket last time I saw her. I pop in a few times a year.'

'You don't suppose,' Georgia said hopefully, 'we could pop in this afternoon?'

He considered this. 'If you're driving and I can have another pint.'

''Allo, Tom.' The sharp eyes swivelled to them. Ruby was in the conservatory at the retirement home not far from Maidstone in what used to be a village and was now rapidly becoming urban sprawl. Thomas bent over and gave her a kiss. She was so small she almost seemed moulded into her armchair, huddled under a shawl despite the time of year. 'Brought any fags with you?'

'You'll be breaking the law soon as well as storing up trouble for your old age,' he joked, as Peter handed over the packets that Tom had advised them to bring.

She cackled. 'What they goin' to do? Throw me into clink for a year or two? Look good in the papers, wouldn't it?'

'Were you at Woodring Manor all through the war?' Georgia asked when the cigarettes had worked their magic.

'You bet your sweet life I was. Officers and gentlemen? Forget it. Officers maybe. Mind you, they was up all day in the air and ready for a drink or two after. The stuff we had to serve then was half water, no spirits at all. You had to make your own fun then and we did. Cried my eyes out when they closed the station down in '44.'

'Weren't you called up?'

'I was up. Woodring was war work. Good name for it. Employed by the government to look after our lads. So I did. Married one of them after the war. Dead now.'

'A Battle of Britain pilot?'

'No. I met Fred later.'

'Do you remember the battle clearly?'

''Course I do. Those were the days, eh? "We'll meet again",' she crooned. 'We kept our sunny side up, all right. We did our bit for England our way.'

'Do you remember Patrick Fairfax?'

'The one who was killed up at Woodring? Should do. I was there. He was special, he was. Why would anyone want to kill him? I remember him from earlier, *and* the others. They'd all been meeting since the hotel opened up again after the war. Lay derelict for a year or two then Mr Matt bought it. His chums came over every May. Anniversary of the day he bought the hotel, he said, and the day war broke out in earnest. Old Hitler's Blitzkrieg.'

'Mr Fairfax,' Georgia reminded her gently.

'Hot temper had our Patrick. All the boys down in Hell's Bells Club downstairs, them and their women.'

'During the battle?'

'Oh yes, they entertained their lady friends. Supposed to go by curfew time, but a few stayed on, I reckon. Old Arthur knew about it, but he turned the old Nelsonian eye, as they say. Some real ladies there was, as well as the scrubbers. There was one night, Mr Fairfax he had the pick, you see. There they were dancing to a gramophone in the bar, up and down the corridor. Anyway, this young chap turned up, and Mr Fairfax was with this lovely young lady. Hadn't seen her before, staying in the village so they said. A Sunday night it was, and they'd been in the air a lot of the day. It was the day Biggin copped it so badly. Someone said later she was that actress Sylvia Lee. Well, I couldn't take my eyes off her, golden hair coifed up, blue eyes, so graceful and gentle, and a wee bit sad. Mr Fairfax was all over her, and she was dancing away with him. Then this young chap comes in and picks a fight.'

'One of the officers living there?'

'No. Don't remember if he had pips. He was looking for Pilot Officer Fairfax, and when he found him he punched him. Just like in the films. I thought they were all going to attack him but Mr Fairfax stopped them. The young lady was in tears and so Mr Fairfax said he'd go outside with this chap and sort it out. They were out a fair time, then Mr Fairfax came back and said someone should take the young lady home, and the evening sort of broke up. The young lady was still upset. "How's Oliver?" I remember her saying. "How's Oliver?" They all left the bar to see her off, and that's the last I saw of any of them. Closed the bar and that was it.'

Oliver Tanner? Georgia wondered. The LMF sergeant pilot. If so, how *was* Oliver? Could that have been the day he deserted?

'This is the last one,' Peter said. 'If this isn't Alan Purcell I'll eat my Marks and Spencer's hat.'

A dire threat since this was his favourite headgear at present. Peter had been impatiently working his way through the Arthurs in the list supplied to him by Jacob. He had vowed to track him down by the end of July, and since time was running out fast, this was the last day.

'This one is surely it,' he continued. 'I've checked this address. Not a stone's throw from Wierre Effroy where Purcell was shot down. Coincidence? Perhaps, but unlikely.'

She left him to it, unable to bear the suspense, and was rewarded by his smirk of triumph when she returned.

'Bingo. Unfortunately the house is guarded by a stone wall called Alan Purcell.'

'He won't see us?'

'He was furious, I persisted and he reluctantly agreed to

meet you in Boulogne. Would you believe it though, the new address we had is false too. Email him to say what time you'll be there. And make it soon; don't give him a chance to change his mind.'

Meet *you*, she noted without surprise. Not us. Peter never went to France. On principle, he claimed. The principle was that Elena lived there now. No matter that she lived almost at the other end of the country.

'I'll go tomorrow.'

'With Luke?'

'He's too busy with deathwatch beetles.'

Alan Purcell had suggested a restaurant in the square at Boulogne, and so she booked her SpeedFerries ticket, even though this meant taking her car. She parked it by the quay and walked up the hill through the main street of the town. She had plenty of time, and dawdled looking in the shop windows at everything from charcuterie to shoes, enjoying her own company. Her own? Once again, she began to have the feeling that she was being watched. Nonsense, spies nowhere, she joked to herself, and bought a coffee to forget it. As she watched the passers-by through the window, the feeling would not go away, and continuing on her way she looked round uneasily as though all shoppers were out here to get Georgia Marsh rather than baguettes for lunch.

She duly found the restaurant, opposite the old church in the square, and went inside not knowing whom to look for, save an Englishman in his eighties. The Cherub had been his nickname, but he was unlikely to look very cherubic now. She became aware of a man scrutinizing her from a window table and walked over to him, even though he most certainly didn't look English. From his small hunched body and face, one could mentally stick a beret on him and a Gauloise in his mouth and he'd be French. Nevertheless the cool blue eyes summing her up had more than a hint

183

of British reserve, and, she admitted, even a hint of his earlier nickname.

'Miss Marsh?'

'Georgia,' she murmured automatically, doing her own share of summing up.

'An attractive name.'

At least he didn't say it had been 'on his mind', a retort that came all too easily to many people. That was a point in his favour. His movements were slow but controlled, as was his face. Here was another Jan Molkar rather than a Harry Williams. He'd have made a good spy, she thought, unremarkable to look at – and capable of single-minded thought and action.

'May I offer you a drink?' he asked.

'Water for the moment, thank you, and by the way, lunch is on me. It's the least I can do.'

That won a slight smile, but one that didn't reach his eyes. 'I agree, Georgia. You seem to have been exceptionally determined to seek me out to hear my old war stories. I can't see how they would help you in the matter of Patrick Fairfax's death.'

'Did you like him? I realize that's a trite question since you were fighting a war when you knew him, but it's relevant.'

'I did.'

'You admired him?'

'He was a beacon in the darkness of those days. In war one needs that. As I told Jack.'

She realized with shock that he might not have heard the news. This man wasn't the sort to be in contact unless he needed to, and presumably with Jack's visit that had vanished.

'I have bad news,' she said awkwardly. 'You might not know that Jack died.'

He went very still. 'How? When?' he rapped out.

There was no easy way to say it. 'He was murdered in

his home, and his wife believed he had recently been to see you.'

'Do you connect those two elements? If so, Miss Marsh, you might begin to understand why I live a very low-key life.'

'I don't have enough facts to connect them. Do you?' she threw back at him. 'The police have charged a man called Paul Stock, whom you would not know. They believe Jack might have amassed evidence that Paul killed Patrick Fairfax.'

'Do you believe that?'

'No, but I can't explain why. He did have a motive, he was there – and yet it doesn't fit.'

'And for you everything does have to fit?'

'Yes. In this case they have to fit the dell.' The minute she had said it, she regretted it. Why on earth did she have to confuse the issue by mentioning that fatal word? It had its effect though. Alan Purcell's eyes moved as though he were looking at a human being.

'You are referring to the dell at Woodring Manor, of course?' he asked quietly.

'So you remember it?' He hadn't asked which dell or what on earth she was talking about. This was going to sound weird, but she would have to work hard if she was to get anywhere with Alan Purcell. 'It reeks with the atmosphere of decay and death.'

She had his attention now. 'Patrick Fairfax's body was found there,' she continued, 'and my father and I felt strongly that his unsolved murder is crying out to be investigated. I feel there's more to be discovered about his death than was revealed at the time, or even than what we've found so far. We've been talking to Eddie Stubbs, to Sylvia Lee and to the barmaid who used to serve there during the battle. You might remember her, Ruby her name was. She still thinks of you all.'

'She was pretty,' he said absently. 'Yes, I remember her.

We all remember Ruby. She was a dainty little thing. Well able to look after herself, however.'

'I imagine she still is.' No creeping silent watchers would faze her, thought Georgia enviously.

'Please tell me what your interest is in the Battle of Britain period, if it is Patrick's death you are investigating.'

'It's partly because Jack was interested in it, and planning to do a book with Eddie Stubbs, which I imagine is why he came to see you, and partly . . .' She hesitated. 'Because it seems to have been the beginning.'

'Of what?'

'If I knew that, Mr Purcell, I wouldn't be here.'

'I think you would,' he said softly. 'I do think so.' Then, with scarcely a pause, 'Aren't these mussels splendid? That's the reason I live in France of course.'

OK, she could play that game too. 'Not because you're near the home of the people who sheltered you when you were shot down?'

'They are long dead.' He didn't seem surprised at the question.

'Were you shot down twice?' she persisted. 'The accounts we have read suggest that you were shot down in 1944, yet in Jack's biography of Fairfax you were in the same group of evaders as Patrick Fairfax.'

'That was Maurice, my brother. He was captured with Patrick but did not escape from the train. He went to an internment prison, then a POW camp. He survived the war, but only just. He died of tuberculosis in 1949 as a result of his experiences. The line was betrayed of course. I am still in touch with a lady who was a young courier on the line. She was arrested, escaped being shot but spent the rest of the war in Ravensbrück.'

'Who was the traitor?' she asked.

'Who can tell for sure? There are odd stories in that world. The Pat O'Leary line was betrayed by a former sergeant in the British army who had worked on the line himself and saved many lives before he betrayed it. Another line was betrayed by an airman who talked too much. There will always be those who cannot withstand torture, there will always be those who seek money at any price, there will always be . . .' He paused. 'Cowards.'

'Even in 362 Squadron,' she commented.

'I take it you have heard about Oliver Tanner and Joseph Smith.'

'I have. Eddie Stubbs told me you had some sympathy for Tanner. Can you tell me about them?'

'No more than I can tell you about Harry Williams, Daz Dane, Jan Molkar, Matthew Jones or Bob McNee. Or Patrick Fairfax. That door is closed, Georgia. The one for 1975 is open, but any incidental passages that lie within that room are barred. Nor would it be wise for you to follow them.'

A threat? A warning? Either way, she had to ignore it and make a leap in the dark. 'Ruby told me Sylvia Lee was present on the same evening that a young airman called Oliver came to Woodring and that there was a fight. Is that one of these closed passages?'

For the first time Alan looked shaken, and took a moment or two to reply. 'You must talk to Sylvia again, Georgia. I would suggest you tell no one you are visiting her, but relay to her that you have talked to me as I talked to her in 1940. Use those words if you please. '

'I will.'

'I appreciate that.' A pause. 'As I appreciate this local cheese. The riper it becomes, even a small portion of it can spread its smell around. Perhaps the same is true of that dell, Georgia.'

Twelve

A lan Purcell had provided either a milestone or another blind alley. He had told her little or nothing, but what he implied might be a way forward – even if by bringing Sylvia Lee back into the picture she would merely be doubling back in a U-turn. But why should Alan mislead her? He clearly had had no part in the events of 1975. Nevertheless if he were, as it seemed, pointing her back to the Battle of Britain then he might have had as much at stake in 1975 as any of the others. Except that he wasn't there!

Now you see them now you don't, she thought as she boarded the catamaran for the return journey. At least she no longer had the sense of being watched, despite the hordes of shoppers returning with their wine supplies. She couldn't blame them. She had nipped into the wine shop herself at the port, not to mention the charcuterie on the way down the hill. Peter would never have forgiven her if she hadn't come back with several cheeses, an interesting supper for them both, and several cases of wine. His avoidance of France did not extend, thankfully, to its goodies, and she still had hopes of persuading him into a day visit to Boulogne for a lunch. Not many, it was true. A Kentish restaurant with a French chef was probably the closest they would get.

Her purchases were in a way a justification since she still had no idea why Alan Purcell should have cut himself off from his past, especially since he had been an admirer of Fairfax. Choice, she supposed. It was as simple as that. She had asked him if he had any idea as to the cause of Patrick's death, and his reply had been curious: more than harmless moths fly to a bright light. Perhaps it wasn't so curious, when one considered the way stalkers marked down celebs. Stick your head above the parapet, and expect to be shot at as well as cheered. Fairfax was still hero-worshipped by his family to the point that surely no one in it must now recall the real Patrick Fairfax. Jean perhaps? Shades of Queen Victoria and Albert. Albert had grown more saintly as the years passed. Was that true of Fairfax and his admirers? Only Sylvia Lee had said anything about him that spoke of the inner man. She had said that he was gentle and lovable. Had she discovered that in the two brief weeks she'd known him, to such an extent that she still remembered him for it? And if so gentle and lovable, why had she left him with her heart so intact that she married someone else in December that same year? Could the answer be that Patrick had dropped her, rather than the other way around? If so, she couldn't imagine why. Sylvia Lee must have been a trophy girlfriend, so what had happened during those two weeks? 'How's Oliver?' Sylvia had asked, according to Ruby.

Georgia began to feel the slow growth of excitement.

Sylvia looked tired, or perhaps it was that some, at least, of her defences had been dropped. Georgia had needed Alan Purcell's password for Sylvia to agree to see her again. There had been silence on the telephone when Georgia explained. Then a weary 'I understand.'

Now that she was here, however, Sylvia seemed resigned to her presence. 'Have they found Jack Hardcastle's murderer yet?' she asked.

'No. They charged Paul Stock with the murder, but it's been dropped.'

The CPS must have ruled the evidence too flimsy. Such

forensic evidence as there was linked with his story, but not with the murders. There was still unidentified DNA from fibres on Jack's clothing and fingerprints. Nothing had emerged to provide evidence linking Paul to Fairfax's death, not even with the Janet Freeman information. Georgia suspected Pullman blamed them for leading him up a blind alley. In short, Mike had told them on the phone, Pullman was temporarily sulking over the case. Now was the time for the Marshes to save Pullman's career, he had added.

'It is also time to save Marsh & Daughter's career,' Georgia had grumbled when Peter told her.

Peter had been all for her second visit to Sylvia. 'It's a tempting new line, even if it's a hell of a distance away from 1975. It would have to turn a few somersaults to affect that.'

There was one already turning in Georgia's mind, and now that she was here and had given the password, she had to play the card quickly. No stopping to test the water.

'It was Oliver Tanner you were really attached to, wasn't it? Not Patrick Fairfax,' she asked Sylvia. 'It was he you were thinking of when you spoke of his being gentle and lovable.'

Sylvia shifted in the large chair. 'Attached is hardly adequate, although I understand why you use the word. It's kind of you. I loved Oliver deeply, even though I knew him only for a few weeks. Have you ever been lucky enough to meet someone about whom you knew, to use the cliché, that you were made for each other?'

Zac flew through Georgia's mind and was pushed out as her stomach churned.

'If we'd looked in the mirror,' Sylvia continued, 'we would have seen two halves of the same person – not twins, but each other's complement. I met Oliver in the Rose and Crown almost as soon as I came to stay in Town Malling. That was the pub the NCOs used, when they weren't in their own mess. That was a billet on the field, not like Woodring Manor. He seemed somehow apart, not exactly lonely, because he joined in the fun. The squadron had only just flown in, he told me. We started talking about this and that, I told him about the Ivor Novello play I was in, he told me I looked like Evelyn Laye, and I said he looked like Leslie Howard. So we had this running joke – I'd be Evie, and he was Les. Silly, isn't it? That's how it was. We didn't do much socializing, once we'd found each other. Whenever he could get a pass, we'd meet. Sometimes we'd walk in the Douce Manor grounds, but more often we would take bicycles and go out to the river at Teston, or to country pubs. Away from the war, he said. Some of the pilots coped with the war by being with their mates, but a few such as Oliver needed to get away from it. He liked looking at the river trickling by, the birds having their dusk tuck-in, as he used to call it. That would still be the same when the war was no more, when we were no more.'

'Maybe that's like the pilot who wrote "High Flight"; he could touch the hand of God in the sky, side by side with the battle. Did Oliver talk about what went on during the daytime?'

'Never. I thought that was natural, until . . .'

'You heard about the lack of moral fibre.'

'Yes. This is where it gets difficult, Georgia. Patrick warned me about it on the Saturday night at the end of August. He said the CO was seeing Oliver and his friend Joseph Smith the next day. Oliver hadn't wanted to go to the dance, and I couldn't understand why. I persuaded him though. He must have known what was brewing.'

'Had you noticed anything different about him that would explain the LMF charge?'

'He was increasingly silent. I thought it was just because the battle was getting to him, so the real reason came as a terrible shock. When Patrick told me, I was so shaken I spent the rest of the evening with him. I'd met him quite

191

a few times casually and knew he was attracted to me. When I'd calmed down, Oliver had disappeared.

'I had time to think it out, and next day he came to see me in the late afternoon. He'd seen the CO by that time. Joseph had been found guilty; Oliver was to return next morning to know his fate. There was no doubt what it would be, and I was hardly sympathetic. I was only young, not able to see the other side. I saw nothing but myself, how I felt. He began to defend himself, but I didn't believe him. Then he just told me to remember that no one should be judged solely by what they did or did not do in wartime. I flew into another temper, full of empty stupid words and he just walked away. That evening he came up to Woodring Manor. It was a Sunday evening, and we were dancing to a gramophone. I was flirting with Patrick, trying not to think about Oliver. Then suddenly he was there and punching Patrick. I knew it must be about me, and that if they went outside Patrick would surely win. The other pilots wouldn't let me go after them. They said he was a rotten coward and would be leaving tomorrow. I was all mixed up, and when Patrick eventually came back, he said Oliver had left and someone should get me home. He was too shaken to drive me himself, so Alan Purcell took me in the station brake. He was wonderful, talked as though the evening had been perfectly normal, and fights happened all the time. I asked whether I would be able to see Oliver if I stopped at the NCOs' mess, and he said no, but he would probably still be around the next day. But he wasn't. I was told he'd deserted and Joe had already left for the special camp.'

'Was that true?' Georgia had a terrible feeling where this might be leading.

'No. Georgia, I didn't tell you before because there are those alive whom it might hurt. I only tell you now on condition it doesn't appear in your book unless . . .' She hesitated. 'Unless it affects Jack Hardcastle's death, though I can't see how it can.'

Georgia didn't like this condition, but Sylvia was immersed in her story. 'Oliver was dead,' she continued quietly. 'He never left Woodring Manor. It was a terrible accident, when he and Patrick came to blows. Patrick was the stronger physically, and hit Oliver so hard he fell backwards and hit his head on a stone.'

Suspicion once confirmed doesn't shock, Georgia thought. Instead it creeps up and chills the body slowly. She had never met Oliver Tanner but he had lain in the dark shadows almost since they began this case. Now there were glaring questions.

'I'm so sorry,' she began. 'I can see that even now it's distressing for you.'

'It was my fault; I can never forget that.'

'When did you find out about it?'

Georgia thought she sensed a hesitation, but perhaps not for Sylvia answered: 'Two weeks later, through Alan. He came to see me; he felt I should know. I'd been trying to forget Oliver by seeing Patrick, but every time I saw him it reminded me of what had happened. I knew I had to go. Alan said that after we'd left Woodring that night, the other pilots found a car with sufficient petrol in it, and drove the body to the coast. Alan and I talked it over and decided that for everyone's sake, particularly Oliver's parents, we should leave it as it was: that Oliver had apparently deserted and drowned himself because of the disgrace. There was, he told me, no doubt. The verdict had been confirmed the next day and deserted entered after it.'

Georgia had to ask. 'Do you know where exactly Oliver was killed?'

'Does it matter?' Sylvia she asked wearily.

Oh yes, it mattered. 'If you can tell me, yes.'

'He hit his head on one of the rockery stones, near where Patrick was found.'

*　　*　　*

Back to that dell. No wonder it cried out to them so loudly. Two days had passed since Georgia's visit to Sylvia, but still she was thrashing it over with Peter.

'These idyllic bike rides,' he had remarked. 'I wonder if they led to idyllic sex.'

Immediately she thought of her earlier idea that Sylvia's twins might have been Fairfax's. 'She married Norman Lake in December.'

'Her great love affairs are either short-lived, or she needed a husband quickly.'

'Where are we going with this?' Georgia asked crossly. 'That Richard Vane suddenly decided to take up cudgels and kill Fairfax?'

'Perhaps,' he said annoyingly. 'At least this story about Tanner provides an answer to why the pilots are all so close together, although I'm not convinced that's the whole story. It was after all a death that they were concealing from the proper authorities for whatever good reason, as they saw it. Even so, what bearing could that have on Patrick Fairfax's death? If the truth had emerged, there would hardly have been violent repercussions, and Tanner's family would surely have raised a legal scandal rather than set up a personal vendetta. They would have been too old for that in 1975, although his brother could in theory have been there. I don't buy it. Besides, there's one thing we should consider. We began this because of that dell. Does something occur to you?'

'Yes,' Georgia said. She'd been trying to suppress it though. 'Which death was crying out to be reheard? Fairfax's or Tanner's?'

'Back to the drawing board,' Peter said glumly. 'And time might be running out. I had a call from your chum Martin Heywood. He says the 362 gang is getting twitchy.'

'What about?'

'This plan for Battle of Britain Day in September. The publicity launch for the film at Woodring.'

She'd almost forgotten that. So typical of Martin's approach to hold it there. Seek the inner meaning in sound bites.

'It seems they're getting worried by the concentration on Patrick's death, rather than his life,' Peter said. 'He asked what the hell we've been stirring up. He got in quite a state.'

'What did you tell him?'

'I told him by holding it at Woodring he was doing quite a lot of stirring himself. He calmed down then, and said that he'd more or less told them he'd ensure the film would close on the heyday of the aviation club, and that his commentary for the reprint of *This Life, This Death* will focus on his aviation career. Jean Fairfax is apparently happy with that idea, and Martin said he might even get Alan Purcell to come over.'

'He's traced him?' she asked in alarm. She didn't want to be blamed for that.

'No, but he thought there'd be no problem in doing so if he tells the pilots the heat will be off now Paul Stock's been charged. I had great pleasure in telling him he'd also been set free again. Pity Heywood could only have been a toddler when Fairfax was killed. We could have pinned that on him. By the way, he said to tell you the letters seem to have stopped. What did he mean?'

Georgia explained and Peter frowned. 'So perhaps the pilots are getting twitchy with reason. I don't like the sound of this silent stalker of yours. Time to ask ourselves why.'

'Perhaps we have the key in Tanner,' she said, 'and it's time to turn it. And blow what Martin says. Let's tackle the pilots.'

'Which do you fancy? Not Bill. He speaks for the pack. We need a weak link.'

'No,' Georgia replied. 'We need a *strong* link.'

'Jan Molkar,' Peter said.

*   *   *

The more she had thought about it, the better the idea sounded. Jan lived in Kent too, which was a help, albeit in Bexleyheath, the north of the county.

An anonymous place for someone who preferred to be anonymous himself, she thought as she pulled up outside his home five days later. Jan's home was a pleasant 1930s semi-detached, neat, tidy, as anonymous as he, she thought as he welcomed her into a living room which was equally neat and tidy. His accent was still noticeable.

'Tell me, Miss Marsh, why you come to me, not to Bill?' he enquired, not accusingly but intently.

'Because I haven't spoken to you before.' It was partly the truth.

'I am honoured. But I think the reason is more. I was a teacher for many years, and I look for such things. You sought me out because you believe I might be the most objective?'

'That could be,' she acknowledged. Why not?

'In that case, you might perhaps be wrong.' He smiled slightly. 'But please ask me what you wish to know.'

'I have talked to Sylvia Lee, and to Alan Purcell.'

'To Alan?' His eyebrows rose. 'That is more than any of us has done for many years. I last talked to him in 1975 when I telephoned to tell him of Patrick's death.'

'You *telephoned*?' So at least there was some path of contact between them.

'Yes.' Jan did not fall into the trap of answering the question in her voice. 'Alan was very shocked. Indeed we all were. But his death was not due to any one of us. There was no reason that we would wish to kill Patrick.'

'I thought so too, until I heard about Oliver Tanner.'

'Ah.' Jan barely moved. He just became stiller. 'We have talked about this; it seemed unlikely that you had learned about it, but possible.'

'After Patrick's death, you went on meeting, even though you might have felt absolved from having to go to Woodring

Manor any more. It can't have been an easy decision to conceal that death.'

'Absolved? No. We all took that decision, and we must all remember.'

'Why did you?' she asked bluntly.

'It is hard to explain, Miss Marsh, for this is a different age. *You* come from a different age. We saw death every day, and then we were faced with this terrible accident. There were terrible accidents to our friends every day, not all due to the enemy. Collisions, misjudgements, crashes – we lived with those. This was one more. If it had been reported, the squadron would have lost Patrick just at the moment when we most needed him to inspire us with his leadership in the battle. We were scrambled daily and two days later Malling itself was again under attack. Four days earlier, there had been a night raid on the airfield. There was a rumour going round – we blamed those two LMF pilots of whom Tanner was one – that Malling was being specially targeted by Hitler who would continue bombing it until we were all dead. We did not believe it, but the tension was rising. We needed Fairfax. For some weeks he'd been worried about Tanner and Smith's reliability in battle, and here was one of them coming to tell him he was pinching his woman.

'We agreed we would cover the story up. Tanner would have left the next day anyway, and so for him to have apparently deserted rather than face the LMF camp was logical, even that he might have drowned himself. The battle grew even hotter as days passed, and with the immediacy of each new struggle, what happened was forgotten, no matter the hows or whys. It was death. In the First War Tanner would have been shot, I think. And even by our time being LMF was a kind of death.'

'Are you excusing what happened?'

'No, Miss Marsh. I am explaining it. I have no need to excuse it,' he said with dignity. 'I will tell you why. My wife and children were killed in the German raid on Rotterdam, while I fought in Belgium. I saw the Nazis come, the refugees fleeing, civilians killed in terrible circumstances every day, machine-gunned by Stukas, bayoneted like pigs. For evil to flourish it is only necessary for good men to do nothing. To surrender, as Belgium had to, was to do nothing, even though it had good results in the end. Britain was perhaps saved because of the breathing space the surrender of Belgium gave it. I did not see it that way at the time, so I managed to get into France and then to England, where I was interned for several weeks while they worked out whether I was a German spy or not. When I convinced them I was an officer in the Belgian Air Force, they were only too happy to post me to a squadron, for the invasion was pending and they needed all the experienced pilots they had. My wife and children are gone, whether to an unmarked grave or they simply disappeared in the bombing. I never managed to find out. That is something one does not forget. Oliver Tanner was not a pacifist, but he refused to stand beside us to fight evil. He turned away. He died by accident and I am sorry, but I do not hold myself or Patrick responsible.'

'So why go on meeting if Tanner's death meant nothing?'

'I did not say it meant nothing. I said it happened, and that is what we remember. It might have been right or wrong; we judge differently now.'

'The decision was that Alan Purcell took Sylvia Lee home, while some of you drove the body to the coast.'

'Who told you that, Miss Marsh?'

For a moment she did not understand, but then she saw his face, and a terrifying thought came to her. Jan looked his full age now.

'You mean,' she stammered, 'that you didn't take it to the coast? That . . .'

'Yes, Miss Marsh. So far as we know, it is still at Woodring Manor, one of the reasons that Matt bought the hotel. We buried it that night. Even if we had the time, we did not have the petrol to get to the coast and back.'

Oh that dell, would she never be free of it?

'You don't look well, Georgia,' Peter said in concern when she came back from Bexleyheath and reported in. 'Go and lie down. We'll talk later.'

'Now,' she said. She felt sick, and if she spoke out it might help. She pulled herself together and forced herself to tell her father, who listened gravely.

Then he said at last: 'Georgia, there is more bad news, I'm afraid. There was a message on your answer service. A call from a Madame Roseanne Fleurie. She is a friend of Alan Purcell's. She wanted you to know that Monsieur Arthur's home was set on fire yesterday, while he was inside.'

'He's dead?' She felt pitchforked into a crazy world. Surely he couldn't be. That would mean a death directly to be laid at her door.

'No, but he's badly burned, and I gather it's touch and go. He wanted to warn you.'

Thirteen

'It's too great a coincidence,' Georgia said flatly. It was she who had stirred up this terrible hornets' nest. She needed to think clearly, but she was still reeling from the altered scenario that Oliver Tanner's death had brought. The attack on Alan Purcell must surely be another piece of this jigsaw. She had telephoned Madame Fleurie immediately, but there was no more news. Monsieur Arthur was alive, but most of the time unconscious. The police were with him – and so Georgia had no need to ask if there were suspicions that this was no accident.

Peter had been making his own investigations. Jacob was a retired Interpol officer from the Sûreté and, despite his ex status, when he asked questions they were smartly answered. There was little doubt it was an arson attack, Peter had told her. 'The seat of the fire was by a rear window. And petrol was the accelerant.'

'It was my fault,' she told him bleakly.

'Explain how,' Peter challenged her briskly.

'We tracked him down, virtually forced him to meet us, and I was being watched while I walked up to the restaurant.'

'Imagination,' he dismissed briefly. 'You sensed it earlier and therefore were subconsciously waiting for it to happen again.'

'I thought someone was about to push me in front of an underground train when I visited Sylvia.'

A short silence. 'You didn't tell me about that.'

She heard herself trotting out the hackneyed words: 'I didn't want to worry you.'

'We know that there's risk in what we do,' Peter said reasonably. 'All we can do is be aware of it. I am, however, also aware that you're more vulnerable than I am.'

'Are you sure about that?' Her night horrors returned to her in full force.

He took her point. In the right circumstances a man in a wheelchair was an easier target than an active woman. 'Do you want to stop work on this case, and announce the fact to the world?'

'The world might not believe us, and anyway, we're getting somewhere at last. It's the trail we're leaving behind us that worries me.'

'Then we shall have to get a move on before we add to it. Look at this.' He turned his attention to the desk before him.

'Not Suspects Anonymous,' she tried feebly to joke.

'Why not? It's as good as anything else.'

She forced herself to pay attention as he logged on and opened up the software. She watched May 10th 1975 play out before her eyes for the umpteenth time. 'We've been seeing the link as between 1975 and Jack's murder,' she observed at last. 'Suppose it goes deeper than that? That the link is between 1940 and 1975, and that Jack's death was either unrelated or he began to suspect what it was all about?'

Peter looked at her for a moment. 'Tanner? No, too great a time span between the three deaths. On the other hand, the 362 files disappeared from Jack's computer and from his shelves. That does suggest a link of some kind. Jack's murderer wouldn't have had time for planting red herrings. Nevertheless, is a time frame of over sixty years of active violence conceivable?'

A silence while she thought about this. 'Back to carers and minders?'

'Minders of body or soul?'

'Soul?'

'Family reputation anyway.'

'Which family? Paul Stock turns out to be Oliver Tanner's nephew? Mary Fairfax takes a machete to Jack to defend her father's good name? Vincent Blake, whom we've never followed up, turns out to be Ken Lyle's younger brother?'

'Why don't you start looking for proof of all these interesting theories?' Peter suggested mildly. 'How about a trip to the Family Records Office?'

'Ouch. Are you serious?'

'Perfectly. Always do a tidy research job,' Peter said sanctimoniously. 'Do a clean sweep. We might have a look at Paul Stock's origins, as well as the Vanes', the Fairfaxes' and the Tanners'. Even the other pilots' families. Not to mention Ms Freeman's.'

'I'll feel like a peeping Tom by the time I've finished,' Georgia said, appalled.

'Excellent,' her father said irritatingly.

A long silence while she glared at him, and he stared her out. 'When did we tell Luke he could have this book?' Peter asked gloomily.

'Next March.'

'Can we tell him this one's off, and we'll find something else?'

'Coward's way.'

'The LMF way. Are we missing something, Georgia? I'm beginning to think you were right. Suspects Anonymous is fine once you have the evidence to put into it. What it can't do is point us in the right direction to search for it. *Or* suggest what's missing.'

She agreed but nevertheless it didn't stop him logging on, this time to put the new Tanner icon into action. He frowned. 'It's telling us that Sunday September first 1940 ended with Tanner as victim and out of play. Nevertheless, continuing to hit his icon for Monday the second results in a red cross on the screen in the sergeants' mess, which is highlighted to indicate action of some sort.'

'Eddie told me that Joseph Smith left that day and that Tanner's effects were collected by the adjutant.'

'Including his logbook presumably. Now I wonder what happened to that. It belonged to the pilot himself, and was presumably returned to the family. I also wonder,' he added without drawing breath, 'why Purcell is so *very* silent.'

'I didn't know the Tanner story when I met him. There's obviously been at least a tacit taboo on any of them talking about it.'

'In which case,' Peter deftly picked up, 'did Jan tell you the story with Bill's permission, or was he stepping outside agreed limits?'

Georgia thought about this. 'The latter, but knowing Sylvia had told me about her side of what happened.'

'Then why was Alan attacked *after* he'd seen you, not before, if the story wasn't to get around? And how did his attacker know where he was living? Let's assume that someone really was watching you on your Boulogne trip – not in threat to you, but to find out about Purcell. Who knew you were going to meet him?'

'You and Luke, no one else.'

'Sure?'

'Positive. The ferry company knew I was going to Boulogne. No one else did. I doubt if Purcell told anyone.'

'There I agree. How did you make the booking with SpeedFerries? Phone?'

'Internet.'

'How did you tell Luke?'

'Email.' Georgia did a double-take when she saw his expression. 'Come off it, Peter. It's not possible.'

'It is. You could well have a hacker.'

Georgia closed her eyes. This was all she needed. 'All my emails? All of my address book?' She thought back rapidly. Yes, she had emailed Luke, and Jack. She'd been in contact with Sylvia by email too. *And* others.

'If there's a hacker, it has to be someone we know or hired by one of them.'

Visions of six elderly pilots – if one included Eddie – busily worming their way into computers seemed faintly ludicrous to Georgia. 'How would they do it?'

'Through Jack's murderer, Georgia. You'd be in his address book.'

'What now?' She hadn't meant it to come out as a wail, but it did and he looked at her kindly.

'We send for Charlie, but meanwhile we know someone's reading your mail, yes? So we do as with double agents. Send out false intelligence. Fortunately our hacker won't be interested in sabotage, only in knowing what we are up to. Very well, we'll tell him.'

When the internal telephone rang, it was the last straw. She'd just finished a session with Charlie on the telephone, another long conversation with Luke about the house, and preparing back-up files in case the worst happened.

'Where have you been?' Peter's impatient voice demanded when at last she picked it up. He did not stop for an answer. 'I'll tell you what I've been doing. Talking to Oliver Tanner's brother, Robert. Not an easy proposition since he was inclined to deny he had ever had a brother called Oliver. No, I didn't tell him the story, merely that we were interested in Patrick Fairfax's death. He did not howl and say, "It's a fair cop, gov", so I take it that he never had any involvement with 362 Squadron.'

'Can you be sure of that over the telephone?'

'I'd risk it. He was in the army, not the RAF. Oliver was his younger brother, and I gathered it was generally thought at the time that Oliver had done the right thing in disappearing from the family escutcheon, even though his mother never believed in his cowardice – naturally enough. I asked what had happened to Oliver's effects. That produced a reaction. A long pause – you know the sort of thing?'

She did. The feeling that you had gone wrong somewhere or that – and she hoped so in this case – that you had hit a nail on the head.

'He said,' Peter continued, 'that there seemed a lot of interest in these things and that I was the second aviation historian who'd asked about that.'

'Who was the first? Or can I guess?'

'You can. Jack Hardcastle. How do you feel like a chat with Mrs H?'

Susan didn't answer her phone until the following weekend as she'd been away, and as Monday was set aside with great reluctance for visiting the Family Records Office in London, it was Tuesday before Georgia could go to Eynsford. Better that way than discussing it over the phone. Susan needed live contact.

Meanwhile, north London, poring over indexes of births, marriages and deaths, was no place to be on a late August day. Only a week to go and the bank holiday would be here, signalling the imminent arrival of autumn. August should be spent in the sunshine, but nevertheless Georgia obeyed instructions, did a thorough sweep and ordered the certificates. One thing was sure. Sylvia's twins, born in early May 1941, could well have been Oliver Tanner's.

As Georgia drove up and parked by the side of the lane on the Tuesday morning, Bramley House looked desolate, and she tracked this down partly to the fact that the Spitfire and Hurricane had departed from the doorway.

'I couldn't bear them,' Susan said frankly as she led her into the living room. The door of Jack's office was closed. 'They seemed to be mocking me every time I came into the house. It's bad enough waiting all the time for the police to ring, without having too many of Jack's things around. I suppose I'll have to decide what to do about his collection.'

'Take your time,' Georgia advised. 'Are the police any further forth?'

'They don't seem to be. They talked to Eddie Stubbs
again a day or two ago.'

'I'm sorry to pester you again . . .' Georgia began.

'Pester all you like. It's a small price to pay for company.
I think of Jack all the time anyway.'

'Did he ever mention a 362 Squadron pilot called Oliver
Tanner?'

'Not that I remember, but then I didn't know one from
the other.'

'Or Jack meeting or phoning a Robert Tanner?'

Again a no. 'He said,' Georgia explained, 'that he had
sent something – an RAF logbook – to Jack.' She knew it
was all too probable that his killer had taken it. 'Is there
anywhere he might have put it for safe keeping?'

Susan grimaced. 'Safe keeping? Goodness knows. Jack
was a squirrel.'

'No hollow tummies in the wooden Spitfire?' Georgia joked.

Susan managed a smile. 'I think I'd have noticed. Jack
was a straightforward man. He wouldn't think of that.'

'The bank? Storage?'

Susan shook her head.

'What would you have done with it?' Georgia asked in
desperation.

The answer was prompt. 'Copied any pages I wanted and
got the original out of the house. Given it to my son, probably. But before you ask, he hasn't got anything. The police
have checked already.'

'And Michael Hastings only has the disks,' Peter grunted
when Georgia reported back. 'Which makes me wonder if
this logbook is so important.'

'It could be,' Georgia said firmly. 'It's worth checking
anyway.'

'You know what?' Peter looked up in the middle of the
spaghetti puttanesca she had cooked. He was getting gloomy
again, she realized with foreboding, partly through

frustration with Suspects Anonymous. 'I *still* don't think we've got the full story.'

'We're eating supper,' she protested. 'No work. Anyway, we now know there's a corpse in the dell, unless Matt had it removed. That's possible, but unlikely. Isn't that full enough for you?' It certainly was for her.

'No. Something Eddie said set up a train of thought and it's gone, dammit. And what exactly did Purcell imply by "as he spoke to her in 1940"? Fairly weird statement, isn't it?'

'I took it merely to mean that he had told Sylvia the story in 1940. She confirmed it. She told me she left Malling so that she was no longer reminded of Oliver all the time. Then Alan told her what had happened, except for the fact that the body was still in the dell. He spared her that. It wasn't the fact that she was pregnant that made her leave – not that it makes any difference. The twins are almost certainly Tanner's.'

'I agree.'

She sighed. 'So why are you so sure it's not the full story?'

'I told you already. The attack on Alan was after he met you, which implies that the arsonist was not particularly interested in what he told you, but in what *proof* he had. And that might mean more than an accident at the heart of the story.'

Tap, tap, tap. The sticks advanced out of the darkness. What was so terrible that it could have led to Fairfax's murder later? She saw where this was leading and shrank from it. *Murder begets murder.*

She swallowed. 'Are you implying that Patrick Fairfax deliberately murdered Oliver Tanner? Supposition. It wouldn't fit all the facts.'

'Why not?' Peter asked.

'The other pilots wouldn't have helped cover up a murder. For one thing, that would make them accessories after the fact, which could carry the death penalty in those days.'

'They might not have known it was murder. It was getting dark. They were burying him, presumably in a sheet or blanket. Even if they'd had time to be curious, death by hitting one's head on a stone and by other hands crashing the stone down would look the same to the lay eye, especially in the dusk. Especially if the person telling you what had happened was your much admired leader whom everyone trusted.'

'That's possible,' she agreed. In her mind she saw the blood from the stone, seeping into the ground, from what was left of Tanner's head. She saw the whole grisly scene, but there was one inevitable question.

'Why?' she asked. 'Over Sylvia?'

'The trophy girlfriend. A prize. Fairfax could well have thought the prettiest, wittiest girl in town should be his, and not welcomed the idea of being second best to an LMF pilot. It could have been manslaughter; it could have been deliberate murder. We might never know.' Some drumming of fingers on the table followed. 'I'd like to know whether that logbook survived.'

'Why? Tanner wouldn't have recorded anything about Sylvia in that.'

'No, but Jack asked for it specifically. He must have had some reason. Besides, it might give us some insight into the man. He was charged with LMF. How did that reveal itself in the logbook, for example? Did he forge entries? No, he can't have done. Logbooks had to be signed by the intelligence officer, or flight commander.' Peter poured himself another glass of wine as the spaghetti grew slowly colder. 'What exactly did Michael Hastings say when he told us what he held of Jack's possessions?'

Presumably Peter had some reason for going over this old ground. 'As I told Mrs Hardcastle,' Georgia obediently complied, 'he said he had the computer files, but that was all.' Then she had a sudden doubt, thinking again. 'No,' she said slowly, 'didn't he say that what we saw were all the *files* he had?'

'That's my recollection too. And files would not include anything Jack left with him for safe keeping. Such as a logbook.'

Fourteen

It was in their hands at last: Michael Hastings had oblig-
ingly disgorged it, once Susan Hardcastle had spoken the
magic words of consent. Now all they needed were the
magic words to tell them what, if anything, made this
logbook so important that Jack had asked to see it. It was
history, as Peter had remarked. Grey-covered, each page of
the book had columns headed month, date, aircraft type,
serial number, pilot, remarks, flying times etc. Each sortie
was meticulously recorded in Tanner's neat handwriting.
She glanced at one entry: *attacked 3 Me109s; bullet in star-
board wing; engine rough.* This looked like standard stuff.

'Perhaps Jack's interest was only casual,' Georgia said
at last.

'Then why did he secrete it away? He could just have
returned it to Tanner's brother.'

'Did Jack think Tanner had managed to fake the logbook
in some way? Claimed he was flying when he hadn't been?'

'I doubt if that would be possible. These logbooks had
to be signed every month or so. Look, it's initialled here
and there.'

Georgia squinted at it. 'It's unreadable.'

'That's not unusual with officialdom.'

Georgia continued reading when something struck her.
'Look at this entry, Peter. *August sixteenth. Pilot self.
Remarks: raid on airfield by Dorniers. Got Spit out of harm's
way. Attacked, got one.*'

'So?' Peter asked.

'I'm sure that was the day Jean Fairfax told me Patrick had rushed out to save one of the LMF pilots who was frozen with fear in the cockpit. He pulled him out, and took the aircraft up himself.'

'That might have been Joseph Smith, not Tanner.'

'All the same, I'll just check something else.' Georgia turned back to July 20th. *'Remarks: Ju87s over convoy. Attacked Me109 fighter escort. Shot down one.* But according to Jean Fairfax, Patrick rescued the same pilot from certain death; he wasn't even firing, but trying to get the hell out of it.'

Peter logged on to Jack's notes. 'Well, perhaps we're in luck. Joseph Smith only joined the squadron on the twenty-second, so if Jean has her facts right, it was indeed Tanner to whose rescue Patrick did – or did not – come. Where does that get us? Tanner was a fantasist and cooked the books?'

'He couldn't. They had to be initialled.'

He seized the logbook from her and went quickly through it. 'One set of initials only, and that's at the end of July. No more. Either Tanner eluded the check, or routine had gone by the board in the frantic scrum of battle conditions. So there is a question mark – a small one,' he warned.

'Jack wanted this logbook,' Georgia argued. 'He thought enough of its contents to ask Michael Hastings to look after it.'

'He was a thorough man.'

'Then he would have pursued it twenty years ago for the squadron history, not for a general history of the battle years later.' She took the logbook back to skim through it once more. 'Have a look at the last entry, on August thirty-first, the day of the dance.' She thrust the logbook under his nose again. 'The handwriting's changed,' she said. 'It's less neat. Look at this line scored underneath the entry for the first operation, when they were scrambled at twelve fifty p.m. *Raid on Biggin, Heinkels and Dorniers. Attacked Me109 escort. Lyle shot down. No enemy again* (underlined). *Fairfax tally ho!'*

'That doesn't make sense,' Peter said.

'I agree. It did to Tanner though. He's obviously under extreme emotion.'

'Nothing for the next day, the day of his death?'

'Yes, but not a report of an op.'

'What then?'

'A doodle. Look.'

Peter stared at it. 'What is it?'

'I think it could be the dormouse.'

Peter frowned. 'As in *Alice in Wonderland*?'

'Yes, it might be Tenniel's drawing of the Mad Hatter stuffing the dormouse in the teapot. Is Tanner reproaching himself for being asleep at the switch?' she speculated. 'Blaming himself for Lyle's death?'

'Why the mention of Fairfax tally-ho then? That Tenniel picture always worried me as a child,' Peter observed. 'The Mad Hatter seemed to be pushing him in upside down, but whether upside down or not the dormouse went through a rough time.'

'As Tanner did. But, unlike the dormouse, no one listened to his story before stuffing him in the teapot,' Georgia reflected. 'This was probably drawn after he'd seen the CO and learned of the LMF charge. Suppose, just suppose, Tanner wasn't a fantasist and we've got it upside down. *Everyone*, including the CO, had it upside down.'

'I'm not sure I follow,' Peter said politely.

'Not literally,' she said impatiently. 'Suppose the RAF had it upside down, that 362 Squadron *still* has it upside down.'

'Do you mind telling me what you're talking about?'

'Suppose – what a wonderful word.' Her excitement grew. 'Suppose Oliver Tanner is the dormouse, and Fairfax the Mad Hatter. That it wasn't Tanner whom Fairfax helped out of that aircraft on August sixteenth, but Fairfax helped out by Tanner. Oliver wasn't a gung-ho chap. He wouldn't have let down a fellow pilot by saying the fellow couldn't hack it. Fairfax might have done though.'

'Pardon my saying so, Georgia, but you're not thinking straight. Fairfax is on public record as a war hero; he won two major decorations. And you claim there might have been a slight mistake?'

She was determined to go on now, nonsense or not. 'Remember what Eddie said.' Odd facts were beginning to clog together in her mind now. 'These LMF cases begin with rumours going round. Who better to spread them than a popular pilot like Fairfax? He climbs down from the cockpit and says offhandedly, "I say, chaps, better watch young Tanner, he cut me up at the third cloud" or whatever pilots say. The further the ripples spread the more it will be believed. The climate is there. It's not as though it was an orderly line up to see the headmaster when they returned from an operation. The adrenalin was going as they all rushed to dispersal. Angry words, angry accusations, not thinking straight when a chum has been shot down.'

She had set Peter thinking at least. She could tell that from the drumming fingers. 'Far too many unanswered questions, Georgia,' he said briskly. 'First, they both wrote full combat reports. Discrepancies would be tracked down if there were a serious charge against someone.'

'But Tanner wasn't the sort to word combat reports as though he deserved the VC. Or to mention that he saved someone's life under fire. I bet if we read this logbook against Jack's biography and the National Archive records we might find a few discrepancies.'

'We'll do that,' Peter replied briskly. 'You do realize that you might be implying that Fairfax had it in for Tanner in a big way, and that the LMF charge was concocted? I might go along with that, but to take it further and theorize that Fairfax was the real LMF candidate is going overboard.'

She stared at him. 'It sounds crazy, doesn't it? But think about it. When we ask about Fairfax we're always told what a great chap he was and what a magnificent man of the air. *Not* what a great chap he was in a dogfight or in the midst of battle.'

'Wrong. Jack Hardcastle said, according to your notes, that he was a gung-ho leader, taking his section into the midst of the fight.'

She was deflated, but aware that Peter was watching her closely for her reaction. 'Let's read what Jack had to say in his biography.'

'I've a better idea. I'll talk to Bob McNee.'

'Why him?'

'Both Tanner and Patrick were in B Flight, and he was its commander. It would have been he, not Patrick, who put forward the LMF charge.'

She prowled restlessly round the garden for the remainder of the afternoon. Only fifteen days to go before Battle of Britain Day, when the publicity for the film would be kicked off. After that, there'd be no stopping the momentum, even if her theory was right. It would be grist to the mill, not worthy of serious consideration. Peter had announced he needed twenty-four hours at least, so she could either resign herself to the wait, or do some work on her own.

'Georgia?' The call from Peter came exactly on the twenty-four-hour mark.

'You're very prompt.'

'It seemed a good time to call. This is September first, the anniversary of Tanner's death.'

'Can we offer him anything?'

'I think we might. Nothing definite, because Bob McNee's away until next week. Theory still, but credible. In Jack's biography he's full of enthusiasm for the airman *and* the fighter. The gung-ho approach straight into the midst of the enemy formation. By the time of the squadron history, however, he's adding a caveat. The losses in B Flight were high, and one reason, he conjectures, is that the gung-ho approach practised by Patrick could lead to problems. Think of it, Georgia, straight into the middle of a flock of birds and what do they do?'

'Scatter.'

'If they're Messerschmitts, not birds, they scatter to fly round and home in on the rest of the section. Number Two will be close to his leader, so that's not so tricky, but Number Three, the arse-end Charlie, would be a sitting target unless the leader turns to protect him. So would the weavers who protect the whole flight or squadron at the rear. That could be what happened to Lyle, who was Tanner's chum. It would explain Tanner's angry logbook comment *Fairfax Tally-ho*.'

Georgia longed to agree, but surely there was a snag here. 'Fairfax and the tally-ho theory doesn't fit with Fairfax frozen with fear in the face of the bombers coming straight for him on the airfield.'

'Bombers wouldn't scatter. They're coming straight for him, and he's powerless. Even if he gets the Spit up he'd be vulnerable until he gets his speed up. That's a different ball game to being up already, and being able to take action of some sort.'

Another problem. 'What about the aircraft he shot down and had confirmed? He won decorations for that.'

'Gongs could be awarded for general performance, not just particular incidents. And the claims procedure wasn't straightforward. You couldn't just say I shot down twelve enemy aircraft today and have them credited to you. There had to be confirmation of some sort from fellow pilots, so some are never going to be confirmed, and some might be confirmed when it wasn't your shot at all. Suppose two are shooting and one doesn't live to tell the tale. Fairfax says to the Spy, "I got one over the Channel"; his fellow pilot Joe Bloggs saw one go down and only one is claimed, so the claimer gets it. I'm not saying Fairfax didn't shoot any down; he well could have, even if he was shooting in a blind panic.'

'So we're saying the jury's out over which, if either, was

the true LMF candidate.' Georgia thought this through. 'I
go for Fairfax. If Tanner were a fantasist, why was Fairfax
so keen to continue the fight outside that night?'

'Because of Sylvia's feelings,' Peter replied, changing
sides to the defence.

'Really? It was a bit late for Tanner to make a fuss about
that. Why didn't he object at the dance the night before?'
She was on the attack now. 'He'd already had a spat with
Fairfax at dispersal over Lyle's death that day. Moreover if
Tanner were LMF, that basically means he avoids conflict.
Does that sound like a sergeant pilot who comes storming
up to accost a superior officer in the holy of holies, the officers' mess, merely to accuse him of taking his girl – who
would surely have left him anyway after the LMF declara-
tion. He'd have slunk away with his tail between his legs,
not come to square up to Fairfax. No, Peter, think of it this
way.' She was sure of her ground now. 'At last Oliver had
realized what had been happening. Lyle's death had brought
it to a head. Fairfax had been building up a climate in which
his own shortcomings would be unnoticed in the fuss over
Tanner. The fact that he spent a lot of time with engine
trouble and had a tendency to abandon the weavers and arse-
end Charlies would go unnoticed if he were prompt enough
in accusing Tanner – whom, incidentally, he had noticed
had an exceptionally pretty girlfriend. He was also the pilot
who had rescued him in the attack on the airfield on August
sixteenth. That's why Patrick took Oliver's appearance at
Woodring Manor seriously enough to want to settle the matter
outside. He'd just have ordered him away if he was willing
for everyone to know what Oliver had to say.'

Her words were tumbling over each other now as she
rushed on. 'They had to sort this out alone. What's more,
Peter, this is an issue that makes the accident thesis look
even less likely. Surely there really was motive for murder
here. If Tanner began shouting the odds publicly that Fairfax
wasn't all he was cracked up to be, the CO would have to

look into it, war or no war, and however popular Fairfax was deemed for general morale. He couldn't overlook such a serious charge as that. Once their memories were jolted the other pilots would begin to think, remember things that they might not otherwise have done. Come on, Peter, admit it. You know it makes sense.'

'We'll look into it further.' Peter must have heard her exasperated sigh. 'We need facts and figures, though. Incidentally, what about Fairfax's evasion and his later career? How do they fit in?'

'Fairfax was sent for a rest after 362 left Malling at the end of October 1940, by which time he was a flight commander. Then he did some instructing, after which he was back on active service as a squadron leader at Tangmere the following summer. But it was only a month before he was shot down—'

'Any proof of that? Could he have deliberately crash-landed?'

'Possible, I suppose. There would only be his word for it. But that would have meant a long journey home and only if he were lucky.'

'Or instant arrest and POW camp.'

'But it wasn't like that.' Georgia frowned, less sure now that she had it right. 'His evasion and escape were a great deed of derring-do. Martin Heywood offered me his co-escaper's account. I'll take him up on it.'

'Careful whom you ask for anything, Georgia, especially on this theory. Remember Heywood is producing a film, not to mention this new edition of *This Life, This Death*. He has an axe to grind.'

'Point taken, but he'd be even less pleased if we substantiated this theory and came out with it *after* it was too late to do anything about it. Anyway, Hugo Barnaby's account isn't going to say anything anti-Fairfax.'

'Then why do you want it?'

'I don't know,' she answered with surprise. 'To be

thorough, perhaps; to see that everything fits the pattern. It would explain why there was such animated discussion about Fairfax writing his memoirs.'

'True. Then for the sake of thoroughness, should we not consult the whole of the magic circle about your theory, not just Bob McNee?'

She considered this. 'Most definitely not. It's interesting that although Tom Armstrong didn't like going to those reunions, he *did* go, and that suggests to me that the closeness of the unit is because they believe, rightly or wrongly that it was an accident. If it was murder, and they suspected it, then they would all have distanced themselves as did Alan Purcell. Moreover, Bill Dane is hardly likely to have taken holy orders if he'd condoned murder. An accident is bad enough. Before we've gathered definite proof, I don't think we should ruin their image of Patrick.'

She managed to catch Martin Heywood on the telephone that evening, who promised to email the report to her the next day.

'How are you doing?' he asked.

'Several lines still to follow up,' she said brightly, 'but progressing. We want to do an introductory chapter about Patrick, which is why the evasion line is interesting to us.' Make it as vague as possible, she decided.

'I'll be publishing before you at this rate,' he commented. With Martin this didn't sound like a light-hearted comment. She could almost hear the relief in his voice that he wouldn't have to share the Fairfax limelight. She might have felt the same in his shoes. She toyed with the idea that his passion for his subject had led him to murder Jack, and reluctantly abandoned it. Intense though he was, even Martin Heywood wouldn't kill for the sake of a film.

'Let's hope our two books don't conflict on what happened,' she said lightly.

'They won't,' he said flatly.

How marvellous certainty was, she thought. He and Jean Fairfax both. So sure of their gods.

'Are you coming to Woodring on the fifteenth?' he continued. 'The tickets were sent out yesterday. Everyone who is anyone who knew Patrick Fairfax or can write about him is coming, as well as the cast, family and friends. We're planning a lot of the old stagers to be present, including the 362 collection and every film critic. The management are letting us rig out a conference room for extracts from the film so we'll virtually be taking the hotel over.'

'It sounds splendid. Thank you,' she said sincerely.

'So there's a smoking gun pointing at us,' Peter replied when she went next door to tell him about the Woodring event. 'Call it our deadline. Did he ask about Purcell?'

'No. He probably thinks we've given up on him.'

'Hum,' was all Peter said.

Only two weeks to go. Two weeks to devote to loose ends and gather fresh evidence. The birth certificates were due but hadn't arrived yet. There were combat reports to be read at the National Archives, squadron operation books, evasion reports, and so much else.

Hugo Barnaby's story was, as predicted, full of praise for Patrick Fairfax. 'The sun shines forth from Fairfax with every move,' she reported to Peter.

'No yellow streaks?'

'No. Fairfax was put through a rough time by the Vichy police inquisition squads and was determined to escape. Fairfax saw him through thick and thin to Spain, then to Gibraltar, where they were interrogated and packed off home.'

'How does Barnaby know about the rough time?'

'Not explained. He might have seen him afterwards, all roughed up.'

'Or perhaps Fairfax told him of the grilling and made a little self-inflicted blood go a long way.'

'You mean leopards don't change their spots, even yellow ones,' Georgia said. That was true. Perhaps there was something odd about this evasion story. 'We can't *paint* spots on without evidence. But what do we consider evidence? A handwritten account of what a rotter Fairfax was?'

'Why not?' Peter snapped back. *'That's* what Eddie said. I remember now. He wrote a diary, he said. He was always scribbling, they all were. So it's odds on that Tanner wrote something of the sort. Where is it?' he roared.

Ten days to go. Wherever the diary was, it wasn't with his brother. Nor with Eddie Stubbs, whom she met in a Dover pub.

'Very nice too.' Eddie drained his pint appreciatively.

Georgia was on tenterhooks as she was at last able to ask, 'You said you *all* wrote diaries.'

'Did I? Maybe.'

'Did Tanner keep one?'

He paused for an agonizing moment or two. 'Yeah. I think he did.'

'Did Jack ever give you the idea that he was especially interested in Tanner?'

A sideways look. 'Why would he? LMFs played a small part. Told you that.'

Different tack then. 'I know you liked Patrick Fairfax, Eddie. Did you ever fly in his section?'

'Once or twice. I was usually in A Flight. Fairfax was B Flight.'

'And Oliver Tanner?'

'With Fairfax. Often flew arse-end Charlie to him.'

'Did Tanner ever talk about Fairfax to you or to Vic?'

'About what?' Eddie carefully licked his lips.

'His flying abilities.'

'Look, Georgia. I worked for the Gas Board after the war, see? We were sent out in teams. You did your job, whether standard repairs or emergency, you came back and had a cuppa. You didn't gas – pardon the pun – about what

219

a cock-up old Tom made of such and such a job. You talked about Arsenal or Chelsea, or the latest film, that sort of thing. Same in the war, only there it were different. Believe me, once you got down and got the line-shooting out of your system in dispersal you didn't even want to think about what happened till the next time.'

'What about *in* dispersal though?' she persisted.

'Too busy unwinding, seeing the Spy, seeing who was back down and who wasn't. So if you want me to say I remember talk about Fairfax, I can't. I wasn't in his mess. I tell you something, Joe Smith used to try it on, and we didn't believe a sausage he said. Not a great surprise when he went LMF, I can tell you. Tanner was different – a dark horse. Only time I saw him off his guard was after that dance. Said something about Fairfax having pinched his girl. Off his trolley, Vic and me thought.'

If only he'd mentioned that earlier. Now it was old hat. 'Did you ever hear details about what he'd done or not done to deserve the LMF charge?'

'I wouldn't, not being LMF myself.'

I'm just going round in circles, she thought in despair. Wasting time while it was ticking away towards their deadline.

'Mind you,' he went on, just as she had given up, 'I'll admit Fairfax was a line-shooter, but then,' he added hastily, 'he would be. He'd a lot to shoot about. It was his nature, meant nothing.'

'What did he line-shoot about?'

'How many he'd shot down, that sort of thing. Jack was asking that. I told him one I remembered. He claimed one for the day Lyle died, but it was Lyle's, so Vic told me. He was quite sure about that. Still, Fairfax could have been mistaken, or perhaps Vic was. Easily happened up there. That was Spy's job to sort out.'

Unless, Georgia thought, the pilot who really shot it down was dead.

'Do you remember Tanner crossing Fairfax's path before the death of Lyle?'

'Not that I know of.' Eddie paused. 'No, I'm wrong. They had a spat almost as soon as we arrived. We flew in on July twentieth, had our photo taken and then it was "how would you like to scramble now, lads?" My memory isn't what it was, but afterwards Patrick was letting off steam at dispersal about bailing out one of the novices, who tried to peel away to get away from the scrum only to find himself with half the Luftwaffe making for him. Then Tanner came in and must have overheard; he said something like, "Tell me, sir. This sounds interesting." Patrick went for him, tore him off a strip for insolence and after he'd gone he explained it was Tanner he'd saved.'

'Could that have been the start of the rumours about LMF?'

'How would I know? We watched out for him, that's all. Blimey, it were a long time back.'

'Why didn't Fairfax act earlier? Couldn't he have made sure he didn't fly with Tanner?'

'How? Only by splitting on him to the flight commander or CO and we needed every pilot we could keep, even duff ones. Patrick must have reckoned it was best to keep him where he could keep an eye on him, in his section most of the time. He was a great guy.' Eddie stared at her defiantly.

Nine days to go. 'I'm emailing Luke that I'm going to France the day after tomorrow,' she told Peter.

'And are you?'

'No. I'm going tomorrow. I cancelled the ferry crossing for Friday and rebooked one by telephone.'

'This will only work once,' Peter warned her.

'Then this is the one. I'll do an email cover-up afterwards to explain why I wasn't there.'

She had to force herself to overcome the weird feelings that were aroused when she sent out false messages, imagining

221

who the silent reader might be. What would they make of it, would they see right through it?

With their deadline looming she seemed constantly on edge. Paul Stock had flummoxed her by turning up unexpectedly on her doorstep yesterday. He told her apologetically that Susan Hardcastle had mentioned the logbook.

Georgia had silently cursed. Why hadn't she asked Susan to keep the logbook's appearance confidential? On the other hand, why should Paul be interested in it? Reluctantly she had taken him to see Peter, who had been surprisingly accommodating.

'Here,' he said, passing it over. 'You're welcome to look at it. Can't loan it to you because we're not yet finished.'

'Haven't you found what you were looking for?' Paul asked. 'Or can't you tell me? I presume I'm still prime suspect for Jack's murder and therefore, by a process of reasoning, for Fairfax's too. All because my one-time wife had a sordid affair with Fairfax. And at that hotel. Convenient, I suppose, which always meant convenient for Patrick Fairfax.'

She seized her opportunity. 'I thought you liked him.'

'Everyone did, until it came to the crunch. With me the crunch came.'

'The 362 pilots went through a lot with him without any apparent crunch.'

'*With* him? Lucky the Spits were single-seaters. I wouldn't like to have flown a bomber with him, I can tell you. He was a fair-weather flyer. When the storms came, you were apt to find yourself in the clouds alone.'

'Like Miss Prism, I'm sure you speak metaphorically,' Peter said blandly.

'No,' had been Paul's blunt reply. 'We were pleasure flying at the club, but in the war they weren't. You know his reputation, and decorations are seldom won for steady flying. The spectacular one-off was his style in everything, including women. I'm surprised that Jean hung on so long. I suppose only because she was a long-term worshipper and they're valuable. When you look in the mirror they tell you that the face you see is exactly as you see it yourself. It would take courage to point out the warts to Patrick Fairfax.'

'And there were warts? There's nothing to suggest that in Jack's biography.'

'His book was a lot of crap, and I told him so. He didn't like it.'

'So if I were to ask you if there was any doubt about Fairfax's worthiness for having won his decorations?'

'I'd be the first to want you to prove it. That's what Jack was on about when he asked me over that evening. He said he wanted to talk about Patrick, that he was beginning to think I was right and that he wasn't the great hero he's cracked up to be. I hadn't got that far along the line, but then I began to think. He was a great flyer; flying didn't scare him, but blazing guns might have done. Ironic that he was shot in the end.'

'Did you tell the police this?'

'I began to. Then I could see I might be digging an even deeper hole for myself. So what's going on?'

'Did Jack mention Oliver Tanner?'

'Yes – that's why I wanted to see the logbook.'

'Good of him to drop by,' Peter said drily when Paul had left, obviously disappointed that the logbook, as well as Marsh & Daughter, had revealed so little.

Eight days. Driving off the ferry in Calais brought back memories of her last visit to France. This time she knew the net must surely be closing, even if it wasn't clear around whom. Madame Fleurie lived in the hinterland of Calais in the small town of Guines. It was here, Georgia remembered, that Henry VIII had stayed before the Field of Cloth of Gold with his vast retinues and no expense spared, a display of nationalism which today was sneered at. Was today's alternative – military power – preferable? At least no one could be blown to bits by cloth of gold.

Guines' days of grandeur were over now, but Madame Fleurie lived near a pleasant canal. Her apartment on the first floor had a view across to its banks where townsfolk were strolling. She was younger than the five pilots, a spry eighty-two, Georgia was informed, but even so she immediately guessed that this was Alan's 'friend', the courier from the Garibaldi line.

'Many children my age were,' Madame explained, when Georgia asked her about it. 'We were not so instantly suspect as our parents were, but we understood what we must do, and why.'

'And your parents?'

'Shot after the line was betrayed. I was sent to Ravensbrück concentration camp, where I kept out of sight so far as I could.'

'And that's how you survived?'

'Survived?' She shrugged. 'One returns home, and one sees one's neighbours. Nothing seems changed except so many dear faces gone. And then the questions. Could it be that one who betrayed you, or this one? We have a phrase – *résistant de quarante-quatre* – to describe those who helped the cause only after the Germans had left.'

'You led the group that included Patrick Fairfax and Maurice Purcell?'

'*Oui*, madame. I took them from Amiens to the last safe house before the Pyrenees mountain pass. When Monsieur Fairfax crashed, he was brought to my parents' home, near Etaples. There were already two other airmen there and an army sergeant. Patrick, he was charming. They were there for several weeks; we were not so organized in 1941 as we became later. You have heard of the Abbé Carpentier?'

'No,' Georgia admitted.

'A priest who made false documents for the Garibaldi line. Also then for the Pat O'Leary line. Alas, when that was betrayed he too died, most horribly.'

'Were you with Patrick's group when they were arrested?'

'*Non*. I had taken them to meet the guide for the crossing of the mountains, and it was then that it was stopped.'

'By betrayal or by a routine check?'

'We do not know, but after the capture, we were all arrested, certainly betrayed, perhaps by one of our own, but Monsieur Arthur and I believed that one of our charges talked. When the Vichy took you for interrogation, the Gestapo was not far away. It was hard for the servicemen to remember that for us the penalty is death, but for them only a POW camp. Bad enough, but not death.'

'You talked about it with Monsieur Arthur?'

'*Oui*. Often. His brother was in that group. When we meet our charges, we see where there are signs of fear, who we can trust and who perhaps not. Some are content to let us lead, others wish to interfere. That was not possible for not only were our lives at stake, but those of the other charges. We wanted to get the pilots and other servicemen back to England so that they can fight the Germans for us. My parents go through the First War. We all knew what to do when war came again. We had to resist in whatever way was open to us.'

'Do you know which of them might have betrayed you?'

'Ah, we know, Miss Marsh. Monsieur Arthur and I. His brother told him. It was Monsieur Fairfax, and already I had suspected that. But Alan will tell you when we see him. Shall we go?'

The end of the trail must be approaching, Georgia thought, even though it was not yet in sight. It was inevitable now. What happened then would be a different matter. The truth did not always result in a book, however.

'We will take my car, Georgia.'

Madame Fleurie had a lovely way of pronouncing her name, though the car drive was less attractive. She approached driving with all the dash and determination that she must have shown as a teenage courier. At least they were heading for a hospital, Georgia thought wryly.

225

There was still a policeman on guard outside Alan's door in the hospital, but Madame Fleurie was clearly a frequent visitor for he barely looked up as she approached. To Georgia's relief Alan was sitting up in bed, and although bandaged he looked in better shape than she had feared.

He managed a smile in greeting. 'As you can see, Georgia, rumours of my pending death have been greatly exaggerated. I regret to say that even you came under suspicion from Roseanne, however.' He indicated Madame Fleurie.

'It is natural,' Georgia said, as Madame cackled. 'How is your recovery going?'

'Physically the burns will mostly heal. Mentally – it is one more sign.'

'Of what?' she asked gently.

'Of the reasons I left England. Roseanne tells me it is time to speak. The fire sets me free to do so.'

At last. Even so, Georgia realized she must tread carefully. 'About what happened on September first 1940 at Woodring?'

'Of course,' he said gravely. 'When I learned what happened then, I could not bear the responsibility of holding such a secret. I too was a coward. I walked away.'

'Too?' she queried guardedly.

'Wasn't Oliver Tanner accused of lack of moral fibre?' Now for it. 'But that wasn't justified, was it?'

His eyes flickered. 'Did Sylvia tell you that? Please tell me. Don't be afraid to speak out. I have a wonderful ability to keep my own counsel when necessary, and being close to death because of my age only adds to that.'

'No. Sylvia spoke of an accident, but my father and I have a theory that Oliver Tanner was deliberately killed by Patrick Fairfax and that the main reason was that it was not he, but Fairfax, who was guilty of LMF.'

It was out now, and with it her last long shot.

'That is a belief that I have had for some time, Georgia.' His face relaxed.

'Tell her, Alan,' Madame Fleurie commanded.

'You are favoured, Georgia. Roseanne now trusts you.' He smiled when Madame Fleurie scowled at his gentle mockery. 'It was my brother who told me about Patrick,' Alan continued. 'He had medical training, and knew Patrick was lying about being beaten up by the Vichy. So it was no surprise that only two pilots escaped from that train. Fairfax needed a grateful witness. There were even shots at the side of the railtrack, to make it seem as if it were a real escape. My brother knew it was not. Those doors opened and shut too conveniently. Fairfax was lucky. No such arrangements would have been possible when the Gestapo took over later.

'My brother's POW camp, where they were sent after the Germans occupied Vichy, was not in Germany itself but in Poland where conditions were much harsher,' Alan continued. 'Two of the men died in captivity, and in 1949 my brother died too. His tuberculosis was sparked off by the last bitter winter in the camp. Already suspicious of Fairfax, I made it my business to look into his career and came to the same belief as you, Georgia. I told Sylvia what I had discovered since I knew how much she had loved Oliver Tanner. It came as an enormous shock to her. To be told that Oliver had died at Patrick's hand had been bad enough, but to suspect he had been deliberately murdered and why was quite terrible.'

'Why did you still say nothing publicly then?'

Madame Fleurie glanced at Alan, as if again giving him permission to speak. 'We would not begin the witchhunt; we would not hurt those that loved him. Roseanne had seen enough of that in France, and I would not distress my comrades from 362. Sylvia agreed.'

'But you had told her the truth.'

'Yes. I went to see her after the war ended. I told her exactly what I felt about Patrick, and she too decided that since there was only suspicion and no proof of murder that we should do nothing.' He looked at Roseanne, who again nodded. 'I had a great affection for Patrick,' Alan continued. 'I believe he was a good man with one big fault. He wanted – needed – to be liked, to be admired. Most of us do, but for him it was an obsession. He had to believe himself worthy of that admiration, he had to be the best. It was, I truly believe, fear of losing that respect that drove him to his impulsive, desperate act, because Tanner knew the truth. He had saved him on 362's first day in action, and again in August. Patrick forced himself to go straight into the heart of the oncoming enemy fighters, guns blazing, even though he had a horror of guns, but the effort required made him forget that those he was leading needed his support.

'Tanner must have stood by while rumours circulated about himself, but when he had to listen to Fairfax insinuating he was responsible for Lyle's death, he might have snapped. He came storming up to Woodring after seeing the CO the next day. Patrick would have realized it had to be sorted out, especially since Sylvia was there, whom he was convinced that he and he alone deserved. Tanner was always there; Tanner could cast aspersions on his reputation if he chose; Tanner knew his weaknesses.'

'But murder—' Georgia began.

'We believed it an accident at the time, Georgia,' Alan interrupted. 'I hadn't seen the body, my fellow pilots had, and it was only in talking about it later that one of them mentioned the position of the body, and how it had looked. My brother, who had just returned from the camp, told me it seemed wrong for a blow to the back of the head caused by a fall.'

'And now, do you still have that affection for Patrick?'

'I'm not sure I can answer that. What I am sure of is that Patrick, being the man he was, genuinely believed he had shot down those planes himself, that he *was* the daring pilot who went straight in for the kill. He was a brilliant man of the air, and he must therefore, in his view, also be the greatest battle hero. After the war, when I had a chance to read *This Life, This Death*, I talked to Patrick about Tanner and his death.'

'That was brave,' Georgia said sincerely.

'Far from it, alas. I can only say that if Patrick did indeed murder Tanner he had no memory of it. He believed his own tale, that he had killed him by accident in righteous fury over putting the lives of his fellow pilots at risk. I didn't believe that, but I swear that he did. Just as Patrick firmly believed that Tanner was LMF, because he couldn't face the fact that it was he who could not face the guns.'

'He still should be judged,' Georgia said.

'Then so should I,' Alan said. 'I walked away; I came to France. I too am a coward. Which of us can throw the first stone, Georgia?'

She could not answer him; it needed thinking about. 'There's a film ready to be released next year and on September fifteenth, in eight days' time, the producer is officially launching the publicity for it. Patrick will be a household name again. There'll be a celebration at Woodring Manor, the press will be there, the pilots interviewed. What are my father and I to do? We know the story, but we can't tell it without proof. And there is the question of Patrick's death.'

'You mean do I know who killed Patrick?' He smiled. 'Fortunately for me I am excluded. Your zealous police could find no evidence that I was there, for the best of reasons. I was not. Nor can I believe that any of my old friends from 362 Squadron would have taken it into their heads to kill him.'

Still getting nowhere. 'Someone,' she said firmly, 'is anxious about what we might find out about Fairfax's death. Someone set your house on fire and nearly killed you. Someone killed Jack Hardcastle. Someone hacked into my computer in order to be able to silence you and perhaps my father and myself as well. He or she is still out there. Where will you go, if you don't speak out?'

'Madame Fleurie and I are good friends. She is to look

after me, and we who have seen such horror in our lives acquired the strength to survive. And as for your question about evidence, I think you will find that Oliver Tanner is the root of this business.'

'We still need proof.'

'Once you are there, so may the proof be.' He slumped back against the pillows and it was clear that she should go.

Six days to go. 'He's holding something back,' Peter said gloomily. 'He must be. Purcell looked into this thoroughly at the end of the war. So why won't he cough it up?'

'He seemed to imply that *we* need to do some more work.'

'He's right. We don't know who killed Fairfax, for a start. Yesterday evening I managed to speak to Bob McNee at last.'

'Did he toe the party line?'

'Yes. I hammered him over Tanner and Fairfax though. He did tell me Patrick had come straight to him at dispersal on the day of the dance, accusing Tanner of being responsible for Lyle's death, and that was far from the first time he'd made formal allegations of his behaviour in battle. He'd decided he was going to the CO about it, and asked Patrick to gather all the evidence he could. Patrick tried to dissuade him, but he was adamant. He said it happened once too often and that was that.'

'So presumably when the CO talked to Tanner,' Georgia reasoned, 'Tanner would hardly have taken it lying down. He'd have put forward his side of the case. That's why the verdict was postponed. And that's why Tanner was so furious that Sunday evening. And now?'

'Now we have six days left. If we come up with evidence after that, it would be a two-day wonder, but it would be the film and book that would survive in the long term. High Noon is coming fast, Georgia.'

Fifteen

The day was here. Somehow Marsh & Daughter had survived the whirlwind and reached Woodring Manor. September had vanished for Georgia while she and Peter had grappled with the ramifications of the Fairfax case. Just as on every Christmas Eve, however, there came a point where one had to decide it was over, not another parcel to be tied, not another decoration to be hung, not another card written. That, as the boy had remarked in the A.A. Milne poem, once clad in his waterproofs and Wellington boots, is that. And she had declared it last night.

'I agree,' Peter had said thankfully. He was looking tired this morning, she thought, and she was doubly glad that Luke was going to be there too. He had been spending so much time whistling between Haden Shaw and South Malling that she had hesitated to ask him. Peter had had no such compunction.

'A publisher needs to keep an eye on his investment,' Luke had quoth merrily when they met in the car park.

'Medlars?' she asked, deliberately misunderstanding.

'Signed and sealed,' he said offhandedly. 'Completion by November. Just in time for Christmas.'

'But . . .' she began, unable to face the idea of yet another whirlwind.

'Later,' Luke said firmly. 'Work first. Remember I have an interest in this book too, if it ever gets written.'

That was the question. Would it? Today was crunch time, and yet Marsh & Daughter were helpless to influence the course of the day. That was in police hands. They were the deus ex machina who would descend from the skies to decide the issue. Or not descend at all. That was the worst scenario. If they failed to show – which meant they hadn't made their case – Marsh & Daughter would achieve only a Pyrrhic victory of knowledge without resolution. And Jack's murderer might yet walk free. There were obligations to be met to others who had risked a great deal to help them. Not least an obligation to Susan Hardcastle.

That was why they were here. Two days ago she and Peter had met Pullman and his counterpart from Downs Area, DI Jennings, now in charge of the Fairfax case, plus Mike Gilroy who, for all his placidity, couldn't bear to be left out. For good measure, Christopher Manners had also been there. She and Peter had both left with a sense of anti-climax, however. The pace of the last two weeks had dissolved, understandably enough, into a world of maybes and ifs, dependent on fingerprint matches, footprint matches, labs coming up with the right answers, and procedural OKs. Where Patrick Fairfax was concerned, there had been over sixty years of ifs and buts, and now what might be the last effective chance of justice for Oliver Tanner might be slipping away.

Today would bring problems either way. If – and it was a big if – the police had their warrant, it was going to cause great distress. Indeed they might even postpone their arrival for that reason. Oliver Tanner's reputation meant nothing to them, only the killer of Jack Hardcastle and, in Jennings' case, Patrick Fairfax. All the accumulated evidence they had amassed in the last week would be for nothing. At last the final certificates had arrived through Family Records and at last avenues miraculously unblocked themselves.

'We owe this case to the tying-up of loose ends,' Peter had said complacently last night.

'And to Charlie,' she had pointed out.

He had arrived to clean up her hard disk, and wisely or

unwisely she had expressed her doubts about Suspects Anonymous fairly forcefully. He had been highly indignant and marched her next door for a joint session with Peter.

'Confidential information,' she had muttered. 'Data Protection Act and all that.'

'Nonsense. I'm a service provider. Even MI6 has to have its computers serviced. I'm an invisible shadow. I don't count,' Charlie said crossly. 'And look at this, Georgia. No wonder you don't get much out of Suspects Anonymous.' He was scanning the folder lists. 'From what little you've told me, these Burglar Bill icons are your suspects, rights?'

'Right.'

'Who do you count as suspects?'

'Those who had opportunity and motive.'

'Quite,' Charlie snarled. 'I knew you'd be using it all wrong. You've qualified it. How do you know who had motives? Everyone present should go in, until disqualified.'

'Define everyone,' she countered.

'The postman, the dustman, the head chef, the plumber's mate, the owner's Auntie Maud if she was upstairs in the rocking chair. Otherwise you're looking at the case upside down – only why *you* can envisage someone wanting to murder your victim. Bit limited, isn't it?'

Peter had sat smugly by as Georgia defended her wicket. 'Of course we've considered someone could have been there, but not recognized. Alan Purcell for example.'

'No, Georgia,' Peter said patiently, 'Charlie means not *could* have been there, but *was* there, although not recognized as a possible player in the game.'

She was there now. How could she have been so blind? 'You mean G. K. Chesterton's postman theory. The man who escapes notice. And that suggests—'

'The barman,' she finished in triumphant unison with Peter. Of course. So blindingly obvious when one thought about it – like the million-pound question on the TV quiz show.

And that had been the beginning of the end. It had seemed so simple when they had discussed it between themselves, even with the police, but now faced with the reality of what revelation of the truth might mean, it wasn't so simple at all.

As she walked into the marquee, the first person she saw was Jean Fairfax queening it at Martin Heywood's side, poor woman. Close behind her was her bodyguard Mary. A myriad unknown faces, of course, but here and there a familiar one. She saw Sylvia Lee with Helen at her side, plus an unknown man – brother Harvey perhaps? Seated round one of the tables were six other familiar figures. 362 Squadron was here in force, including Eddie Stubbs. Did that suggest a symbolic equality after all these years, or a unity in the face of what they might perceive – rightly – as a threat? Or did it mean nothing? She was getting hyper-sensitive, she decided.

The day's official plan was straightforward, according to the programme thrust into her hand by a PR lady. An official welcome from Martin, now in his element, then a buffet lunch followed by a screening of extracts from the film in the improvised cinema in one of the conference rooms – this one was in the converted stable block. After that there would be a press free-for-all. Publicity packs were to be seen everywhere.

'I miss David Niven. He always looked good in an Irvin jacket,' Luke whispered ruefully as the film extracts began in the cinema.

'I bet Sylvia does too,' she whispered back. The female lead was a sultry beauty called Sharon Cross, who in Georgia's view looked as if she lived up to her surname, but perhaps she was only being soulful.

Leo Jakes, the star of the film, was well cast as Patrick, she thought, looking much like the real Patrick and possessing his charm and sexiness. Sexiness, that is, to the world at large. Not to her. She preferred Luke. Unbidden,

Zac reminded her of his particular brand of sexiness. Time had moved on, she told him. What was sexy at twenty-four was less so over ten years later. Then why are we having this conversation, Zac enquired gently. Go away, she ordered him, and surprisingly he did.

It wasn't her style of film but she had to admire the expertise with which Patrick had been brought back to life. She was even gripped by the extracts from his student life, then the war hero, then the jewel in the crown: the aviation club. He came over as a man of vision as well as action. The film gave a good overview, so far as she could judge, cleverly twisting past values to accord with something recognizable today.

Even Paul Stock was impressed when she met him after the presentation. He was with Jean Fairfax, who raised a cool eyebrow of welcome to Georgia as if daring her to comment adversely, and then departed with Cerberus.

'As the only one here who hated his guts,' Paul quipped, once Jean was out of earshot, 'I was impressed. Maybe I could get to like the fellow.'

Janet Freeman had strolled up to join them. 'Why not? I did,' she countered coolly. 'I came to tell you someone was enquiring for you at the desk, Georgia.'

'Did he have a gun in his hand?' she was tempted to ask. But then, the answer might be yes.

'There,' Janet pointed to a casually dressed young man walking towards Peter, who was just emerging from the conference room. Curious, Georgia left Luke with Paul and Janet, and went to join them.

'My daughter, Georgia. She met your grandmother,' Peter said to the young man. 'Madame Fleurie's grandson, Philippe,' he explained.

'Monsieur Arthur?' she immediately asked him, alarmed. Had he come to tell her he had died?

'He is well,' Philippe said hastily. 'This is from him.' Georgia glanced at Peter, her heartbeat quickening in sudden hope as Philippe produced from his canvas holdall an old-fashioned ledger and a smaller bound notebook. 'You are to see these, if you please, and do what you wish with them. They were in my grandmother's house, and therefore not burned. He asked you please to greet his old comrades.'

Georgia handed the smaller notebook to Peter, and quickly looked inside the ledger. What she saw there made her heart race. Columns, dates, careful entries in one handwriting: Alan's. There were lists of operations, and Fairfax and Tanner's names, and source notes.

'*Merci, merci*,' she heard herself babbling, even as she turned to see what treasure Peter might be holding. He seemed glued to the notebook, and she peered over his shoulder. Dates – and a familiar handwriting.

'Tanner's diary,' Peter almost choked. 'The real McCoy. You take this, Georgia.' Peter handed her the diary. 'Leave the ledger with me. I'll look after Philippe and wait for the police.'

It was three o'clock now and there was no sign of them. She began to panic. The afternoon was scheduled to end in two hours' time, and perhaps this meant the police weren't coming. Or were they deliberately leaving it late to avoid the full glare of the press?

She had to read this diary, for there, if anywhere, would be the evidence they needed. She needed a place where she wouldn't be disturbed by curious eyes. Inside the hotel? No, she would see this story through and go where it had begun. No one would pry on her there. Besides, it would be a test for her.

When she came to the point in the path where she had stopped in May, however, she regretted her decision. It seemed unnecessary, even melodramatic, but it would be equally melodramatic to turn back. The leaves were falling now, and without the bluebells the dell seemed a forlorn place indeed. It was in all probability still the grave of Oliver Tanner and it was all she could do not to turn and run. With a great effort of will, she sat down on a rock and opened the diary. Immediately she forgot her surroundings:

> Airfield under fire again today. One of the airmen copped it. Joe took a shovel to help fill the craters in; he's bearing up well. Unlike our noble section leader. Straight for the quickest way through and no matter what happens to the rest of us. Does he even think? Probably not. Two days ago I found him stuck in the cockpit staring glassy-eyed at the black specks heading for us. He blanks out, I reckon. Doesn't remember a thing about it afterwards. Hauled him out, pushed him to the shelters, and jumped into the crate myself. Only just made it.

Another entry caught her attention.

> Who is Sylvia? She is the best of me. She is my life, the reason to see this bloody war through, so that we can roam this green and pleasant land without jackboots bearing down on us. Last night . . . ah, last night!

'I thought I might find you here.'
Georgia froze. What a fool she'd been.
'Is that Purcell's file so-called proof?' Martin Heywood continued easily. 'I realized you'd tracked him down. Well done. Shall I take it?' He sounded as casual as if they were speaking on the phone and yet she was terrified. He was standing between her and the only accessible way out of the dell. His voice offered no threat, but his body language suggested otherwise.
'Here.' He held out his hand. 'Give it to me.' He moved further towards her, and trying not to display fear she stood up, retreating slowly down the dell.
'I didn't believe a word of this nonsense,' he continued,

'when Jack told me he had doubts about Patrick's place in history. And I still don't believe it now. You do know Patrick was my grandfather, don't you?'

'Yes,' she managed to say. Talk, that was the best way. *Talk*. 'But only when I saw your mother's maiden name on the birth certificate. I'd forgotten she was divorced. I thought of your brother's children being involved, but not hers. Foolish of me.'

'What was foolish was to believe all these lies about Patrick. You saw the truth today on that screen and that truth isn't going to be wrecked by any dirt you or that devil Purcell can throw at it. It's too late.' He moved impatiently towards her, and involuntarily she stepped back again.

Talk, she commanded herself.

'I presume it was you who hacked into my computer and kept a watch on me?'

'My son, actually. He's a bright lad. He's here today because he believes in the family name too.'

'You let him follow Purcell home and set fire to his house?' She was appalled.

'No. I did that. That rubbish you're holding has to be destroyed. Jack told me Purcell had some kind of nonsense he called proof. I had to act. I couldn't let him besmirch Patrick's name. Or you.'

She saw his fist coming out, she saw him lunging towards her, then the pain as the blow struck and she felt herself tumbling downwards and hitting the ground, with something jabbing sharply into her. His voice above her almost pleading, 'I have to have that diary. You see that, don't you? I have to have it.' It must have been lying beneath her, for she felt herself being hauled up. *The cavalry, where are the cavalry?* Crazy thoughts jumped around in her spinning head as another fist hit her.

She opened her eyes and something seemed to crash into her head. Then she remembered the dell. She wasn't there any more; she was in a room – no, a tent, and it was Luke, not Martin Heywood who was bending over her now. She seemed to be lying on a couch – the first-aid tent?

'My lovely,' he said, kissing her lightly. Even that hurt.

'The cavalry,' she managed to stammer.

'They came. Now keep quiet.'

'The diary – did he get it?'

'No. The police did.'

'The mounted police cavalry?' This wasn't making sense but her head couldn't cope with it.

'No. The ordinary sort, I'm afraid. They picked Heywood off the ground where he was investigating the dell's soil content.'

'Then who was the cavalry? Me? Did I hit him?' She had to get to the bottom of this.

'I was the cavalry, my pet.'

'Oh, Luke.' She closed her eyes again.

When she next woke up she was much clearer. 'Where's Dad?' For some reason that seemed easier to say than Peter.

'Talking to the St John's ambulance chaps who want to cart you off for a check-up, and to the police who need a statement from you. They seemed to think I was the one who knocked you out, so you might put them clear on that. They've got his nibs though.'

'Is it,' she asked, trying to keep the wobble out of her voice in case she burst into tears, 'acceptable for a publisher to interfere in his author's research? What about moral rights?'

'You can't claim any. You're about to become an immoral woman and move in with someone you aren't married to. Yet.'

She considered this proposition. It sounded a pleasant, homely idea. One thing was for sure: Zac wouldn't have joined the cavalry.

'. . . keep your own house or office, at least for a while,' Luke seemed to be saying. 'Not too many nights working late though. Anyway, Medlars won't be fit for habitation right away. We might be looking at Christmas if we're lucky.'

Christmas. A Christmas tree. With lights on it and a fairy at the top. Like the ones Peter and Elena had dressed for her as a child. And for Rick. Unbidden, the tears began to roll down her cheeks.

'Don't you like Christmas?' he teased.

'Yes,' she managed to say. 'I do.'

Sunday lunch never tasted better than when someone else cooked it. Today Luke had. Or rather he'd arranged with the White Lion to send their best over when he arrived at Haden Shaw. The hospital had insisted on keeping her in overnight and sent her away with Luke on condition she rushed straight back in at the slightest ominous symptom. Eating lunch was not forbidden. Nor was talking. Provided, Luke said, she didn't do too much herself. Mike had promised to look in to tell them what had happened after her dramatic disappearance yesterday.

'DI Jennings arrested Heywood for assault on you. Pullman was most grateful to you, Georgia. While Heywood's being held, he has a chance of sorting out the other matter.'

'Jack's murder,' she said.

'Correct. They're expecting a match for his nibs' tenprints and DNA for that. Tenprints already here, DNA takes a little longer but before tomorrow's out it should be OK.'

'Has he confessed?'

'Not even to assaulting you. Apparently you got in the way of his fist while he was demonstrating a left punch at your request,' Mike told her straight-faced. 'Alternatively it was self-defence.'

'My guess,' Peter said, 'is that Jack warned him when he first mentioned the film that he thought Fairfax's reputation was suspect. Heywood must have watched him like a hawk after that. Of course, Jack probably didn't have the benefit of knowing he was talking to Fairfax's grandson, otherwise he might have held his horses, knowing how besotted Jean Fairfax is about his memory. Heywood is even more of a fanatic than his grandmother.'

'It's often left to the next generation to carry the flame, so Mary Fairfax remarked,' Georgia said. 'Not the sons or daughters, but the grandchildren.'

'Quite. When Heywood saw you talking to that boy he was on your case. He knew it must be the diary and Purcell's records that Jack had told him about. Luckily Luke managed to remove the diary from Heywood's grasp before he could eat it,' Mike said straight-faced.

'I said something to him ages ago that must have made him think I was on to this question of Fairfax's reputation.' At Tangmere, she remembered wryly. Just a few idle words misinterpreted, a man killed, a house burnt down and its owner badly burned, not to mention two punches to her face as a result. 'But at one point he was anxious to help me,' she pointed out, struggling to work it out.

'Of course,' Peter said, 'but only to draw you out. He must have been desperate to find out where Purcell lived and what lines we were working on. He thought you might tell him if he cosied up to you.'

'Ugh,' Georgia said. 'But he did send Barnaby's statement.'

'Which supported Fairfax's noble nature. Barnaby was the other evader who was given a free pass to Blighty. It probably included a cruise liner from Bordeaux, rather than a stiff climb over the mountains.'

'All the same, murder and attempted murder on Heywood's part seem over the top, even if both were spur of the moment reactions.'

'Not to him. He firmly believed and still does that this is a dirty-tricks campaign to throw mud at the Fairfax name, in some misguided attempt to make excuses for Oliver Tanner.'

Georgia's thoughts went sickeningly to Jean Fairfax. 'How is she?' she asked.

'As you might expect. Furious. All your fault. The worst is still to come. They think he's only arrested for assault at present. There was much discussion amongst the pilots afterwards, but I doubt if it touched the Fairfaxes.'

'At least some of the truth about Patrick will have to come out if Heywood's charged with murder or even with manslaughter.'

'I don't think they would believe it. Heywood doesn't, so why should they? It's all part of the conspiracy against the man they love. It's knocking heroes time, they will argue to themselves.'

'There'll be enough proof now. The press will leap on it during the trial.'

'Will they? Isn't there something you're forgetting, Georgia?' Mike asked.

She was. It must be the bruises and bumps to blame.

'The motive for Hardcastle's murder doesn't depend on its proof, only that Jack made these allegations,' Mike continued. 'And . . .'

Georgia could finish that for herself. 'No one has yet been accused of Fairfax's murder. And of that, Heywood most certainly can't be guilty.'

Georgia was amused to see Peter's reaction to welcoming Sylvia Lee to Haden Shaw. She and Helen had stayed the night at Woodring Manor in view of the attack on Georgia and Martin's Heywood's subsequent arrest. Now Sylvia had taken the initiative, and suggested that if convenient they would drive over to see them later that afternoon.

They arrived an hour or so after Mike had left, and Peter almost glowed in a severe attack of fan dottiness. Sylvia,

Georgia thought, had the effect of lighting up the room as though the breath and romance of Fifties' romantic musicals had swept in with her. It seemed amazing that an elderly lady of eighty-six could still convey this, but charm, once possessed, seldom departed. Even Luke was fussing around, more than normally assiduous in settling their guests in comfortable chairs. There were even strawberry tarts – how did he manage that in September? An appeal to Pat Mulworthy? A special crop grown overnight? Or did he whip them up himself while she wasn't looking?

'Georgia dear.' Sylvia leaned forward. 'It was all my fault.'

'That I won these?' Georgia managed to laugh, pointing to her battle wounds.

'Because I didn't – I couldn't – tell you the full story. If I could have done, perhaps this wouldn't have happened.'

'I doubt,' Georgia said, 'if it would have made any difference. Alan would still have been attacked, and perhaps I would too. Fortunately Martin Heywood didn't know about your involvement.'

'He still doesn't know.' Sylvia said. 'The story was mine, and Helen's, and even partly Richard's. What I told you was true so far as it went. I loved Oliver very much and . . . Helen?'

'Go ahead,' Helen said comfortingly. She took her hand like a mother to her child rather than the other way around.

'Helen and her twin were Oliver's children. You might have guessed that, or that they were Patrick's. That's a distressing thought. I was still too close to Oliver even to have thought of another man in that way. I told you what happened when I went to the dance with Oliver on the Saturday night. Oliver said he wanted to talk to me about it, but Patrick scooped me up and took me away. I wasn't sorry. I couldn't bear even to think of it. All those pilots I'd known who'd lost their lives – maybe, I told myself, they'd lost them because of Oliver. I'm not proud of what

I did, but who knows? If I were nineteen again, I might do exactly the same.

'Late the following afternoon, Oliver came to see me and tried to explain. He'd just seen the CO and would be getting his verdict the next day. Again, it sounded like excuses. He said false rumours had been circulating for weeks, because one of the pilots had it in for him. I still couldn't believe him. He said he didn't expect me to understand, but it was all in his diary. He wanted me to look after it for him if he were sent away to camp. We had an awful row, and I flounced off, though I took the diary as he asked. That evening Patrick had said I should come to Woodring Manor to take my mind off it; I didn't want to, but I went. I felt so wretched. And then Oliver came, out of the blue, demanding to speak to Patrick. Naturally I thought he'd come to find me and not finding me at home, hitched a lift and came up to Woodring. The fight broke out and Alan took me home. I didn't hear any more about Oliver except that Patrick told me he'd deserted before he could be formally charged.

'Two weeks later Alan came to see me, concerned that I was still seeing Patrick. He told me that Oliver had been accidentally killed that evening, and he assumed as I did that the fight was about me. You can imagine how I felt. I just wanted out. I thought I'd been completely mistaken about Oliver, and appalled though I was at his death I just wanted to blot everything out. I pushed the diary into Alan's hands, and decided to go.

'Two weeks later, back in London, I realized I was pregnant. Norman Lake was a dear man. He was shortly to be called up, he was very fond of me, and when I told him my story, he suggested we should be married. In those days that seemed the right solution. The children were born five months later, by which time Norman was in the forces. At the end of the war Alan came to see me. He told me what the diary had contained, and the evidence that he had collected to support it. He also told me that he thought it possible that Oliver had been deliberately murdered, but that there was no proof of that.'

She paused. 'That much you might know or have guessed. Now for the hard part. You have met Helen, but you never asked about her twin, Hilary, who died eight years ago in New Zealand. When the twins were twenty-one I told them the truth about their father and about the LMF charge, I told them it was a mistake and that he was really a brave man and a kind and gentle one too. Neither appeared to react strongly to the news, and I assumed therefore that it had been quietly stored away and forgotten. That was 1962 after all, over twenty years since Oliver had died. It was never mentioned again. Then one day Richard came home from the aviation club very puzzled because he'd seen Hilary working at Woodring Manor Hotel.'

'As a barman,' Peter said.

Sylvia looked at him. 'Yes.'

'I'd assumed,' Georgia said ruefully, 'that Hilary was Helen's sister. It was only when I saw the full birth certificate that I realized otherwise. The index only gave the name Hilary.'

'I'm afraid we let you assume that,' Sylvia confessed. 'You saw the photograph of the two babies and naturally assumed them both girls. I was exceedingly anxious to keep Hilary from suspicion so I let you continue to do so. He was, after all, my son – Oliver's son. We asked Hilary what he was doing there – this was several weeks before the murder. It was just the coincidence rather than the job itself that surprised us. He had never settled to anything and seemed content to drift from job to job. He had his own flat in north London, so we were never quite sure what he was doing. We had no idea he was working at Woodring under a false name, of course.'

'Did your husband see him there the afternoon Fairfax died?' Peter asked.

'Yes. But naturally he thought nothing of it by that time. He had a few words with him, but had left long before Patrick was killed. Hilary had told us he was there simply because Richard had talked so much about the aviation club and the hotel that he thought he'd come down to see them. He hadn't realized it was so closely connected with his father's old squadron.'

She looked at them in appeal. 'When we heard about Patrick's death, naturally we talked to him about it, and it was then he told us he was working under a false name, but that was nothing. He often did it, he said. It made things easier. We wondered *what* things of course, but with Hilary one didn't enquire too far. He had this way of staring at you and just shutting up, going inside himself. We were uneasy, but felt reassured because he went on working at the hotel. If he'd been implicated, Richard reasoned that he would have run away immediately. We waited and waited for someone to be arrested but no one was. Hilary told us that Matt Jones was the chief suspect, and Richard said that was entirely likely. But later Hilary suddenly disappeared and we had a letter to say he was working his passage to New Zealand. I think we guessed then, and . . .' She looked at her daughter. 'Helen did too.'

'You want me to tell them, Ma?' Helen asked doubtfully.

'Yes,' Sylvia replied firmly. 'This is the time. Georgia and Peter can decide how much to put in their book and how much to omit. When Jack Hardcastle came to see me not long before he died, I wasn't prepared, but now I am. We both have to be.'

Helen took a deep breath. 'Mum was wrong. I took it OK – after all, I didn't know the full story about Fairfax, but Hilary was obsessed with it. I know twins are supposed to be close, but we weren't close in everything. I could tell when Hilary was lying and when he was genuine, but his thought processes were a mystery to me. We complemented each other rather than duplicating. Does that make sense?'

Peter nodded.

'After Mum told us about Oliver, I thought it was tragic but it was in the past. It didn't seem to bear much reference to me; I wanted to go forward. Hilary was different; he kept wondering what our father was really like. *If* Mum was telling us the truth. And if so, there must be more to find out. He was always one for absolutes was Hilary. All coward or all hero. He seemed to forget it after a while, and I thought he was over it, but in the 1970s with the new thirty-year rule at the Public Record Office over releasing records I discovered he spent hours there, poring over documents. One day he was very excited. A chap called Joseph Smith, who'd been in the same squadron, told him he reckoned Fairfax was inclined to be yellow himself, and that Oliver had been the cat's whiskers. It was then that Hilary left home and I lost close touch. Then a year or so after Fairfax's death, this New Zealand plan came out of the blue. It turned out that Hilary was gay. We heard from him occasionally, but never saw him again. Then we heard he'd died.'

Georgia looked at Sylvia's face and realized how much this was costing her.

'He hadn't left a will,' Helen continued, 'so I had to go over to New Zealand to sort it out. His partner had found a holdall stuffed full of papers and thought we should have them. It was packed with information about 362, and a sort of journal that Hilary had kept of his researches, full of hatred for Patrick Fairfax – and of what had happened that day. You can copy it if you wish.' She delved into her handbag and produced it.

'You're sure about this?' Georgia asked Sylvia.

'Yes,' she said.

Georgia opened the journal and turned to May 10th 1975.

So I gave him the message that his dollybird was waiting in the rockery garden for him. Nice touch.

That's where I reckon he killed my dad. Thanks, chum. And the same to you. May it was, and the bluebells were ringing. Really pretty. Only it was drizzling. What the hell's she gone there for? Fairfax muttered. I'd seen a picture of Mum and him together in the hotel gardens – what kind of a creep would let that happen? He'd only murdered my dad a week or two before. Sick, really sick. I took my time; I'd brought ammo with me, took the gun out of the cupboard in the bar and walked after him.

He stopped short when he reached that dell and she wasn't there, so I ran up to him. Sorry, just met her, I said. She'll be here in a minute or two. His sort never question a mere barman. Why should I lie, he'd think. I'll tell you why. Because he did. Lied and lied and lied about my dad. I'll never forget his face when he turned and saw the gun. Oh boy. What the devil . . . That's for Oliver Tanner, I said, cutting across him. That did it. Fear? He was yellow. As yellow as a Texas rose, was old Patrick. This is for my dad, I said, and pulled the trigger.

Epilogue

Georgia stood by Peter's wheelchair at the back of St Mary the Virgin's church in West Malling as the coffin with the skeletal remains of Oliver Tanner was borne down the aisle on its way to a private burial. Only Sylvia and her family and Oliver's brother would be present at that, but it was fitting that the short memorial service should be held here, in the presence of his former squadron members. Georgia didn't know what had passed between them. All that had appeared in the press was a notice that the film was postponed due to production difficulties, and that there would be a note on the squadron records about the removal of an LMF charge on a pilot called Oliver Tanner. The new edition of *This Life, This Death* had been cancelled. One reputation restored, and one still officially intact.

She watched as Sylvia, a small figure in black, followed the coffin with Helen and Robert Tanner, and then came the five pilots, their wives and carers. With them were Eddie Stubbs and Alan Purcell, leaning heavily on his stick. The pilots knew the truth now – and it had been Alan who had broken the news to them. What exactly he had told them, she had no idea. Not the whole truth, perhaps, but enough of it to reinstate Tanner's memory.

She and Peter followed them out into the churchyard, where Eddie stopped to speak to them. 'We're off for a noggin at Woodring Manor. Why don't you come? The chaps all want you to.' The six other pilots stopped too and gathered round, nodding their confirmation.

An olive branch. 'We had no choice,' Georgia said. 'I'm sorry.'

Bill Dane put his hand on her arm. 'It's we who are to blame, not you. We refused to see it. We saw Patrick that night, we saw the terror on his face; we thought it was an accident, you know. Even now, we can't believe it was murder – not planned at least. All we can say is that many pilots crashed during the war without graves save the ruins of their aircraft. To us Oliver was LMF, which put us all at risk. Our other friends who had died deserved our sympathy more, we felt. Now we know that is not true, and it's too late.'

'A rock crashed down on his head,' she said quietly. How could she and Peter go to Woodring with them in those circumstances?

He regarded her gravely. 'Why do you think we have met all these years?'

'You were drawn together by this secret hanging over you.'

'No. That would have driven us apart, not kept us together. The main reason was Patrick. Worthy, or unworthy as we now know, *then* he kept us together. As Alan says, he believed himself a brave man and therefore unified us with his presence. And for that, we may owe him our lives.'

'Will you go on meeting?'

'I believe we shall. Yes, I do believe that, so long as we are able. We'll go on now for Tanner's sake. Eddie will join us, of course, and Alan too when he is able. And we trust that today you and Peter will do that too.'

She wanted to walk away, be rid of the case, not to have to think about the dell. But there was a book to be written. King Arthur must be banished from Peter's desk. And there was a house to move into, a house called Medlars. A house with a permanent ramp for wheelchairs. A house without ghosts. A house with Luke. She had all this before her. Could she walk away from what she and Peter had stirred up?

She glanced at Peter, who nodded. 'Thank you,' she said. 'We'd love to join you.'